a novel by COLLEEN CLAYTON

poppy

LITTLE, BROWN AND COMPANY
New York Boston

Copyright © 2012 by Colleen Clayton

Poppy
Hachette Book Group
237 Park Avenue, New York, NY 10017
For more of your favorite series and novels, visit our website at www.pickapoppy.com

Poppy is an imprint of Little, Brown and Company.
The Poppy name and logo are trademarks of Hachette Book Group, Inc.

The publisher is not responsible for websites (or their content) that are not owned by the publisher.

First Edition: October 2012

Library of Congress Cataloging-in-Publication Data

Clayton, Colleen.
What happens next : a novel / by Colleen Clayton. — 1st ed.
p. cm.
Summary: The stress of hiding a horrific incident that she can neither remember nor completely forget leads sixteen-year-old Cassidy "Sid" Murphy to become alienated from her friends, obsess about weight loss, and draw close to Corey "the Living Stoner" Livingston.
ISBN 978-0-316-19868-4
[1. Interpersonal relations — Fiction. 2. Emotional problems — Fiction. 3. Eating disorders — Fiction. 4. Date rape — Fiction. 5. High schools — Fiction. 6. Schools — Fiction. 7. Family life — Ohio — Fiction.] I. Title.
PZ7.C57916Wh 2012   [Fic]—dc23   2012001554

10 9 8 7 6 5 4 3 2 1
RRD-C
Printed in the United States of America

For Mary

1

It's four in the morning and I'm sitting on my porch steps waiting for my friends. The streetlight casts a pale glow over my yard and I'm so exhausted that the snow is starting to shape-shift into an enormous feather bed and soft cotton sheets. I should go back inside where it's warm and wait by the window, but I'm more tired than I am cold, so I guess I'll just stay where I am, hunkered down like a frozen gargoyle.

I didn't fall asleep until almost two. I just laid there imagining Kirsten, Paige, and me on the slopes, ski bunnies on the rampage; no parents, hot guys everywhere. When the alarm went off, I didn't even hear it. My mom came in and shook me awake—*Get up already, jeez, it's all you've talked about for weeks*—then stalked back to her room like a zombie.

Finally they pull in. I grab my stuff and head toward the clownmobile that sits all candy-apple-red at the end of my driveway. It's a car designed specifically for amusement or torture. Clowns, contortion artists, and Kirsten Lee Vanderhoff—these are the people who buy MINI Coopers.

Paige has shotgun so I stuff all five-foot-nine of me into the cramped, but thankfully empty, backseat.

"Is there time for a nap?" I groan.

Paige tries to hand a cup of hot coffee and a paper bag back to me. I wrestle with my duffel, stuffing it into the tiny space next to me, and then take the coffee and bag from her.

"Rise and shine," Paige says, singsongy, "no naps allowed. The party has officially started."

Paige is bright-eyed and bushy-tailed as usual: makeup on, hair done, a whole raring-to-go-I'm-just-happy-to-be-alive look on her face.

"What's in the bag?" I ask, setting it on top of my duffel and taking a sip of the best coffee ever poured.

"Breakfast. A clementine and a muffin," Paige says.

Kirsten looks at me through the rearview mirror and says, "Compliments of Paige Daniels, Future Soccer Mom of America."

"Shut up, brat, or I'll tell your mom you're speeding again," Paige says.

"No, I'm not," Kirsten argues.

"Yes, you are," I say, "and there's a cop up ahead in the Malloy's parking lot so slow down."

"Shit," Kirsten says, pressing down on the brake too quickly.

Kirsten already has four points on her license. If she gets two more, her parents are going to dump her from the insurance and bury her keys in the yard till she's twenty. We pass the cop, all of us quiet and holding our breath, staring straight ahead like he can read our minds or something. He doesn't pull out when we pass him, so we relax and Kirsten turns on some music. Paige pulls out a wet nap from her purse and wipes off the coffee that slopped down her hand. The hot coffee and the music and my friends' stupidity—it all starts to work its magic and wake me up.

She'll deny it, but Paige loves being the Type A Goody Two-Shoes of our merry trio. She's always there to pick up the slack and remember the details. I mean, wet naps? Kirsten's right— Paige is going to make some six-year-old soccer star very happy someday. Some people find her tireless perk and nerdish tendencies a turnoff. Not me. I dig nerdy little Paige. Especially since I skipped breakfast and have a three-hour bus ride ahead of me. I bite into my muffin. Banana nut. Yum.

We get to the school lot, park the car, throw our bags onto the luggage heap, and climb aboard our assigned bus, which is freezing cold. I grab us a seat as far back from the PTA chaperones as possible, a few seats up from the Callahan brothers, who are sprawled out in the backseat like two kings. Sean's a junior and Devon's a senior and they're both on the wrestling team. They're pretty good-looking; not drop-dead-gorgeous-hand-me-a-towel-because-I'm-drooling kind of hot, but decent enough.

"Ladies, plenty of room back here," Sean says, patting his

legs and winking at Kirsten. Of the three of us, Kirsten usually gets the most guy attention. She's blond, and she has a nice body and a great smile. Paige is pretty cute, too. She's super tiny—about five feet tall and ninety pounds, like a little bookworm pixie. She only just got contacts last year, after spending the first fourteen sporting thick-rimmed goggles. It took Kirsten and me ambushing her in the mall and dragging her into LensCrafters to finally make her ditch them. Still, even without the goggles, she radiates this I-heart-Harry-Potter type of vibe—like the glasses disappeared from her face but resurfaced in her personality or something.

"Yeah, you'd like that, Sean," Kirsten says, smiling, "but, sorry. Older brother already beat ya to it."

"Oooh, burn," Devon says, laughing as he reaches over to punch his brother.

The Callahan boys are notorious in our town. There're eight of them altogether, and not a female among them, except for their mom. Kirsten hooked up with Patrick Callahan last year at his graduation party. The Callahan graduation parties are legendary keggers, and there's one practically every year.

"It's all good," Sean says, "there's always more brotherly love where that came from."

"Yeah, I'll bet," Kirsten says, rolling her eyes at Sean, then squeezing into the seat with Paige and me.

"Brothers comparing notes over the dinner table," I mumble, "that's what you need."

"Exactly," she says.

Paige is squashed between us like a loaf of bread. I could seriously put Paige on my lap and never even know she was there. Still, I move closer to the window to give her more room.

"What the hell, man, I can see my breath," Paige says, blowing out a stream of vapor. "There should be a law against this—child endangerment, inhumane traveling conditions—something."

The PTA chaperones start clapping their hands and barking orders, taking roll call, and passing out lift tickets. Then the bus takes off. After about twenty minutes, the heater finally kicks on, and before long the bus goes from meat locker-on-wheels to rolling crematorium. It becomes so suffocating and hot that the excitement and chatter cease altogether. By the time we cross the Ohio border and into Pennsylvania, everyone is sitting in roasted agony, staring into the thick, sweaty silence.

"I'm so hot, I think I feel cold," Paige says, gazing into the void, her voice limp, her hairline soaked.

I look up toward the front of the bus at the back of Mrs. Winthrop's head. She's the lead chaperone and gave everyone strict instructions not to open the windows. She's about two hundred fifty pounds and is sporting that *Kate Plus* 8-But-A-Bit-Too-Late hairstyle that went out ages ago, swinging that fringe like she invented it.

"That's it," I say. "I don't care what that PTA bitch said, I'm opening a window."

I lean up and slide down the pane and call out, "Opening up a window, Mrs. Winthrop. People are getting queasy back here."

Immediately, every window on the bus is snapped down and an audible wave of relief sweeps through the aisles. "Just till it cools down! And no throwing things out the window, not even gum! Arms and legs inside, people!" Mrs. Winthrop yells out to no one in particular

"Legs inside?" Kirsten groans. "Are we five?"

"Thank god we're not stuck in that woman's group," I say.

"Yep. Dodged a bullet there," Paige says. "Once we get to the lodge, we'll be under the not-so-watchful eye of Cougar Di."

Kirsten adds, "And then the fun can begin."

Cougar Di is Taylor Anderson's mom and the chaperone for our condo group. Her real name is Diane Mason but she also goes by The Former Mrs. Phil Anderson of Anderson's Custom Paint & Tile or The Former Mrs. Rick Sheffield of Sheffield & Zuckerman, Attorneys-at-Law. She's a navel-pierced, botoxed, gold-digging, career divorcée who thinks she's Taylor's hot big sister rather than her mom. The original Real Housewife of Cuyahoga County, and she's all ours for the weekend.

"Can you imagine being stuck in a condo with Mrs. Winthrop?" I say. "The Queen Bee Nazi of the PTA? It would ruin the whole trip."

"I heard a rumor she's brewing up some kind of game night at their place," Kirsten says. "She brought a slew of prehistoric board games—Parcheesi, backgammon—and she's setting up stations around the condo for some kind of weird relay."

"*Gak.* Poor Ellen," Paige says. "She's been stuck with that woman every day since birth. She must be mortified."

"Uh-huh," Kirsten mumbles, rifling through her coat pockets, then holding up a compact mirror and sliding on tinted lip balm. "These are the times when I'm actually grateful to be the by-product of upper-middle-class alcoholism."

She snaps her compact shut and smiles matter-of-factly.

"Doesn't count if it's expensive, right?"

I laugh, even though technically it's not funny because it's so completely true. Kirsten's parents spend their nights and weekends smashed on imported wine and Grey Goose martinis, fighting like two drunken pit bulls. I know it really bothers Kirsten about her parents, so I throw a bit of my own dirty laundry into the mix, spread around the misery, so she doesn't feel like a leper.

"I know what you mean; times like these, I'm happy I have a deadbeat dad. No time to chaperone when there's only one parent and she's busting her hump to feed the kiddies."

Paige sits uncomfortably quiet. I give her a playful shoulder shove.

"What's your excuse, Miss Perfect?"

"Yeah," Kirsten adds, bumping her shoulder against Paige, too. "Where are your parents in all this? Judge and Delores are always looking to bust up your good time."

Paige shrugs, halfheartedly trying to defend her paranoid, overbearing parents. "They're not that bad."

Kirsten looks at me with her eyebrows raised. Maybe Judge and Delores have decided to loosen the apron strings?

A moment of silence passes. Then Paige comes clean: "Bible retreat in Columbus or they'd totally be here—Parcheesi and backgammon in tow."

We all bust out laughing. Then we settle in and relax quietly inside of our friendship, safe in the knowledge that when it comes to the family ideal, all three of us got screwed.

2

We arrive at the resort around eight a.m. Our condo has direct slope access. Just walk out the back door, slap on your skis, and slide downhill. We hit the powder at eight thirty sharp, and by eight thirty-one, it is apparent to all who witness the carnage that I suck entirely.

Usually I'm more athletic than either Kirsten or Paige, but apparently skiing is not my forte. Three hundred bucks down the drain. Kirsten's parents, despite being high-functioning alcoholics, make decent bank. Paige's family is also fairly well off, so it's not a big deal for them to spend three hundred dollars. I had to beg my broke-ass mother to let me join the ski club this year, and all I got for Christmas was a homemade gift certificate wrapped in a neck warmer: *SKI CLUB MEMBERSHIP WORTH 300 CLAMS. NO REFUNDS.*

Kirsten and Paige push me to the bunny hill and work patiently alongside me for two hours, instructing me on various novice techniques that go by precious names like "making pizza slices" and "cooking French fries." None of their hard work and patience is paying off. For the hundredth time, I unscrew my limbs, dust myself off, and look up at my friends' faces.

"It was better, I swear," Kirsten says, helping me up.

"Right." I say. "Face it, I'm a ski bunny reject. A ski-ject."

"But you stayed up a whole six seconds that time!" Paige says, nodding her head up and down, beaming a little too enthusiastically.

They're trying hard to be nice but I know it isn't fair. They'd be doing some world-class skiing right now if it weren't for me. Zigzagging down black-diamond runs with menacing names like CPR Gully and Body Bag Drop-Off.

"Why don't you guys go on ahead?" I offer. "I'll be okay here on the bunny hill."

"What? No, it's fine. You're getting the hang of it! Really!" Kirsten says.

I look at her flatly.

"Uh, Kirsten, I don't know if you've noticed, but we've been here for two hours. For two solid hours, every trip down that tiny lump of hill has ended with me tumbling into a crumpled heap at the bottom. You guys paid good money to be here and shouldn't be stuck babysitting the ski-impaired all day."

Paige's smile disappears. "But you'll be all alone."

"There are other kids from school here," I say. "I do have other friends besides you two." I look around for a familiar face. "Look," I say, pointing over toward the lift line at a group of snotty girls from school. "My fellow cheerleaders are right over there, just waiting to welcome me into the fold."

Starsha Lexington, Amber Franks, and the rest of the squad are huddled together like a package of pink marshmallows. They see me pointing at them, scowl, and then turn into themselves to whisper. They're probably sending up prayers to the Barbie gods in hopes that I break my legs so Cameron Fitzpatrick can finally be restored to her rightful place on the squad—the place that I callously snatched out from under her last year when I had the unmitigated gall to try out for cheerleading.

"You get onto that ski lift with Starsha," Kirsten says, "you better chain yourself to the seat, sister. Otherwise you're goin' down. *All* the way down."

We laugh, but I still feel like a ski bunny reject holding back her two best friends, who've been skiing since they were in diapers.

"Seriously, guys," I say, "I need a break anyway. I'll go to the lodge and get a hot cocoa or something. I'll find someone to hang with. I'll text you later for lunch or something."

"Are you sure?" they say.

"Yes! Now go! Have fun!"

I shoo them away from me and they slide effortlessly off toward the black-diamond runs. As I watch them disappear around a thicket of trees, I think about how excruciatingly long this weekend just became.

I don't go for hot cocoa.

I dig my heels in, determined to get it done.

I've been called a lot of things in my life—fat, obnoxious, snarky—but never a quitter. I work hard at the bunny hill, and after about an hour, my body starts cooperating a bit. I do finally start to get the hang of it. I think the pressure of being watched and critiqued was affecting my confidence. I head toward the intermediate runs, skipping the easy trails altogether. Unless I plan to spend the next two days alone, I need to step it up.

Sweaty and nervous, I get into the lift line at Snowshoe Dip. I look around at people and notice a hot specimen in the crowd. Is he staring at me?

Snowboarding tweens to the left.

Geezers to the right.

Yes.

I'm pretty sure he is staring at me.

I take off my gloves and casually run my hand over my face, sure that I have something disgusting smeared across it. The slopes are packed and the grouchy crone running the crowded lift shouts out for single skiers, pairing people up if they're alone. Staring Hot Guy bustles through the crowd and plants himself next to me.

"Hey there, how's it going?" he says, smiling directly at me, beaming with that self-confidence that only the truly gorgeous or truly disturbed seem to possess. I force an awkward smile before looking down at my skis.

Our turn is up. We both stumble forward, shuffling like mad to beat the bench that is fast approaching our rear. Staring Hot

Guy grabs my arm and nearly sends us both crashing to the ground but then right at the last second, the seat clips the backs of our knees and scoops us up in a tangle of skis and poles. He starts laughing, which makes me laugh, too. *Ho! Ho! Ho!* We are both laughing away, hanging on for dear life, up, up, and away we go, just the two of us, suspended in midair for the next ten minutes.

When we settle into the seat, he pulls down the safety bar, leans in, and flashes his Colgate smile. "Apologies. I don't usually maul unsuspecting females in public. I'm new to this skiing bit."

"Don't worry," I say. "I stink, too."

"Dax Windsor. I'd shake your hand but I'm afraid I'll lose a glove or a pole."

He looks below us at the snowy ground, which is getting farther and farther away.

"Cassidy Murphy. Or... um, Sid."

"Nice to meet you, Cassidy Murphy."

I say his name in my head. *Dax Windsor.* It is beyond a doubt the coolest name I've ever heard in real life. He proceeds to talk my ear off the whole way up. Not that I mind this, of course, because, well, did I mention that he's hot? ·

"So, where you from, Sid? No, wait, let me guess. I can already tell you're a Midwesterner, but if you answer *three* questions then I'll tell you within one hundred miles where you're from."

"Oh, like what's the capital of your state or who's your congressman?" I say with friendly sarcasm. Not that I would know the answer to that second question if he *did* ask it.

"No, not ones that are dead giveaways. General questions about what you call things and how you say things. I'm taking a course on shedding accents and perfecting the non-regional American dialect. I'm studying broadcasting at Central U. I can pinpoint accents and vernacular down to under a hundred miles."

"Okay. Shoot."

Then, slow and deliberate, he asks, "What do you call a carbonated beverage that comes in a can?"

"Pop."

"Okay, you're from western Pennsylvania, Ohio, Indiana, Illinois, Wisconsin, or Michigan."

"But which one? That's a lot of territory you're covering there."

"Oh, you don't think I can do it?"

"No, it's not that, I'm just saying that you—" The more I talk, the more I am giving him information, so I cut myself off, zip my mouth shut, and pretend to throw the key over the side of the bench.

"Oh, a wiseass. All right. Number two: Is it a drinking fountain, water fountain, or bubbler?"

Bubbler? What the hell is a bubbler? And my confused expression gives me away.

"Cross out Wisconsin," he says smugly. "So which is it? Water fountain or drinking fountain?"

"Water fountain."

"Okay, I already know the answer from the way you said water, but I'll go ahead with the last question. Shits and giggles."

"Well, if you already know the answer, then tell me where I'm from, smart guy."

"But then the fun is over, and I want to hear you say it."

"Say what?"

"The answer to the last question."

I mull this over for a second.

"Okay, I know," I say. "Write it down ahead of time, and when I answer the question, we'll see if you're right."

I hand him my poles, reach into my pocket, and pull out a tiny pencil that I accidentally filched when I was filling out my ski rental forms. Then I fish around for some paper until I find a piece in my snow pants.

"Okay, here. Write it on the back of this receipt," I instruct, handing him the pencil and paper.

I hold his poles while he writes his guess down.

"So what if I guess correctly after only two questions? Do I win something?" he asks.

"You win the satisfaction of knowing you are Master of the Universal Accent or whatever you called it. Anchor of the Year!"

"Nah, that's not good enough. I want you to promise to come to a party."

My heart jumps.

"A party?"

"Yeah. At my roommate's uncle's condo tomorrow night. We

have this dinner thing tonight, but Tony's uncle's leaving in the morning. My roommates and I are planning the mother of all blowouts. Bring your friends, roomies, sisters, whatever. So long as it's female and at least *half* as gorgeous as you." Then he bumps his knee against mine, grins, and says, "Just kidding. You can bring your ugly friends, too."

"Ha, ha," I say dryly, but on the inside I'm jumping up and down, screaming, *Hooray!*

"No, for real, if I guess right, you have to come."

He looks at me and he is not joking. It's a real invite. I start to get panicky as my mind races in circles. A party? I just met this guy. He's in college. He looks like he's in his twenties. He said "roomies," so he thinks I'm in college, too. Holy crap! Somebody pinch me. What do I do? Do I tell him how old I am? That I'm a sixteen-year-old junior who rode in on a big yellow bus with the rest of the ski club from Lakewood High? That I have a curfew and if I'm caught breaking it, it means deep shit trouble and a guaranteed suspension? How do I politely decline without looking like a toddler freak? Did I mention that he is hot?

"Okay, deal."

And I say it, not having the slightest clue how I will go about *honoring* said deal if I lose the bet. I guess I'm hoping deep down that he'll guess Pittsburgh or Detroit and I'll be off the hook.

"Cool. All right, here we go. Ready?"

"Ready."

"And no cheating by throwing in a fake British accent or something."

I nod.

"Okay. What does C-A-N-D-Y spell?"

"Candy," I say, biting down on that first syllable to where it sounds like *Kyandy*.

I am trying to fool him into guessing Chicago.

He flips over the receipt. It says, *Cleveland Rocks!!!*

"You're good," I say, looking at him wide-eyed.

"Yep, all that from the way you said one little word. *Candy?*" he says smoothly while pulling out a half roll of Life Savers, offering me one.

My favorite flavor peeks out the unwrapped end. Lime green. He takes the next one, cherry red, and pops it into his mouth.

"Two-twelve Snowbird Trail. Be there by nine, little girl."

My stomach leaps when he calls me "little girl." My heart hammers away inside my chest as I look out at the snowy mountain passing below us. I say nothing for the next few seconds as I ponder my unanticipated situation. This is the best-looking guy I have ever seen up close and he is interested in *me*—goofy, loudmouthed Sid Murphy, with my crazy red hair, bubble butt, and obnoxious laugh. The busty cheerleader who was put on the squad solely to hold up bony-ass princesses like Starsha Lexington and Amber Franks. Always stuck at the bottom of the pyramid while the *real* cheerleaders dive gracefully from the top like size-zero Christmas stars, right into the arms of good old dependable Sid. I mean, I'm not the girl who reels in the big fish. I'm the funny sidekick who gets the leftovers. I'm Sid Murphy: Designated Driver, Best Friend, and eternal Wingman.

"Okay. I'll be there," I say.

Dax leans in, smiles mysteriously, and raises one eyebrow. "You'd better come. Remember, I know where you live."

It's during the lean-in that I smell it—liquor mixed with cherry Life Saver.

"Oh, my god! Have you been drinking?" I ask, laughing.

He scrunches up one eye, makes a pinchy "little bit" motion with his fingers, and then puts a forefinger to his lips.

"Shhhhh. Don't tell the snow patrol."

I look behind me at the mountain below. We aren't on the wussy hills anymore. It's a long, long, steep way down.

I turn back to him.

"Are you crazy?"

"Certifiable," he says, then pulls out a flask from his coat pocket, twists off the cap, and takes a long pull of what I can only assume to be hard liquor.

"You're gonna kill yourself."

"Liquid courage, baby," he says, wincing as he swallows another mouthful. "Whooo. That's the stuff."

He holds the flask out to me.

"Wanna lil' nip?"

"No! I can't be skiing drunk! I'd be maimed!" I say playfully, turning my blushing face away from him to hide my shock.

I look over at the top of the forest passing next to me. Some free spirit had removed her bra and tossed it up into the top branches of a giant pine tree. Seventy feet in the air, it clings there, frozen stiff, for the world to see.

He continues to work on me.

"Come on. It'll relax you, improve your game. We'll be doing double diamonds by noon."

I eye him suspiciously, then look down at his flask, then back up at his face.

God, that face.

I cave, take the flask and rock back a tiny sip, and start coughing as the fiery liquid lights up my pipes.

"What is that? Gasoline?" I sputter, handing the flask back.

"Gasoline? I *beg* your pardon," he says, slapping me on the back a few times, and then takes another long drink before putting it away.

Neither of us has realized that the end of the line is fast approaching until the guy running the top of the lift leans out of his control booth and screams, "Lift up your bar already! Jesus!"

As Dax lifts the safety bar and readies his poles, he says, "That's High Glen single malt scotch you're drinking, aged fifteen years, little missy."

Little. Missy. Double. Stomach leap.

And with that, he jumps off the lift and slides effortlessly down and around the operator's booth. I stumble off and come to a ragged stop at the top of the mountain.

"Otherwise known as liquid courage!" he yells, and takes off down the hill at top speed howling, "Yeeeee-haaaww!"

We spend the whole day together skiing and falling and laughing our asses off. I text the girls and tell them to have lunch without me, that I've met someone.

They text back: **Where r u? We want 2 meet him!**

I turn off my phone and go have lunch with Dax. If they come, they'll ruin things by mentioning high school and asking him his age. I know I should ask him myself, but the stupid, selfish part of me doesn't want to know. The stupid, selfish part of me doesn't care how old Dax Windsor is because, well, I'm having fun with a hot guy for once in my life and screw it, I don't wanna know.

I mean...he's probably not that much older.

He buys me a Coke and a burger and we split a tray of chili-cheese fries at this ski-in cafeteria place. We talk about his classes and his dickhead roommates and my friends and books we've read, shows we like. I keep my end of it all very vague and noncommittal so he can't pin me down to anything age-related.

Around five, it starts getting darker, and I can no longer avoid the fact that I am, indeed, not on a dream vacation with Dax Windsor, Sexiest Man Alive, but on a ski trip with my stupid high school. I need to check in or they'll send the fun-sucking PTA mom-patrol out hunting for me.

Dax makes me promise again to come to his party the next night. He gives me a sweet little peck on the cheek—quick, like he's almost embarrassed—and then he skis away, saying, "Nine o'clock. Remember, I know where you live!"

I text the girls and head back to the condo.

3

It's Saturday evening, and despite my best efforts, I have had zero luck talking Kirsten and Paige into sneaking out with me for the party. I tried to enjoy the day skiing with them, suffered through black-diamond runs, and nearly broke every bone in my body to get on their good sides. I kept looking for Dax on the slopes, thinking that maybe if the girls actually met him, he could charm them into coming. But it's a big resort, and if you don't know where to look, it's impossible to find someone.

It's dinnertime and I have severe butterflies. I can barely eat. This is a shame, because the buffet in the main lodge looks and smells like some kind of cinematic food mirage: a sprawling wonderland of animal-shaped breads; a three-tiered fountain of rippling chocolate; a team of smiling, puffy-hatted chef-people carving up juicy slabs of roast beef; and smack dab in the middle of everything is a revolving ice sculpture of a giant Yeti on skis. It's a culinary opus, indeed.

Yet none of it appeals to me. I load up my plate and pick, pick, pick, pretending to be interested in Kirsten and Paige's conversation about some boys we go to school with who are staying in another condo, but all I can think about is Dax and the party. I push the food around on my plate and think about how blue his eyes are. After a while, a roll of bread shaped like a headless bear comes waddling onto my plate.

"Hello there, Sid. Have you seen my head? It was just here a minute ago..."

Kirsten is trying to make me laugh. I force a smile.

"All right, seriously," she says, irritated, tossing the headless bear onto her plate. "You said he goes to college in New York. So let's just forget for a moment that Mr. Perfect lives two states away. I mean, you don't even know the guy. Plus, he's old. He's probably married with, like, fifty kids."

"He's not old-old," I say. "He's in college. And please, like you should talk. Uh...Patrick Callahan?"

"Right. I hooked up with Pat when he'd just graduated and I was a sophomore. He's two years older and I've known him since elementary school. Your college man is a total stranger. I mean, you look older than sixteen, I'll give you that, but you're still just sixteen. Your mom's cool, but she's not that cool."

Paige comes walking back from one of her numerous trips up to the five-star feeding trough. She has a tapeworm, I swear. Also, she doesn't like a messy plate, so she only picks out about two or three items at a time. All her food is sectioned off into neat symmetrical piles on her plate. As she sits down, she catches only the last bit of conversation but instantly knows what we're talking about. She shakes out her napkin and lays it gently on her lap.

"She's right, Sid. Sorry. A college guy? Katherine would freak."

"Uh, yah. And I mean completely out," Kirsten adds, piercing a grape tomato with her fork and sliding it into her mouth.

I hate to admit it, but they're right. My mom might let me date a college freshman, but Dax looks older than that. Twenty at least. But I don't care. And…well…maybe he's not in his twenties. Maybe he's like me. Maybe he just looks older than he really is. Kirsten spreads some butter onto her headless bear and keeps on talking.

"There are a ton of guys here from school. Go for Rafe Summers or Joey Thacker. Both are single and conveniently still in high school."

I glare at her.

"Oh, yes, that's it, Rafe Summers and Joey Thacker. I'll just call them right up." I reach dramatically into the coat hanging on the back of my chair and pull out my cell. I start banging away at random numbers, concentrating extra hard.

"What's old Rafey's number again? Oh, hello there! Is this Rafe Summers? The guy who pushed me off the slide in fourth grade? Split both my knees open?"

I punch in some more numbers. "Joey! Baby! Cassidy Murphy. You know, *Sid*. The girl you called the Amazon Leprechaun every day of middle school?"

I shoot Kirsten the dirty eyeball. "...Along with every awful name he and his friends could think up that contained the word *tit*."

I slam the phone down on the table. "Yes, let me just give them a shout. I'm sure they'll be thrilled to hear from Tits McGee, or Murphy McTitties, or Siddy-Siddy-Big-Fat-Titty."

Paige starts choking on her applesauce, trying not to laugh.

"Oh, please, that was ages ago," Kirsten argues, also trying not to laugh. "And they gave you shit back then because none of them had ever seen an actual live girl-boob yet. And everyone knows redheads are sitting ducks when they're young. But when guys grow up, they think redheads are hot. Especially ones with big racks."

"Thank you, Miss Beauty 101," I say, settling back into my chair and folding my arms over my ample chest. Then I gesture toward her with my hand. "Oh, please. Do go on. I'm learning so many new and insightful things about myself."

"Sorry, but she's got a point," Paige says. "You know we love your crazy red hair, but a redheaded middle schooler with big boobs? Might as well have a target tattooed on your forehead. And since your hair is curly, you were triple-screwed." Then she shrugs. "But guys grow out of that stuff. Eventually, they learn to appreciate the rarer breeds—girls who look different from everyone else."

I'm seriously going to knock their heads together. It's like they've ripped a page from my mother's Puberty Pep Talk Manual and are reading it word for word. Katherine would be so proud. I sigh and look down at my food while they continue to diagnose my sickly excuse of a love life. The puddle of gravy in my volcano of mashed potatoes is starting to form a skin.

"Also," Paige says, "I think it was because you were taller than every boy in the state of Ohio. It made them feel like you could beat them up or something. Emasculating. That means—"

"I know what it means!"

"Anyway, they've caught up with you now." Then she pauses, scrunches her nose a little. "Well, Rafe has, anyway."

That's it, I've heard enough. I stab my fork into a piece of prime rib, pick up my knife, and start sawing at it like it's a fallen tree branch.

Kirsten gives me a teasing shove to the head. "Come on, lighten up already."

I shove the beef into my mouth and carry on talking with my mouth full. I don't care if it's piggish. No boys here like me anyway.

"Height, boobs, hair? Those are the least of my worries," I say, pointing my fork toward my backside. "Presently, it's the ass that's the problem. No teenage boy wants to date a girl with a fatter ass than his."

"Hold on, girlie. You are not fat," Paige says. "You're voluptuous. Stacked. I mean, if you're fat, then Scarlett Johansson's a beast. Yeah, you're built big, but in a good way. Hourglassy. Like a fifties pinup girl or that plus-size girl who placed third in *America's Next Top Model*. Oh! Or that chick with the blue hair on *Dark Realms*. She's totally hot."

I look at her like she's crazy. "Who?"

She stutters, "You know, on, um, Syfy. Velandra, I think her name is? Or Selandra...something like that. You have her eyes, come to think of it. Big, green, witchy Medusa eyes. Only *her* eyes have the power to bewilder. She can stun you into a life of endless stupidity with just one—" She stops, stumbles, and starts walking it back.

"—I mean, I've only seen it once or twice while babysitting the Newman kids. They're really into it." And suddenly, she has become deeply interested in removing the lip gloss smudge on her water glass.

I smile.

"Uh-huh. Just blew your cover, gamer girl," I say.

"For like the millionth time," Kirsten adds, laughing.

"I'm not a gamer!" Paige barks.

"Please, gamer," I say. "Come out of your gamer closet already. Coast is clear. Nobody cares."

"Oh, I can name two people who'd care," Kirsten says. "Judge and Delores might call in an exorcist if they found her stash of fantasy novels. They'd chain her to the bed and chant, *Out, demons! I compel you!* until her head started spinning."

I can't help laughing. It's true; Paige's parents think fantasy novels and role-playing games are some kind of gateway to devil worship. Like pretending you're a wizard or fairy will turn you crazy in the head, and after too much exposure you'll be drinking your own blood and stabbing cats with jeweled daggers. They think Halloween is the devil's birthday and don't have cable for fear of the fantastical creatures that might come charging out of the TV screen—vampires, witches, clairvoyant teens who commune with the dead. Even superheroes and talking Disney animals are suspect.

Paige's eyes flatten into a glare. Her jaw tightens and she lets out a dramatic, irritated nose-sigh. She's trying to appear mad, but she knows that exorcist comment was funny. She'll laugh about it later.

I pat Paige on the knee and try to get her to break. With a wicked grin I whisper, "Don't worry, gamer girl, your secret's safe with us."

"Oooh, burn," Kirsten says, diving into a big bite of potatoes and laughing even harder.

Paige wipes her mouth in a huff, crumples her napkin, and throws it on the table.

She leans toward Kirsten. "I'm sorry, but how did we start talking about this, again? Oh, I remember. We were talking about Sid's unique ability to repel even the most idiotic of teenage boys."

Kirsten slaps the table. "Oooh, double burn. Good one, P."

"Yeah," I say, tearing a piece of bread off with my teeth. "But then we switched topics to your unique ability to attract half-orc magic users."

Paige's eyes narrow even more; she's starting to get mad for real. And I'm starting to get vicious for real. But I can't help it—it makes me feel better, pointing out someone else's freakishness.

"Okay, let's not fight," Kirsten says. "We're all friends here, remember?"

We sit and sulk for a minute. Finally, I speak.

"Sorry, runt," I mumble. "You know I love ya. Even if you're a closet gamer."

"Me too," she mumbles back. "Even if you're a Siddy-Siddy-Big-Fat-Titty."

We all start laughing and I eventually have to cover up my big, obnoxious mouth with my hand. It's pretty fancy in here, and our classmates at other tables are shooting me dirty looks.

"Okay. Seriously, let's think," Kirsten says. "Who do we know who is a) available or b) willing to cheat on and then dump their girlfriend for Sid?"

"Uh, nobody. Trust me," I say, picking up my water goblet and taking a swig. "I've scoured the yearbook quite thoroughly."

And that's the suck-ass truth of it. The only males who have ever shown interest in me were and are, like Dax Windsor, older. A problem since age eleven. Yes, you heard me, eleven. The summer I turned eleven, I was attacked by mutant hormones. They invaded my body and sent all the baby fat in my belly, limbs, and face screaming directly into my boobs, hips, and ass. I filled out so fast, I actually got stretch marks. The boys my own age either dove for cover or sat around thinking up funny tit names to call me. But I'd get all kinds of lusty looks from older guys—teachers, coaches, neighbors, old farts in grocery stores. As if the height and hair weren't enough? It was humiliating shopping for a C cup in the sixth grade, and then a double D by eighth.

Kirsten finally gets it that I'm stuck on Dax and won't be moving an inch toward her line of thinking.

"All right, if you're so crazy about this Dexter guy—"

"Dax!"

"Dax...then why didn't you get his cell number? That way you could've met up with him today instead of sneaking out after curfew."

"Because his cell won't pick up a signal here so he didn't bother bringing it." I pick my cell up and wave it around. "We're in the mountains, Kirsten. I'm working off one bar over here, two if I stand on one leg and hold it over my head. Your cell shits out every time you try to call home. So if I don't show up tonight, Dax Windsor is nothing more than a distant memory. I'll never see him again."

"Well, you can Facebook him when you get home," she says, digging into her mashed potatoes with finality. "Because no way are you going to some frat party after curfew alone. I'll hog-tie you and sit on you all night if I have to."

Screw it, I give up. They aren't going and I'm too chicken to go alone, so that's the end of it. I push my plate away, get up, and skulk over to the dessert bar. I start piling it on higher than Snow Ridge Mountain.

~

Dinner ends and everyone goes back to the condos. After a while, Cougar Di becomes so engrossed in gossiping with her daughter's friends and playing the role of Cool Mom that she is completely unaware of the illegal behavior going on around her—oblivious to the cooler of beer hidden in the woods out back and the fact that couples are making out in every corner of the house.

I grab a pop from the fridge and head toward the basement. I open the wrong door, the door to a pantry, and interrupt a couple of lovebirds in the early stages of molesting one another.

"God. Creep much, Ginger Bitch?" the girl says, yanking her top down.

It's my fellow cheerleader and archnemesis, Starsha Lexington. Ginger Bitch is her favorite name for me these days.

Oh, how Starsha Lexington hates me. And not just because I bumped Cameron Fitzpatrick from the cheerleading squad. Starsha's hatred of me dates back to the first week of kindergarten, when I was playing Food Channel Hostess in the play kitchen. I must have looked like I was having too good of a time, because she tried to take over my cooking show, and when I wouldn't let her, she grabbed me by the hair. I grabbed her back and we went careening into the toy refrigerator, all the fake plastic vegetables and dishes spilling everywhere. We both started crying, were sent to opposing time-out corners, and glowered at each other from across the room.

Not much has changed. Starsha glowers at me and I glower back. She and Tate have lipstick smeared all over their mouths and chins.

"Eck, gross," I mumble, and shut the door.

I get to the basement and survey the landscape. Misery sets in when I realize how my night's going to play out from here. Some senior boys are shooting pool and playing foosball in the lower rec room while a gaggle of junior girls, Kirsten and Paige included, buzz around them like bees at a honey pot. I slump into a papasan chair and sulk.

I think about the Puberty Pep Talks—what my mom and Kirsten and Paige say about older guys appreciating girls who look different, fair-skinned redheads with curly hair. Big, tall, busty girls with meat on their bones.

I look around the basement again. At all the boys who love all the girls with their perfectly straight, flatironed blond and brunette hair and perfectly proportioned bodies. Whatever maturity switch that is supposed to go off in boys' brains about dating "the rarer breeds" has definitely not kicked in yet. While most boys are pretty nice to me in general now, none of them look at me in that attracted kind of way. Not the way Dax looked at me yesterday.

As nine o'clock looms nearer, I get more and more anxious and more and more disgusted with the people around me. By ten after nine, an over-the-shoulder demon has popped out and is full-throttle duking it out with her angel counterpart on the other side.

Go to the party!

No, you can't!

Go to the party!

But you musn't!

The evil side of me steps it up. The demon says, *It's nine fifteen and you're still sittin' here? Go big or go home, already.*

And that's all I need. When I see that Kirsten and Paige are fully distracted, I slip back upstairs, grab my coat, and sneak out a side door. Off I go, into the night, to find my Prince Charming.

After about ten minutes of walking, my phone starts popping

off like the Fourth of July. Kirsten and Paige are texting the hell out of me.

U get back here!

Im going 2 kill u!

Sid 4 real

pleez? :)

Then, finally: **ur a Br@ dont b 2 L8 xxoo K & Pg**

I text Kirsten back: **Unlock the back door 4 me <3 u guys xxoo Sid**

When I finally find Snowbird Trail, it's already nine thirty, but I can see from a distance that something is off. No loud music, no cars. No sign with a big arrow and the words COLLEGE PARTY THIS WAY! It is just a dark, quiet condo, nestled among some trees with other dark, quiet condos.

Then it hits me.

I've screwed up the address.

Or, even worse, I've fallen for the classic fake-out. Only instead of a fake phone number, I got an entire fake invite and fake address. I turn around to go back, my dreams dashed, when I hear someone calling to me. It's him.

"Hey, stranger! I thought you were blowing me off!"

I smile widely in the darkness. Blow this Adonis dreamboat off? Not a chance.

I make my way down the walkway and up the front steps and sit down next to him—not too close, not too far—on a wooden porch swing.

"Nah, dinner ran late, and I had trouble finding it," I say.

All the moisture in my mouth funnels directly down into my palms. It's twenty-nine degrees outside, and my exposed hands are dripping with sweat. I put them in my pockets before the sweat starts hardening into sweat-cicles.

"So what happened to the party? Where is everyone?" I ask.

"Ah, my friend's uncle's flight got canceled because of the snow in Denver and he ended up staying here an extra night. We had to shit-can it. They went to The Owl's Nest for a drink. You want to go meet them?"

He wants to go for a drink. At a bar. Well, he's not nineteen or twenty. And I'm not even old enough for an R movie yet, sooo...

"No, I probably should just get back then."

Damn. What a bust.

"Well, come in for a little. We can hang out—watch a movie or something lame like that."

Ugh. It's time to end the charade. It's not fair to lie anymore, pretend to be something I'm not.

"Um, look," I say, sighing. "I should probably tell you something. I probably should have told you yesterday, but, I don't know, I just didn't. Anyhow—"

I pause and look at his stunning face one last time before breaking the news. He has the bluest eyes.

"What?" he says.

I open my mouth and try to speak, but can't.

"Hey, you're scaring me," he says. "Are you an escaped convict? A serial killer or something?"

I laugh weakly.

"No, I'm not a serial killer. Not that I know of, anyway."

"Then it can't be that bad."

I shift in my seat and then finally blurt it out: "I'm only sixteen. I'm in high school."

I bite my lower lip and looked up timidly through a spiral of hair. He says nothing for what seems like a long time.

"Is that it?"

"Yeah. But I'll be seventeen in July," I offer.

He looks at me a second longer and then busts out laughing. I sigh. His laughter is a good sign. At least he doesn't hate me for deceiving him. Even if he tells me to get lost, it's a relief to get it over with.

"But it's just a couple of years, that's nothing," he says, laughing.

He's only eighteen, maybe a young nineteen.

I laugh out loud. Really hard. I cover my mouth and try to stifle the Incomparable Sid Murphy Cackling Guffaw.

Then I stop short.

"But the bar? I mean, if you're only nineteen—"

"Almost nineteen," he says, raising a finger. "Never heard of a fake ID?"

Duh, Sid.

"Ahhhh. The fake ID," I say.

Whew. Okay, just two years. This is good. Great, even. God, what a load off. He gets up and opens the front door, stretching an arm out for me to go in.

"Walk into my parlor, mademoiselle. I think *Law & Order* is about to start."

And then he finally remarks on my hair. He didn't mention

it in all the hours that we spent skiing together. He doesn't give me the compliment directly but says it in kind of a way that comes across as thinking out loud. While I am walking past him, he gently takes a coil of my hair between his thumb and finger and when it is stretched to the limit, he releases it, and back it springs.

"Man. Spectacular," he says. "These things, they go on forever."

And in I go.

The love of my young life following behind me.

4

I sit bolt upright, startled with that feeling of being displaced. I should be looking at a poster of Paul McCartney in his twenties or a framed picture of me, my mom, and my little brother fishing off Kelleys Island. Instead, I am staring at an unfamiliar painting of a winter scene. A giant buck with thorny antlers looks down on me with caramel-yellow eyes.

I look around, disoriented.

I'm in someone's bedroom, in someone's bed, and I don't know how I got here. Then I remember and it all comes crashing down in a thousand jagged pieces. I jerk back the covers, relieved to see that all of my clothes are still on. The clock on the nightstand says seven a.m. The bus leaves in an hour.

I call out, my throat dry, my voice cracking.

"Dax?"

No answer.

When I try to get up, a sharp pain blooms behind my left eye and spreads over my head. I can't feel anything from the neck down because the pain is so severe it leaves the rest of me numb. I stumble out of the bedroom, into an alcove, and make my way down a small winding staircase. At the bottom of the steps, I call out to him again. Still no answer.

My coat hangs over a hook near the front door where my boots are sitting, lined up perfectly, right where I left them last night. I pull them on and open the door. It's still dark out, but the sky is brightening in the east.

As I walk, my phone buzzes inside my coat pocket, then beeps with a low battery alert. Kirsten has filled my inbox with texts and messages, but my phone dies before I can call her back. I hurry through lanes that all look the same, all gingerbread houses, row after row.

I finally locate the correct condo; I can tell it's the right one by the police cruiser sitting out front. I sneak around to try the side door. Locked. As I turn to sneak around to the back entry, the door swings open. Cougar Di stands before me, hands on her hips, eyes on fire. A burly police officer steps up behind her. He sees me and his eyes move up a tick, taking in the giant nest of red curls, which I am sure are sticking out in all directions, lending me the appearance of a giant cracked-out Little Orphan Annie.

Diane says through gritted teeth, "Girlfriend, you're in big trouble."

When I walk into the condo, Kirsten and Paige are sitting on the couch in the living room. Their faces are sunken and swollen at the same time. When Kirsten sees me she cries out with this strangled sigh of relief, a sort of whimper that's been knotted up in dread. Paige bursts into tears and they both run over and grab me into a hug. Neither of them can speak because they're sobbing so hard.

I should comfort them, tell them something to stop their tears, but I don't know what to say. And what's worse, I don't hug them back; my arms just hang limp at my sides. I don't know what's happened or what's happening, and I can't think straight. My head is throbbing so hard I can actually hear it. Like two bass drums, my brain pounds against the insides of my ears. Kirsten and Paige's sobbing and clinging won't settle into me the right way; their distress and relief at seeing me won't go into my heart and mind the way they're supposed to. I'm queasy and hot and smothered and I think I might faint or throw up or explode if I don't get out from under their suffocating embrace. They feel my resistance. I'm not exactly pushing them off me, but my body language is clear. They ease away at the same time.

"Where were you? What happened? Why didn't you call?" Kirsten says, wiping her eyes and nose on her sleeve. "We called you all night *long*!"

On that last word, her voice changes, the fear and dread replaced by something else. I see it in her face, too. In a split second, her expression goes from weeping and frenzied into an expression completely unflinching in its resolve.

Kirsten wants answers.

And I don't have any.

I look away, turn my focus to Paige. She's wiping her face, too. And her eyes, while not quite as determined as Kirsten's, are also filled with immediacy, a need for answers.

"Are you okay?" Paige asks. "What happened?"

I start to say "I don't know" but am cut off by PTA Nazi Mom, who comes barreling over.

"Yes. What happened? Where were you, Sid? The girls said you went to meet some boy. You went to a party. Is that true? Are you okay? You look hungover. Were you drinking?"

"I—yeah. I mean, no. I didn't drink. I went to—I met this—" but I'm cut off again when the officer butts in.

"I'll need you to make a formal statement about this."

"Okay, girls, go to the bus," Mrs. Winthrop says, ushering Kirsten and Paige toward the door.

Mrs. Winthrop yells out, "Everybody! On the bus, we're running late!" then turns back to me and says, "Sid, come sit down in the kitchen so we can get to the bottom of this."

I sit at the kitchen table, facing Mrs. Winthrop, Cougar Di, and the officer. Tate Andrews and Hunter Brady walk by with a group of guys, all of them carrying skis and luggage.

"Rock on, Sister Red! Didja get laid?" Tate calls out.

"Boys!" Mrs. Winthrop barks.

They laugh and funnel out the front door with the rest of the kids.

Someone has already packed my stuff. My bag is sitting on the table and I'm being chewed out like I've killed someone. I nod, but I can't absorb what Mrs. Winthrop is saying—the throbbing in my skull is too loud. Am I dreaming this? I think my head is going to blow off my neck.

"We finally got the truth out of Paige and Kirsten about a half hour ago when Diane did a head count for the bus. A party? You know that is completely reckless. Do you have any idea what could have happened? You're lucky you're not dead. We were so worried, and your mother is absolutely beside herself. She's actually on her way here."

My mom. Oh, Jesus.

They call my mom and let me talk to her for a minute. Her voice is all keyed up, and my dead grandmother's thick Irish brogue is surfacing. My mom was born here, in America, but her parents were from Dublin, so when she gets upset, her voice takes on this hint of an accent. I do my best to calm her down. She's literally about to fall apart with terror and relief and anger and whatever else a panic-stricken mother feels when she gets a phone call from her missing child. I do the: *Yes, I'm fine. I'm fine. It's a big misunderstanding, I'll talk to you when I get home, turn around and go home, I'm fine, I'm fine.* Then we hang up. The relief of getting off the phone is followed by a stab of anxiety, because I know I've only postponed what is sure to be a very ugly ordeal later on.

As I'm telling the chaperones and the officer how I met a guy on the ski lift who invited me to his condo, I start to regain feeling in my body. Right around the part of the story where I am entering Dax's condo, I stop.

"Can I use the restroom?" I ask.

Mrs. Winthrop sighs.

"Fine, but hurry up. We have to get going."

I go into a half-bath off the kitchen, remove my coat, and start to realize what has happened to me. My sweater is on inside out and I'm bleeding. My period isn't for another few weeks, and it's never hurt like this before.

"You okay in there?" Mrs. Winthrop asks, knocking on the door.

"Uh...yeah," I stammer. "Just a minute."

I don't have the time or sense to think about what I should do. I clean myself up and walk out, trying my best to mask the shaking of my limbs by folding my arms across my chest. A voice inside me screams: *Open your mouth! Tell this PTA mom what happened! You need to go to a hospital!* But overtopping the voice is the awful banging in my head. A sick regret washes over me in rising waves until I'm drowning in thoughts of: *What have you done?* I walk back to the table, sit down, and tell them what happened.

"We watched TV and fell asleep," I say.

I tell them what I pray happened, what I desperately wish would have happened. And I spin the yarn—I am the Sleeping Beauty who slept too long. I pump the pedal on my little spinning wheel and weave us all a Sleeping Beauty fairy tale. My heart is pounding and I want to run away so badly, but the *What have you done?* voice calls out to me. Softer this time. It whispers to me from that hollow pit in my stomach, that place where fear lives, and it talks me through it. It helps me believe my own lies.

...You can wrap the Fairy Tale Lie around you like a blanket.

You can bring it to life with inflection and embellishment, and when it all fits, you can just click your heels together and poof!, *it will become real. You'll be home in your bed saying it was all a dream, it was all a dream. . . .*

When Mrs. Winthrop and the officer and Cougar Di are satisfied and convinced and thoroughly disgusted with Sid Murphy and her selfish, selfish choices, the officer hands down my punishment. I can see from his name badge that he is isn't real police. He's resort security officer Barry C. Mayfield of the eight-dollars-an-hour-with-no-benefits set. Barry fills out a form detailing a curfew violation, rips it off the tablet, and hands it to me. We head out of the condo and onto the buses. I look for Kirsten and Paige but Mrs. Winthrop instructs me to sit up front with her and Diane. She doesn't want any more, as she puts it, *shenanigans* out of me. I sit down in the front seat with Cougar Di, while across the aisle, Mrs. Winthrop sits surrounded by a sea of disposable bags filled with souvenirs, snacks, books, and knitting supplies.

"You can take this up with your mother and Principal Watson when we get home," Mrs. Winthrop says, pulling out an issue of the Oprah magazine and peeling down the wrapper of a Snickers bar. "I'm done stressing about it. Honest to Pete, I don't know why I volunteer for these things."

Cougar Di pulls out a nail file from her purple croc-skinned purse and starts sanding away. She looks at me sideways and whispers, "Sorry, kid. But you really had us worried," and shoots me a half smile. She's trying to be nice. I return the awkward smile and then lean my head against the seat and close my eyes.

When we pull in, I can see my mom's car sitting front and center at the school curb. I seriously don't know what I'm going to say to her. I've spent three hours stuck between Cougar Di and Mrs. Winthrop, trying to get the words right in my head, because I need to tell my mom the truth. I'm going to tell my mom the truth.

The bus pulls around back. I step off and the terror ripping through me launches me into a delusional dream state. I just stand on the sidewalk, a river of brightly colored ski jackets flooding past me in a blurry current. I try to pick out Kirsten's and Paige's jackets but I can't; the world has become a hundred melted crayons. But Starsha and Amber? Oh, they slide by in slow motion, Starsha's fuchsia jacket blazing in the sunlight, her mouth stretching into a sneer when she sees me. "You are fuuuucked, Ginger Bitch," she says, with a slow sort of dullness. "Totally and completely fuuuucked." She and Amber laugh, then disappear into the Technicolor swarm.

I squeeze my eyes shut and snap myself out of it. I force my legs to force the rest of me to go find my mom. As I'm about to walk around the building, I hear someone calling me from the crowd. It's Kirsten. But I can't deal with her and Paige right now. I need to find my mom. I need to get in the car and go home. I want to be in my bedroom, in my bed, and I want to be there now.

I round the building and there she is, without my little brother—thank god—leaning against the car. Her face is like

Kirsten's and Paige's, sunken and swollen at the same time. Her face is beaten in two from crying.

I walk toward her and psych myself up and commit to telling the truth. I'm just going to get into that car and say it. Just tell her what happened and go from there. She'll drive me to the police station, or to the hospital, or to the cliffs at Nelson Ledges; to wherever it is that mothers and daughters go when something too horrible for words happens.

I walk up and stand to face her. She looks up at me and her eyes tell me that she doesn't know how to feel, that she's waiting for me to tell her something.

Horror or anger—the choice is mine.

And out it comes: "I-met-a-guy-we-went-to-his-condo-and-watched-TV-and-I-was-exhausted-from-skiing-all-day-and-fell-asleep."

So there you have it—my mouth, my mind, and my heart choose anger. They choose anger because anger passes. Anger passes because my mother knows exactly what to do with it. Katherine is the master of anger; she dominates anger. She takes anger in her hands and twists its neck, ripping its head off. She throws anger against the wall and stomps it to death. Her voice rises, it changes, it conjures up ghosts and cusses in a spitting Irish brogue. Then, when she's tapped out empty, she picks anger up between a thumb and a forefinger and carries it outside and drops it in the trash. On her way back, she scoops up forgiveness like a bouquet, sniffs it deep and arranges it in a vase. She sets forgiveness down, shining in the middle of everything.

So anger? I can give her anger.

But horror? I can't give my mom that, because horror doesn't pass. Horror is forever.

I hold my breath tightly and watch the anger rise up in my mom's eyes as "What in the goddamn bloody hell were you thinking?" comes screeching out, and I'm thankful for it. I breathe out and a calmness seeps in because I'm thankful that I don't have to watch my mom fall to her knees and cry forever.

"Mom, I'm so, so sorry," I say, over and over. And I listen to her anger the whole drive home, looking out my side mirror at all the things in the world getting smaller. My dead grandmother's biting Irish brogue rears up, that voice that's been boiled into my mother's DNA fills every space of the car. Her anger is like music; a familiar, raging, beautiful song that I can cling to. I cling to my mom's anger like a raft. I hang on tight and leave horror behind me.

5

I've showered. Thoroughly. And that's all I'm going to say about that.

It's Sunday evening about five. My mom went to the grocery store and I'm babysitting my six-year-old little brother, Liam. Or pretending to, anyway. I stick him in front of Nickelodeon with three juice boxes, a wet rag, and a box of Fiddle Faddle. I tell him he can eat the whole thing and I won't tell so long as he doesn't wipe his fingers on the drapes or move a single inch from the couch. It's almost dark out and I just lie on my bed and look out the window, opening and shutting my eyes to the tune of the landline ringing downstairs. Rinnng! Open. Rinnng! Shut. Over and over until, thankfully, it goes silent and my eyes stay closed.

It's Kirsten or Paige—I know from the customized ringtone. They'll be calling back in another fifteen minutes or so.

I open my eyes and continue the game, waiting for the phone to start up again. I'm trying to gather mental snapshots of the dimming sky, collecting the pictures and laying them out in my mind, so I can remember and make sense of it. So I can figure out how the world went dark right in front of me.

But I can't do it. It isn't working. All I see when I close my eyes is blinding snow followed by everything that came after. The ski trip plays and replays in a circular, endless loop in my mind.

The last thing I remember about last night was standing in the condo kitchen talking to him. Then the sound of breaking glass and the sensation of being carried. I was leaning against the countertop, holding a glass of ginger ale that Dax, or whoever he was, had poured for me. Things went blurry and the glass slipped from my hand, crashed into pieces at my feet. And I was falling, and then floating, being lifted.

Then nothing. Just the white hotness of snow and the jolt of being pierced by those caramel-yellow eyes.

I've tried all the mind games I can think of to reason my way out of it. Like, *If a tree falls in the woods and no one hears it, then did it really make a sound?* Some would argue no. If they're right, then if a person who is raped can't remember it, maybe it didn't really happen. And trust me when I tell you that I don't remember it. At all. Not a single solitary moment of it.

Breaking glass. Falling and floating. Caramel-yellow eyes.

These are the things I know.

It's Monday. I get up from bed at six thirty just as if I were going to school. *No sleeping in,* my mom said, *this isn't a vacation.* I go into the bathroom, pass by the mirror, but only see a flash of red on my way to the shower. I don't look in mirrors now unless I have to, and it's not necessarily because of some deep-seated Freudianesque type shame, although that may have something to do with it. It's because I can't look in the mirror and not have the Truth staring back at me. Literally.

My mother was the first to notice it, in the car when she picked me up yesterday. She'd finished with the screaming and our faces were soaked with tears, our noses were running, and I turned to reach into the backseat for some tissues. "What happened to your hair?" she said, and reached out to finger my curls. I flipped down the visor mirror and that's when I saw it.

One long spiral snipped.

Man. Spectacular. These things, they go on forever.

And now he has a piece of it.

It's Wednesday, the third day of my four-day suspension. It would have been five days, but I haven't been in trouble since middle school. I had a reputation for being a scrapper back then, but I haven't had so much as a detention in high school, and I keep a respectable grade point average. The guidance counselor went to bat for me and the principal let me off a little by cutting my suspension down by a day and adding a detention instead.

I'm grounded, of course, and being indoors is unbearable. Every moment feels like the roof and walls are caving in on me, and the only thing that gives me any real relief is stepping outside into the cold air. But then my mom gets upset because I'm supposed to be grounded, which meant "confinement" the last time she checked.

She's forgiven me, though; the forgiveness bloomed right away, just like always. In the middle of that first night, I felt her tiptoe into my room and crawl into my bed to lay down beside me. I pretended to be asleep. It was comforting to know she was there. She reached out and put her hand on my back like she used to do when I was little. To make sure I was breathing. To make sure I was warm and safe and real.

But I'm still grounded. Katherine hasn't budged an inch on that. Paige and Kirsten are grounded, too. Worse yet, they both got slapped with a week of detentions for covering for me, for knowing I snuck out and not telling a chaperone. Their moms called the house and spoke to my mom. Mrs. Vanderhoff and Mrs. Daniels? Not happy ladies. Especially Mrs. Daniels. Kirsten got her car taken away, but poor Paige—she has no car, no cable, and limited phone and Internet to begin with. There's literally nothing to take. I dread to think what a Paige Daniels grounding might entail. Probably reading the Bible all day long and then copying it by hand. God, I'm such a horrible friend.

I know that I need to call them or pick up the phone and explain myself, but every time the phone rings, I plead with my mother to make excuses, then I go to my room and shut the door. She's tired of lying, so she finally just unplugged the phone from the wall. But not before calling the principal to get the topics for my punishment essays.

The Importance of Curfews... 500-word minimum.

Why Society Needs Rules... 500-word minimum.

Respecting Authority. Peer Pressure. What It Means To Be A Leader.

500.

500.

500.

I only have two days left, and I haven't even started them yet. So I hunker down and get it done. The essay is my true medium; I am a rock star when it comes to mixing bits of information with twenty-dollar words.

With 2,500 words completed in just under four hours, I start my other homework. I jump online for just a moment to e-mail this girl Bethany for calculus assignments, trying not to see the avalanche of e-mails from Kirsten. I can't help it—I start to tally up Kirsten's messages. After eight, I stop. And I don't open them. In fact, I do worse than not open them. I delete them all in one fell swoop.

Check All—Delete—Are You Sure?—Yep.

I feel relieved, staring at my empty inbox, the slate wiped clean and all those blaring unread messages erased. The relief lasts exactly one second before I feel worse.

I push the guilt into the back of my mind and go back to cleaning the house. I spent Monday and Tuesday cleaning the garage and basement per my mom's instructions. She didn't say anything about cleaning before she left for work today, but I clean anyway, without being asked. Anything to keep moving. I clean everything that can possibly be cleaned and I wash, fold, and put away every piece of laundry we own. I organize every drawer, closet, and cabinet in the house. There's a foot of snow on the ground and no gardening to be done, but trust me, if it were spring, I'd be out there in a giant sun hat and gloves, digging and yanking at every weed in sight.

When there is nothing left for me to do, I lie down, exhausted, and pray for the sleep that never comes. I just lay in bed until anxiety overtakes me. Anxiety creeps in on little cat feet and lurks over me. *Get up and move,* it hisses, *or I'll suffocate you.*

Night comes, and I finally crack around three a.m. I decide I am going outside in the morning; I don't care if I get caught. I'll suffer any punishment she can think of if it means I can be outside and moving. The last time I was truly safe, I was outside and moving.

~

Liam is talking but I don't really hear him. We're at the table and I'm sitting in front of a plate of cold scrambled eggs and looking at the half-empty water glass that my mother left on the table before she went to work.

"Huh, Sid?"

I look fuzzily at my little brother.

"What's that, Liam?" I say.

Through a mouthful of toast, he says, "I *saaaaid*, why do they give you days off school if you do something bad?"

I look at him, smacking away innocently. He looks nothing like me, not even one little bit. He is about the most beautiful-looking creature on two feet, with dark, thick hair and eyes so brown they're almost black and olive skin like his dad's. Vincent D'Apolito: certified plumber and former stepdad to Sid Murphy. His name makes him sound like some kind of mob hit man, but really he's just a serial womanizer. He's a good dad, though. Unlike my dad, Vince pays child support and never misses a visit. My dad's never even seen me. Vince lives a few miles away from us and sees Liam every week.

I answer his question.

"Because they're so mad, they don't want to see your face until they've cooled off."

He looks at me with sadness and offers comfort.

"Don't worry, I'm gonna do something bad today so I can stay home to keep you company."

"Oh, yeah? What could you do?"

I ask this knowing full well that Liam doesn't know the first thing about true rebellion. But under my strict tutelage, I may be able to fix this before he reaches middle school.

"I don't know," he says. "I haven't thought of anything good yet. Help me think of something real good. I mean *real bad*."

He scrunches up his face.

"Hmmmm...well, let's see. Maybe you could pull the fire alarm and send everyone screaming out of the building?"

He rolls his eyes and laughs, and a piece of egg falls out of his open mouth. He knows I'm only kidding. I look up at the clock. School will be starting shortly, and he is still in his pajamas and a mess. I get up, pluck him out of the chair, and swoop him over my shoulder.

"Or *maaaaybe* you could cut Madison Kelly's pigtails off. You sit behind her, right?"

"Oooh, yeah!" he says. "I wanna do that one!"

I tickle him and he laughs, kicking and squirming all the way through the house. I dress him and—because he sucks at it—brush his teeth for him. Then I walk him down the street to his elementary school. I watch from the sidewalk as he gets in line at the entrance. Madison Kelly is standing in front of him and turns around to tease him. He looks at me, so I make a scissor snip motion with my fingers, followed by a hard wink and a thumbs-up. He covers his mouth as he walks inside grinning.

I walk back home and look down at the food that I haven't eaten. My stomach lurches. I hate to waste it, so on my way out, I stop and give it to Mrs. Leary's dog. We own a duplex, and she rents the other side from us. She's older than King Tut's grandma, but really sweet. Her dog lives in the garage and has a nice fenced run that he can access from a giant door flap carved into the side.

The dog comes lumbering out of his giant door flap to scarf up the food. He's an Irish wolfhound named Ronan and stands nearly to my chest on all fours. Like I said, I'm five-foot-nine, so that would make him positively the hugest dog ever born. Two gulps and the whole plate is gone. I give Ronan a pat, then shut the gate. He lowers his head and lets out a low *broooof* of a thank-you before moseying back into his freshly cleaned garage.

I walk a few blocks to the business district and stop in front The Diner on Clifton, known for its eclectic and spunky atmosphere. I like the name choice, straight and to the point. I go in and scan a menu at the door. Everything would normally look appetizing, but the thought of eating any of it makes my guts roil. I'm incredibly thirsty all of a sudden, so I order two Red Bulls and a glass of ice. I also order a plain bagel because I feel strange sitting down at a diner with no actual food. I have chosen a table near the window. I take my gloves off, set them in the sill, and sit listening to the clang of dishes and Regina Spektor playing overhead.

The waitress—SHELLEY, it says on her name tag—brings me my bagel and Red Bulls and asks why I'm not in school. I tell her I'm twenty but look young. She has a kind face and is wearing a "Keep it Green" T-shirt and silver earrings that jingle when she moves her head. I want someone to talk to, so I make up a whole story about who I am. How my name is Fiona and I go to Case Western. I'm majoring in ecology. I rent a room from this old widow for practically nothing. I just have to shovel the drive, mow the lawn, and walk the old woman's horse of a dog three times a day. Incidentally, I am also a vegan and don't believe in cars; I only walk, ride my skateboard, or take public transportation. I don't want to leave my carbon footprint on our precious earth.

What a crock. I tell this story to the waitress. I know the words are coming out of my mouth, and on some level, I can hear them, but it feels like they are coming from the girl sitting behind me, like it's someone else's conversation altogether. But the lies feel good. For a moment, I am someone else entirely.

Someone who has never cared about being in love in her whole life. I am someone who cares about real and important things, like carbon footprints. I am someone with lofty purposes who wouldn't try out for cheerleading even if a gun were held to her head, someone who couldn't care less that no boys at school have ever asked her out. A girl who would never fall for a predator's bag of tricks just because she's so desperate for attention.

No, I am not Cassidy Murphy EASY MARK right this second. Not in this diner, at this moment. Right now, I am Fiona-What's-Her-Face-College-Student-Wise-Beyond-Her-Twenty-Years. I am Scholarship Girl, Environmental Warrior, and Caretaker of the Elderly. I am not sitting duck high school *idiot* who was lured in and—

Ow! I wince hard.

I have been rabidly crunching on ice while chewing the fat with Shelley Keep It Green. My brain was elsewhere. It lost track of my mouth and I have bitten into my tongue. Fack! That hurt!

"You okay?"

"Just bit my tongue."

Shelley smiles and walks away. I am left alone again with only the Truth to keep me company. I suck down my Red Bulls. When I am good and torqued up on caffeine and positively brimming with self-loathing, I decide to burn it all off by running. I need to keep moving. I throw down a ten-dollar bill and head back outside. I'm not sure where I want to go and I don't care where I end up so I just pick a direction and keep going straight. I've never run more than a couple of blocks in my life, unless you count the pathetic, lagging sort of running that we're forced to do during the first couple of weeks of pre-season cheer-leading practice. I get two blocks and feel like I'm dying. I stop and lean against a building to spit and heave. My chest feels like I've swallowed a shattered dish, but the immediacy of the pain, the pain that I've created for myself, the pain that I have control over, drives me onward. I rally and keep going until the distant shoreline peeks itself out, surprising me through the backyards of some Lake Road mansions. I stop; bend over, gasping for breath; and think, *Huh, when did they put that there?*

I live in Lakewood, Ohio, and drive by Lake Erie daily. But in winter? I clean forget it's there. It's like a giant invisishield slams down the day after Labor Day and the whole lake just evapo-rates off the map until May. I realize that it's never dawned on me to visit the lake in the dead of winter. I make a turn onto Lake Road and cut through the park until I reach the board-walk, where I collapse onto an empty bench swing, dripping in sweat. Then I stare out at the icy, gray water and wonder if on a clear day you can see all the way to Canada. Some gulls spot me and start milling about, bobbing their heads up and down, squawking for food. I break off pieces of the bagel in my pocket and throw them to the birds. One fat thug in the bunch gets most of the food, and I feel bad when it's gone. Most of the punier birds didn't get a single crumb.

I sit for a while, enjoying the shaky, wobbly feeling in my legs. After a few minutes, I can no longer feel my feet, fingers, or face. They are so cold from the wind off the lake that it doesn't even hurt. I could be frostbitten black for all I know. It's okay, though. I sit awhile longer. Numb is good.

I check my watch. It's eleven, and my mother may call to check on me at lunch. My legs can literally go no farther with the running, and my boobs are killing me. Note to self: Buy a sports bra. I'll need the whole hour to drag myself home. I stop only once on my way back, to look in an art gallery window at a painting of some flowers. Poppies that sit hopeful in a vase, waiting for someone to buy them.

I crawl back into bed, soaked in a cold, frozen sweat and completely fatigued. At the edge of sleep, I think about my life, before.

School.

Friends.

Cheerleading.

Mall.

TV.

Internet.

This is what my life has been for the past several years, and I was happy with it. An ignorant sort of happy, but happy nonetheless. I picture myself watching music videos or shopping now and it makes me feel awkward and glaringly self-aware. Like a fifty-year-old who picks up a dress in the juniors section, then puts it back quickly, hoping no one saw.

I pull the covers over my head and think some more.

I think of a shared joke with my little brother. I think of a single mother who buys suits secondhand so her kids can wear Gap. I think of a dog, grateful for a plate of eggs and a clean garage. I think of a pleasant waitress with jingly earrings. I think of the salty burn in my lungs and the satisfaction of running farther than I ever thought I could run. I think of a forgotten lake and hopeful poppies. I think of how I've lived in Lakewood all of my life and have never seen or felt any of these tiny, beautiful things until now.

It took losing something wonderful and amazing to see them.

It took losing something that, once it's gone, you can never get it back.

Peace.

The irony of this stings me with a sorrow so painful that I have to bite into my fist to keep my heart from ripping in two.

6

Four days of suspension are over. I'm back to school and, apparently, in hot demand. I guess staying out all night on a school trip makes one popular in certain circles. My once-empty inboxes are full again, teeming with tweets, pokes, invites, and adoring chitchat. I finally charged and checked my phone last night, and it practically blew up in my hand from all the activity. People think I'm cool now—even some of my fellow cheerleaders. Not Starsha, but still, a couple of them, anyway. And those boys who never gave me the time of day? Coming out of the woodwork.

I walk through the halls like a goddess—high fives and fist bumps at every turn. I am the poster girl for teenage rebellion, everyone's bad-girl superhero. It's like I'm living in a parallel universe of Lakewood High. It looks the same, smells the same—only in this universe, I am mildly popular.

But Kirsten and Paige? Not a peep from either of them in over a day.

During first period, I get a printout of my new schedule. A new grading period has begun and some of my classes have changed. I look over the list and my eyes land on fourth period. Music appreciation has been swapped out for web page development. Kirsten and I signed up for the class together; couldn't wait to be able to instant message, free and unfettered, for an entire fifty minutes at the end of the day.

I eye the clock all morning while the last period looms.

I have to get it over with. I can't avoid Kirsten and Paige at school, because we're joined at the hips here. And besides, now that avoiding them is no longer an option, part of me is almost glad. I want this to be over. I want things to go back to the way they were.

My heart pounds as the bell rings for last period. I head toward the computer lab. I pass by the art wing and the earthy smell of wet clay fills my nose. Pretty girls with long hair and no makeup, smelling of essential oils, are filing inside one of the rooms for pottery class. "Throwing pots," I think they call it. I wish now that I had channeled my energy into something worthwhile and lasting instead of spending hours in front of the mirror channeling the Dallas Cowboys Cheerleaders.

I go down the steps and stand around the corner from the

computer lab, pasted against the wall like a cat burglar. I take a breath, peel myself off the wall, and go to get it over with. The teacher, Mr. Roudabush, points me in the direction of the last empty cubicle and begins yammering on about templates versus blank slates. I sit down in front of the monitor, fire up the engine, and punch in my school network user name: *ItGirlz2*.

Lame, I know. Kirsten, Paige, and I chose our user names so they would match. Kirsten came up with this theory in ninth grade that if we formed an alliance and called it something cool then it would catch on with the masses and slingshot us over Ordinary and smack dab into Popular. It's been two years and no one knows who the *ItGirlz* are but us.

I send a message to *ItGirlz1*, Kirsten, across the room.

K, can we talk?

She writes back.

4 days go by & now u wanna talk? Gr8. Fn. Go. Tlk.

Her words are like a kick to the chest. My best friend is on the other side of this room, sitting and staring at her screen, waiting for my explanation, waiting for me to tell her what happened and why we're all in so much trouble. My fingers twitch and hover over the keys. Then I press three letters. I sit and stare at his name on my screen. The cursor blinking next to it.

Dax

Blink. Blink. Blink.

That's as far as I get. I can't make my fingers type the other two words. If I type those two words, then it becomes real. It becomes a thing that actually happened instead of a thing I don't remember. Once I type it, the pretending is over. I backspace and erase his name and write:

I'm so sorry. I made a mistake.

She writes back.

Ya think? I'm glad ur sorry Sid but do u know how scard Pg & I were? It was awful. And wots w/the disappearing act? WTF? U could have @ least called or e-mailed.

And then I mess up big time. I tell her my mom took my phone and computer so I couldn't message or call. She writes,

Bshit! Bethany Morris told Pg u e-mailed her for calc assignments so I know u saw mine & Pgs messages! Did u even read them? I called ur landline at least 50 times! When someone would finally pick up it was ur mom saying u were sleeping or doing h-work or in the shower or whatever. U might be grounded but ur moms no prison guard. She would have let u talk if u wanted. U were hiding out. So don't even try it.

We got a wk of detention incl. Sat! And 2 top it all off? Pg. & I got kicked out of ski club! U may not care about skiing Sid but Pg & I do! We LIVE 4 ski club and U RUINED IT!

It's like she's thrown a knife at me from across the room. I sit working up the nerve to tell her. I need to tell her the truth, or some kind of version of it, something to make this better. I can't lose my two best friends over this. After a long moment of radio silence, as I'm trying to think of something to say, she scrolls out a couple lines of angry question marks:

???

???

Followed by:

Gr8. Later, Sid. Don't call me or e-mail. I don't need ur bshit.

I spend a few more moments trying to figure out what to do. I need to talk to Kirsten and Paige in person. In private. I'm too exposed here. If I tell Kirsten now she might freak out. And then everyone will know.

Can u come over after sch? I need 2 talk 2 u in person.

I hit the send button.

A notice pops up.

User has blocked this sender.

The classic freeze-out.

Roudabush is making his rounds. I look back over our exchange. We're supposed to be working on a template and following along with the lesson. I try to close out of the message box but the screen won't budge. *Blink, blink, blink*...nothing. My computer has frozen up and won't drop the message box.

I quickly shut off the computer to get rid of the messages just as he gets to me, not bothering to power down first. Roudabush sees me do this and nearly faints. It takes most of the period for the aide to get my computer working properly again, and I get an F for the day.

When Roudabush tells me my computer is fixed, I sit down and immediately get a ding in my inbox, and for a second I'm hopeful that it's Kirsten. It's not. It's Tate Andrews. Starsha's on-again-off-again-friends-with-benefits-love-you-hate-you-forever is e-mailing me from across the way.

Prty @ Hunter B's beach house this w-end. Catawba Isl. Wanna go?

Soooooo Tate Andrews, the LHS Football Romeo, wants to take Ski Slut Murphy to a party at a beach house Friday night. Uh-huh, I'll just bet he does.

7

My mother is about five minutes late picking me up, and I wait in front of the school, the icy wind whipping me from all sides. I open the car door and slide into the automatically warmed seat. I smell spices and see a takeout bag at my feet. My brother waves from the back and screams, "Hi, Sid! I missed youuuu!"

He has headphones on and is watching a superhero movie on the portable DVD player that hooks onto the back of my seat. I wave back and settle inside. I am relieved and glad to see them.

Mom leans over and kisses my cheek—no grudges, no worries, just love.

"How was it? Bad?" she asks, looking at my weary face.

"Uh, bad would be a step *up* from the day I had. More like awful, I'd say."

"Oh, honey," she says, reaching over and patting my leg. "Don't worry. Hang in there. It'll blow over. Wait and see, a month from now it'll be like the ski trip never happened. People will forget about it altogether."

"Yeah," I say, hoping she's right but knowing she's not.

And besides, even if she is right? Even if, given time, other people forget about the ski trip, I won't be forgetting it anytime soon. That trip has set up permanent base camp in my brain; it's going to be playing on auto-repeat for quite a while.

"You wanna talk about it?" she asks.

"Not particularly," I say with a sigh.

"Well, I have something to cheer you up. I ordered Indian. I thought we could play Tinker. It's a Tudor on Lighthouse Road. There's a glass conservatory that overlooks the lake."

"Cool."

Ever since my mother became a real estate agent, we'll sometimes go to empty houses together and play a game she named Tinker, the Irish term for a gypsy. When there is an especially swank or interesting unoccupied house that she needs to ready for showing, she will take us with her and we will spread a picnic out in the nicest room and pretend we just moved in. We have to eat on the floor, because our truckloads of expensive furniture haven't arrived yet. Liam thinks Tinker is the greatest game ever—running around fancy new McMansions or spooky old Tudors, hiding in bare cupboards or under stairs. It's fun for me, too, knocking around someone else's house, admiring roof-top views or commenting on god-awful wallpaper choices. We haven't done it together in a long time, and I am up for anything that doesn't involve a computer, a TV, or being stuck some-where with my own thoughts for too long.

"Oooh," my mom says. "Man candy, two o'clock."

I look ahead and see a runner—male, extremely fit, longish hair hidden under a navy ski cap. As we pass him, my mom toots the horn and scares the hell out of him.

I roll my eyes and grin.

"Perv."

She smiles like she's won something.

While we drive, I lean my head against the seat and look over at my mother, who is driving and smiling at nothing in particu-lar. She is so pretty, her chestnut hair pulled back in a pony. Dapples of sun hit her smooth skin and I think about how young she looks and about how young she was when she had me. I think about when I was really little, before her second marriage, when it was just the two of us in a shitty little apartment, and our heat was turned off because she couldn't pay the bill. She carried me around all day, me clinging to her like a fat little monkey, her wrapping her thick robe around the both of us and tying it up tight. *Climb inside my robe where it's warm, we'll pre-tend we live in the zoo...*

And now I need to roll down the window and catch a good gust of winter air on my face; the past is giving me a flush. I like thinking about my mom, Liam, and me, the way we are now. The Three Musketeers. Playing Tinker. Plus, the smell of the

Indian food is doing strange things to my stomach. I haven't eaten much all day, so I should be starving, but the smell is making me sick.

And here we are, the Tudor on Lighthouse Road.

We take our shoes off and leave them on the front porch by the door. They just had the floors polished and my mom doesn't want to get the place scuffed up or dirty. I lift Liam up and let him do the keyless lock code that is hidden under an ornate metal plate with the house number on it. The code is easy; it's always easy on the nicer houses. 4321 enter. God, how do these people make their millions?

This house is seriously one of my mother's finer listings. The kind you get maybe once a year if you're lucky. Three floors, a winding staircase, and an amazing view of the lake from a glass conservatory. She'd make a killing in commission if she could sell it. Thirty grand at least. I think about all the things the Murphys could buy with that kind of cabbage: a European vacation for Katherine, a pool for Liam, and a breast reduction for Sid.

We go into the conservatory and spread our blanket out on the marble tile. She opens the takeout containers and dishes out our food while I plug in the CD player and put on The Beatles. Even though I'm still not hungry, I eat a little bit.

"That's all?" my mom says, looking at my nearly full plate.

"I didn't know we'd be eating so early," I say. "I had two burritos for lunch."

Lie. I just don't want it right now. Food and I are not seeing eye-to-eye these days, and I don't want her asking me questions about it. I've actually lost a few pounds and, frankly, I don't want to find them again.

"You can heat it up later," she says. "Indian is always better the second time around."

Then we talk and laugh and I feel calmer and happier than I have in a long time. Something about being in someone else's house and living an imaginary life for a while. We clean up the containers, then look out the conservatory windows. We look across the lake, vast like an ocean, my mom, Liam, and me. We fantasize about our new home and life. My mom scoots closer to me, Liam nestled into the front of her. She leans her head on my shoulder. I can smell Liam's strawberry-scented kid shampoo mixed with my mom's soap-and-water perfume, and there is nothing better in the world than that.

When we are talked out and our butts hurt from sitting on the floor, my mom says, "Well, back to reality. Gotta get to work now," and pulls out her clipboard and camera.

She walks around taking pictures and writing notes to herself. I play hide-and-seek with Liam. I tell him to go hide as I stroll in and out of the empty rooms pretending to look for him, while knowing the whole time exactly where he is. He is hiding in a pantry in the kitchen, which, for some reason, is always the first place he heads in every house. I walk around saying, "Hmmmmm? Where could he be? My, my, he's disappeared altogether…"

While I am walking around pretending to look, I come upon a turret room. A turret is a room that looks like a castle tower from the outside. This one is different, though, because on the inside, it's painted top-to-bottom with a mural. I've seen other houses with murals, but they're usually in kids' rooms. New moms love to crank out a mural of an underwater kingdom or traveling circus train. Not this mural, though. This mural is the real deal—a serious artist painted this room. It's a scene of a quiet forest reaching up toward a warm, pastel sky.

I stretch out on the floor and look up at it. After a few moments, I get this floaty feeling in my stomach, and I can feel myself being pulled upward, like I'm being lifted into the sky. But something inside me hesitates. I squeeze my eyes shut to block the feeling out. It hurts to look at this forest and sky somehow, because deep down, I know they're not real. Before the tears come, I sit up and go to find Liam for real.

When I get to the pantry, I hear him shuffling around inside, trying desperately to be quiet, but, being six, completely incapable of it. I stomp over extra loud.

"Well, this is the last place I can look! I sure hope he's in there, or he might be lost forever!"

I try to open the door, but it's stuck. Or locked. I rattle it.

"Liam, you in there? Open the door, I found you."

My voice is getting a nervous high pitch to it. Liam says nothing; instead, he just laughs.

"No, seriously, Liam, open the door."

"Sid?" he says.

"Yeah, Liam, it's Sid, open the door."

I feel him turning the knob, but the door will not budge.

"I can't open it. It won't open," he says with a calmness that I find unsettling. If it were me in this closet, I would be clawing at the door, trying to kick it in, and screaming my head off.

"Don't worry, I'm right here, I'm gonna get it open."

I'm shaking and rattling the door like a maniac. A hysteria has come over me, as if Liam were in some life-threatening situation. Like this thin door, separating us by two inches, is some kind of serious danger to him. Danger tantamount to a car dangling over a cliff with him inside the trunk or a tornado bearing down about to swallow him up. A predator leading him away with a kind word and some candy...

Magically, the door just opens out of nowhere.

I fall to my knees, grab Liam, and smash him into my chest, hugging him tight.

"Oh, Liam, that scared me. I'm so sorry. Were you scared?" I say, pulling back to look at him.

"Don't cry," he says. "It's okay, I wasn't scared. I knew you'd get me out."

"Yeah. I did," I say, wiping my eyes and smiling.

He looks at me, concentrating closely, his eyes zoning in on my left cheek. Like there's something on my face. I pause and start to raise my hand to my cheek, to see what's wrong, when he smacks me hard across the chops and yells, "Tag, you're it!" before running out of the room squealing.

This is a gag I taught him, sort of like when you say, "There's something on your shirt," and the person looks down and you run a forefinger up their face and say, "Made ya look!" Only I zone in on someone's face, preferably the forehead, and then thwack them a good one, scream, "Tag! You're it!" and take off running.

He has gotten me good; I have never fallen for my own gag until now.

"Oh, little boy! You better ruuun!" I yell, and I can hear him squealing through the house, running to find Mom's legs so he can hide behind them.

I find the two of them stretched out in a huge, empty, marble tub in the master bath. Mom's notebook and camera are on the window ledge and she's singing "Some Day My Prince Will Come," schmaltzy and overblown, like poor, pitiful Snow White. Liam is clinging to her chest, smiling at me sideways with one eye. I lean on the doorframe and look at them. He whispers into her ear and she listens hard, smiling at whatever it is he's saying. It makes my throat ache to look at them.

I look at my mother's familiar face, smiling and listening to Liam's secret, and it makes me wonder how I could have sold her so short. How could I have not told my mom what happened to me when I'd had the chance? My mother could have handled it. The horror, I mean. If I'd told her, she would have felt it, certainly. The horror would have driven her to her knees.

But not forever.

She would have grabbed on to that anger she knows so well and hauled herself up, then grabbed onto me and pulled me up with her.

I think about this. And I almost, *almost* start to tell.

I mean if you can't tell your own mother, who on earth can you tell? My jaws are tight and locked and I am concentrating so hard. I open my mouth just a little bit and almost get the words to come out... *Mom, I need to talk to you about something later when we're alone. I need to tell you something about the ski trip...*

But they don't come. The words won't come.

She glances up and notices me looking at her so hard. Our eyes meet and I am hoping so much that she heard my thoughts and that she'll pull me aside later and ask me what's wrong.

But she can't hear my thoughts; she misreads my expression and bursts out laughing.

"The owners are out of state and no one has the combination but us! Don't look so tense, silly girl! Climb on in, the water's fine!"

The moment passes. I force a bent smile and climb in with them. I snuggle up to my mom and brother. I join in when they start singing along to the music that is seeping up through the floorboards. We sing "Can't Buy Me Love" at the top of our lungs.

8

On the way down the steps to web page development, Tate Andrews sidles up next to me. "So you're coming to Hunter's, right? I'll pick you up around six."

He is so eager and sure of himself. Like rejection by Sid Murphy is not even a possibility.

"Uh, no. I can't," I say, speeding down the steps and rounding the corner.

He speeds up, too.

"If it's about Starsha, don't worry. She and I, we kind of have an agreement. Besides, she's going to Toronto with her parents for the weekend, so it's cool."

I glance over at his perfect jawline. At his trademark hair, sitting perfectly styled in that messy-on-purpose-I-use-man-product kind of way. I look at this dumb jock who's never given me the time of day. He thinks he's going to take Sid Murphy to some island in the middle of Lake Erie in the dead of winter and pour a six-pack down her throat. He's gonna screw himself a ginger, then tell everyone on Monday how much bigger her boobs are up close. I almost go nuclear on him but decide against it. I don't need more drama. I've had enough drama to last me a hundred years.

"Sorry, I have this family thing."

I screw up my lips, raise my shoulders, and try to appear bummed that I am unable to attend the festivities. His expression tells me that he is unmoved by thoughts of Murphy family bonding.

"Well, get out of it," he says. "You just got invited to a party at Hunter's beach house. By me."

I fantasize briefly about punching him in the balls.

And that's when Starsha, who clearly heard Tate's last remark, comes waltzing up to join us. And then, because God hates me, Kirsten strolls by, too.

Starsha, Tate, and I are standing right outside the computer lab just as she passes. She sees the three of us huddled together, and a look of disgust flickers in her eyes right before she heads inside. She thinks I'm chumming it up with Starsha and Tate now.

"Tate, what are you doing?" Starsha says. "Hunter's party is not a Callahan Kegger, it's exclusive. TBP only."

Yes, they call themselves that. TBP—which is short for *The Beautiful People*. An überpopular, Starsha/Tate–led faction of

Lakewood High clones. This unforeseen bit of theatrics forces me to recount my history with Starsha, and the Sid/Starsha film of nostalgia plays on fast-forward in my brain. The primary years spent taunting me about my hair and height; the middle years spent taunting me about my premature boobs and ever-expanding rear; and then, finally, the fit she threw last year when I made it for cheerleading and Cameron Fitzpatrick, cheerleader since fifth grade, did not. I remember the campaign of terror designed to make me quit so that Cameron, relegated to first alternate, could be reunited with her beloved pom-poms. How Starsha called me fat at every practice and declared that cheerleading was for girls size three or smaller, that red hair was ugly, kinky red hair was super ugly, and I wasn't just fat, I was obese. I remember cheer camp last summer when I had to stay in a dorm room by myself because Starsha wouldn't let anyone bunk with me and forced everyone to treat me like a piece of breathing shit all day, every day for a solid week. I remember how my real friends, Kirsten and Paige, sent me a bouquet of sunflowers for moral support with a note attached: *For the best cheerleader ever! Keep on kicking!* I remember the relief when, after camp, Starsha finally threw in the towel, accepted the fact that I wasn't going anywhere, and started rationalizing my usefulness by sticking me at the bottom of all the pyramids.

It's not glamorous, being the brawn at the bottom of the pyramids, but at least she didn't break me. At least I didn't quit. And things have cooled off somewhat. Mostly it's just catty, harmless banter, the two of us being immature and thriving off our lifelong repartee. It's been one of my fondest high school pastimes, actually, fighting with Starsha. When you've got best friends like Kirsten and Paige, it makes the shitty part of high school almost fun...the fighting with mean girls and not being popular, I mean. Well, it used to make it fun.

Tate looks at Starsha. "What do you care, anyway? It's not like you'll be all busted up about it, sitting in Toronto with your dickhead boyfriend, *Bradley*."

"Really, Tate? You want to do this here? He's my parents' friend's son. You're being a child."

Then she points for him to go into the lab. He lets out a snort and slumps inside. Starsha turns and finally addresses me directly.

"You'll have to excuse Tate," she says. "All that football has damaged his already fragile brain functioning."

"Whatever," I say, turning to walk inside. Barbie and Ken are making my skin itch.

"Wait. I wanted to talk to you," she says, following behind me. "It's important."

I sit down at my cubicle, turn on my computer, and pray she'll wrap it up quick. My appetite for sparring with Starsha has reached its limit. It's dried up, really. I haven't slept in days, and I'm just too tired to deal with her.

"Well. I just thought it was my duty to inform you of a few things," she says.

I sigh.

"Great. Go. Talk." I roll my chair back, crossing my arms and looking up at her.

She sits a little on my desk, blocking me from my keyboard.

Her hair and outfit and makeup are so perfect that she looks counterfeit, like she's a Photoshopped version of herself.

"You know, your little ski trip escapade made you, for once in your life, kind of interesting," she says, looking up and away, ankles crossed, arms crossed, like she's pondering her own existence and not actually talking to someone.

"Such a blatant disregard for authority was almost impressive. And then dumping Kirsten and that other girl, that little bookmouse, whatever her name is . . . that was a smart move. Really lightened your load. So much so that in a matter of days, you were able to bypass a few rungs on the ladder and secure an invite to an exclusive gathering. Of course, I've rescinded that offer, but—"

I interrupt her with a loud yawn, saying, "Are we done here?"

She looks down at me and smiles. "Almost."

I muscle in and push her bony ass off my keyboard. I punch in my user name, pretending to be busy and completely bored with her.

"Bottom line, Siddy, I don't think it's working out, so we've decided to let you go."

This makes me laugh. I feel a little fight in me after all. "What? Let go from TBP?" I say, feigning disappointment while typing and clicking, pretending to scan for nonexistent files. "But I just got hired. I haven't even started yet, and The Backstabbing Posers are firing me already? Where will I go? How will I live?"

"Cute," she says. "The Backstabbing Posers, that's clever."

Then she sighs and continues.

"Anyhow, I'm not talking about TBP," she says. "I mean, you might have climbed a few rungs, but our group has standards. Pedigree. If we let in every dog who wins a ribbon at the fair, we'll be overrun by mutts. See, no, what I was talking about is your spot on the Golden Bullets. We're letting you go."

The bell rings and people start settling into their cubicles. I roll my eyes, busying myself with pulling up more nonexistent files.

"Yeah, okay. You may think you run things around here, but you're not the cheerleading coach. You can't fire me from the Bullets. Besides, you've already tried getting rid of me once, and you failed, remember? So I guess you'll have to put up with this mutt a while longer. Because this bitch—"

"Oh, you didn't hear?" she says, interrupting me. She leans in close, like we're best friends sharing a secret. She's smiling, and her eyes are twinkling like stars.

"Hear what?" I groan, *tap, tap, tap*ping away at my keyboard.

"Coach wants your uniform by the end of next week. No delinquents allowed."

My fingers freeze and I look at her.

"You're lying," I say, staring at her.

"Really?" she says, getting a little more fiery, whipping out a yellow booklet from her bag. "See, this is called a code of conduct manual. And it's all right here."

She thumbs through the pages and points.

"Section B, paragraph 3: Any student receiving an at-home suspension will be dismissed immediately from all sporting teams and intramurals for the remainder of the semester." She lowers the booklet and leans into my face. "In layman's terms, that means, 'So long, Ginger Bitch, welcome back, Cameron.'"

She walks away, her hips swaying, smiling and blowing a kiss over her shoulder. I sit in my chair, my mouth open like a fool.

Kirsten still has me blocked and I'm too gutless to try to talk to her in person. She and Paige avoid me as though I were carrying typhoid. To chase after them, especially spouting on about the woes of cheerleading, seems desperate and wretched. I sit in my cubicle, stunned. I want to talk to somebody about this, but I can't. I know cheerleading is stupid. I know this. Why should I care, right? I mean, it's cheerleading, for god's sake. You might even wonder why I would do such a stupid thing as try out for cheerleading in the first place. True, I did it because Kirsten dared me to, but I also did it because...

...well...

...I did it because I wanted to be a cheerleader.

Ugh.

So there you have it. I wanted to be a cheerleader.

And I'm good at it. You might think a bigger girl like me wouldn't be capable of a back handspring or a toe touch or a double side split, but you'd be wrong. Because this one is very capable of it. Liam's dad taught me how to do a back handspring in the fifth grade, and I never forgot it. So sue me. I wanted to wear a cute uniform and shake pom-poms and possibly have a boy or two look at me for a change. A fat lot of good it did me.

No boy has ever looked at me in my uniform and thought anything but, *Wow! That's one big-ass cheerleader!*

It's so stupid, I know. Especially now, after what's happened.

But still, it irks me that I've been kicked off. Not because I won't get to cheer anymore; I'll get over that. In fact, I'm already over it. I was over it three games into football season when the sparkle wore off and I realized that the view from the pyramid was exactly the same as the view from the bleachers. I stayed in it because I couldn't give Starsha and her coven of harpies the satisfaction of seeing me quit. So losing the actual cheering isn't what's bothering me. What's bothering me is that *he* took it from me.

He took my most precious thing, and now he's taken my most stupid, idiotic thing, too. And I get to hear Starsha remind me about it every day for the next eight weeks.

I look over the cubicles, at the tops of people's heads—at Starsha, Kirsten, and Tate.

I cannot sit in this class for the next eight weeks.

I'm throwing up the white flag. I'm embracing something I've always despised: I'm quitting. I am quitting this class. I am dropping web page development.

⁓

"I want to drop web page development for pottery," I say to the guidance counselor, hoping to god he will say yes.

"Sorry. Pottery's full."

He leans back in his chair and puts his hands behind his

head. His carefully groomed soul patch and ornately shaped sideburns cry out to me for acceptance. *See, kids... I'm just like one of you....*

"Okay, then cooking."

"No dice. Canceled—not enough people signed up."

I go moist in the armpits. I cannot sit in that class every day for the next eight weeks. I will go completely cuckoo, rip my hair out, and be hauled out of the computer lab, bald and screaming.

"Well, is anything else available?"

He looks over the catalog on his computer.

"Nope, sorry."

"Is there anything at all that I can do for the period? Office assistant? Writing tutor?"

Long pause.

"Well..."

"What? What is it? I'll take anything."

"Well, all I have available is an open position in the audio-visual department."

"You mean like an aide?" I say, and instantly conjure images of those creepy burnout guys in wifebeaters, the guys who push dusty TVs around the halls, reeking of cigarettes.

"Yes, but you have a pretty good GPA and I don't think that, with the college prep track you're on, AV would be appropr—"

I interrupt him. "I'll take it."

"Yes. Well, while we have almost two thousand kids here at Lakewood and while the audiovisual aides provide a valuable service to the student body—"

He stops abruptly, then continues. "Please, who are we kidding here? We both know they sign up for AV to get out of taking real classes and the school calls it a service because it keeps troublemakers out of their hair for an hour. Computer science courses are much more suited for you. Besides, you'll be stuck down there the whole grading period with only one other student, and you might not like—"

I lean forward and look into his eyes.

"I said, I'll take it."

~

I head to where the audiovisual department is located. Basement level. A land I've not yet ventured to in my two and a half years at Lakewood High. I pass several storage closets; a service elevator; and then, peering in through a little window, what appears to be a sad little "Faculty Only" exercise room containing mismatched free weights and an antiquated treadmill. Finally, at the end of the corridor, I find another door that reads: AUDI ISU L DEPT, and underneath the sign, someone has carved KNOCK OR DIE.

I rap lightly, which causes a flurry of activity on the other side. The door creaks open, and standing before me is Corey Livingston, the biggest stoner at Lakewood High, all six-foot-three, two-hundred-plus pounds of him. He's bleary-eyed, and his tousled, longish hair is sticking up on one side. He's wearing about fifty T-shirts, and the top one, which says SDMF, while technically clean, looks like it was pulled from a Dumpster. He's not fat—not yet, anyway. He's just big and tall, and you know that those love handles he doesn't have yet, they're in there somewhere, waiting patiently for a six-pack of beer or pizza slice too many.

He mumbles while rubbing at his eyes and yawning.

"All the video recorders are signed out until tomorrow."

"I don't need a video recorder. I'm supposed to come down here and help."

"Help what?"

"I have no idea. I don't know what it is you people—I mean— what an audiovisual aide does exactly."

He finally takes a good look at me. His face perks up a bit, like he recognizes me or something. He looks me up and down. Not in a creepy way; more like he can't believe it's me. I get self-conscious of the way I'm dressed: jeans, Abercombie & Fitch hoodie, Chuck Taylors.

I cross my arms over my chest to conceal the big A&F logo emblazoned across the front of me—the "A" and "F" stretched out by the width of my chest, and the "&" sitting all tiny and shrunken in the middle. He probably thinks I'm some bourgeois poser. And why shouldn't he? I'm wearing the uniform, right?

"I know who you are. You're that cheerleader who—"

He stops. His mouth hangs open. I can see the unspoken words ballooning out: *got into all that trouble on the ski trip.*

God, and he smells like cigarettes, too. Gross.

I grunt with disgust, then turn and walk back down the hall. Forget this crap. No way am I spending the next eight weeks with this loser, what with him towering over me in judgment, reeking of Marlboros.

"Wait!"

I stop and turn. He ducks back inside the room, like he needs to get something, and comes back out holding a DVD and a broom.

"You need to take this movie on global warming or some bullshit up to room 208."

He pulls a dollar out of his wallet and tucks it inside the cover of the video. Then he sets the case on the floor and swats the whole thing down the hall with the broom. It almost slides past me before I stop it with my foot.

"And hit the cafeteria on your way back. I need a Dr Pepper."

He walks back into the AV room, shutting the door behind him.

My disgust morphs into rage. I stomp up the steps to room 208 with a thin trickle of steam pouring from my ears. Over my dead body is a hulking loser of the Living Stoner's magnitude going to strip me of my last shreds of self-respect. I bang on the door of room 208, ready to toss the DVD into the room like a Frisbee.

I'm thrown for a loop when Paige opens the door.

We stand looking at each other.

"Hey," I say.

"Hey," she says.

And then the apology comes rolling out.

"I'm so sorry, Paige. What I did was really stupid. I didn't mean to get you in trouble."

She looks behind her at the teacher, who is busy shuffling papers at her desk. The class is working in groups, and it's noisy. Paige steps outside into the hallway to talk to me, leaving the door slightly cracked.

"Look," she says. "I get that you're sorry. But my parents flipped their shit, Sid. I'm in total lockdown."

"Maybe my mom or I could talk to them?" I offer, wincing.

"No, that's not a good idea," she says, looking down, embarrassed.

Then the truth sinks in. The truth about how Paige's parents have never really cared for our friendship. I'd never given them a reason to dislike me, but I've always had this feeling that they'd prefer that Paige ditch me. It has more to do with my mom than anything. Oh, the drive-by digs that Mrs. Daniels has lobbed about my mother being "twice-divorced," about Liam and me being "latchkey kids." Every time I see her, she makes a point of asking if my mom's dating anyone new, chipper-like, as if she cares a particle about my mom and her happiness. She's just digging for dirt. She even referred to Liam as my "*half* brother" once—"How's your little *half* brother doing, Sid?" Paige is mortified by her mom's sneaky little barbs, so she rarely invites me over.

Well, Mrs. Daniels may have not had a legit reason to despise Sid Murphy before, but now she sure does. I practically wrapped that reason up with a shiny bow and a handwritten card that says, *You were right. Like mother, like daughter. Skanks to the bone.*

The teacher calls for Paige, asking who's at the door.

I take the money out of the DVD and hand the video over to Paige.

"Maybe when things cool off," she says timidly, stepping back inside.

I don't say anything back. I walk away, fighting back the tears that are pricking my eyes. As I walk down the hall, I harden my heart and think, *Fine. Be that way. I don't need friends. I don't need anyone.* My determination not to cry grows into anger on the way to grab the Living Stoner's pop from the vending machine. I head back down to the basement—while shaking his Dr Pepper up like a can of spray-paint.

I open the AV door and see him leaned back in a chair, practically sliding down out of the seat with his head thrown back, mouth open. The SDMF shirt is now off, rolled up and covering his eyes. The top shirt is now vintage Billy Idol. I slam the door, and the Living Stoner jumps in his seat. His earbuds are jerked from his head and his shirt mask falls into his lap. Thrash metal is playing so loudly I can hear it from across the room.

"Let's just get it all out now," I say. "Make your comments, your jokes. Get it all out of your system. Let's talk all about how Sid Murphy slept around on the ski trip and is such a big, fat whore, how she was so hell-bent on getting laid and is such a raving slut.... Woo-hoooo!"

I throw my arms over my head and wave them around like a lunatic.

"I don't mind, because I like to talk. In fact, I have lots to say. Like how you, for instance, took a little vacation last year to go to juvie and spent ninety days at Club Cuyahoga for dealing drugs."

He looks at me and starts smiling. He's getting a charge out of my tirade, which makes me even more nuts.

"Oh, you think it's funny? Who are you to judge me, anyway? A half-baked, pothead, ex-juvie thug?"

I rear back to launch the Dr Pepper at him and he throws his arms up over his face.

"Whoa! Killer! Calm down!"

I stop mid-throw and wonder why it is that I'm unloading on this stoner I don't even know. Why him? Why not hunt down the person I really hate, the one who caused all this, and unload on him?

"No. I don't think it's funny. I think *you're* funny," he says. "You wanna try and fight me or something, Murphy? Jesus, settle down."

He clears his throat and his chuckling tapers off.

"Relax, Irish. I mean, we're all guilty of something, right?"

I walk over and set the can of pop in front of him on the table.

"Your Dr Pepper," I say with bitter contempt, "and don't call me Killer, or Irish, or anything that isn't my name. My name? Is Sid."

"Fine, jeez, whatever, *Sid*. Why so much hate? Personally, I think it rocks that one of you cheerleaders finally put down the Kool-Aid and joined the rest of us plebes in our lowly quest for fun."

He pulls back the tab on the can.

I step back as a geyser of Dr Pepper sprays all over him, all over the table, all over the chair and floor. Billy Idol looks out at me and snarls through the brown syrup that has completely coated him and his trusty guitar. Stoner Boy jumps up, arms out to his sides, hair and face dripping, looking down at himself, stunned.

"Holy shit," he says, letting out a cough of a laugh.

Then he looks at me like he can't believe I just did that. And truthfully, I can't believe I just did that either. Wow. He's really sopping wet with Dr Pepper. Maybe I'd better run?

I start to backpedal. "Uh, I...I didn't know—"

"Stop," he says, holding up his hands. "Don't apologize. Because that...was brilliant."

He takes off the Billy Idol shirt and wipes his face with it. Billy is replaced with a long-sleeved plain white T-shirt.

"Well played," he says, smiling and pointing a finger at me. "But when you least expect it? Expect it. Because I've got eight weeks to plot my revenge."

Then he slides his fingers through his hair and sits back down. He leans over and starts slurping up puddles of pop from the table like he's four. I get a good look at his eyes for a few seconds before his bangs fall back down over them. They're brown—big with long lashes.

I turn away so he won't see my face and how hard I'm trying not to smile.

9

I google him sometimes. I don't know why.

I know his name isn't what he said it was. Dax Windsor is not a real person, but he does exist. It's the name of a doctor on a soap opera that was canceled back in the eighties. Can you believe that? When I read that, I wanted to take a sledgehammer to my laptop and then go turn on the oven, crawl inside, and shut the door. God, I am so dumb. His real name could be Rumpelstiltskin for all I know.

But still, I always go back for more. When I'm unable to sleep, most nights actually, I'll fire up the laptop, hop on the Internet, and promise myself that I'm just going to do normal stuff. I promise myself that I'm just going online to check e-mail or IM with the second-string replacement friends I sit with at lunch,

Bethany Morris and Emma Jackson. Cofounders of the LHS Society for Kinder Living, otherwise known as Fanatical Vegans. Usually, though, I just hide out offline on Facebook and stalk Kirsten's and Paige's profiles. They've got new pictures— ones from the ski trip that are all cropped and free of Sid Murphy. There's this one, though, a close-up of the two of them on the ski lift, and I can see a little curl of my hair on Kirsten's shoulder. When I see the curl and the ski lift, things go quickly downhill from there. My fingers become possessed and I start googling horrible things: date rape, drug rape, travel rape, vacation rape, Dax Windsor, Windser, Winzor.

I don't know how it happens. It just does. I search and search for clues to tell me what happened, where he is, who else he has done this to. I find nothing but inner sickness. I get so torn up and panic-stricken that I have to slam my laptop shut and raise my window, stick my head out into the cold night, and try not to scream. I don't know what to do with it, this lack of peace, this need to know. I want it to go away but it won't.

Every night it comes back.

Every night I am searching.

10

It's Friday and last period is over, so I head out of the gym rolling an AV cart back toward the basement. I had the pleasure of running the movie projector during that oh-so-lovely freshman assembly on STDs. It was pretty awful having to sit through that movie for a second time, especially since…well…you know. I mean, I think I'm fine, everything feels normal enough—down south, if you catch my drift—but still, I couldn't wait for that movie to end.

In front of me in the crowded hall are three freshman girls. They're all squeezed together shoulder-to-shoulder, holding their books and gushing about some boys they met at the movie theater. It reminds me of how things used to be with Kirsten, Paige, and me when we were that age. Everything was so exciting back then. It's been a few weeks now, and neither of them has made any attempt to talk to me. I wrote them both, saying I was sorry again. I got no replies, just crickets. I cut down an unfamiliar hallway so I won't have to listen to these three girls being best friends anymore.

I pass by the woodshop, slowing down a bit to peek in the long windows that run horizontally down the wall. The Living Stoner is in there hooking up a stereo system, a tribe of flunkies gathered around him. A piece of paper is being passed around, and the guys are all laughing about it. Right before I reach the end of the window, I see the Living Stoner grab the paper off of a guy in a red sweatshirt. He looks at it, then gives the guy a shove before stuffing it into his back pocket.

Ten bucks says it's his report card.

He's not the brightest bulb in the chandelier, from what I've heard. Bethany and Emma told me all about him. Even though they're a bit kooky with their meat-is-murder-enviro-nutball world views, my lunch buddies seem like reliable sources. I told Bethany I was doing AV instead of computers, and she offered to rub her head against mine, in case I needed to borrow some IQ points after losing them to Corey. She said he used to get made fun of in elementary school when he read out loud. According to her, between the inborn stupidity and the permanent marijuana cloud hovering over his house, Corey Livingston is operating with a dangerously low amount of brain cells. Three to be exact: one for growing pot, one for smoking pot, and one for dealing pot. Then Emma added a fourth: eating, so he can nom after smoking all that pot.

I drop off the cart, and right before I lock the AV door, I see Corey's backpack sitting in a chair. We don't have keys to this room, so I leave it unlocked for him. On my way back up the steps, I run into him.

"AV room's still open; your backpack's in there," I say, hurrying past him and up the steps. My house is technically walking distance from the school, but if I hurry, I can catch the RTA and ride most of the way.

"Sid, wait!" Corey says.

I stop and look down at him from the top of the steps. He just stares up at me from below, saying nothing. I give him this gesture like *What? Spit it out. I'm in a rush, here.*

"I need to talk to you. Tell you something," he says.

"Can it wait?" I say. "Seriously, I have zero seconds to spare right now."

He shakes his head no. And he looks worried. Which makes me worried. Did he accidentally blow up a stereo in the woodshop or something? Am I in trouble, too?

I look ahead at the crowded hallway emptying out. The clock down the hall reads two forty. Even if I run, I probably won't make the two forty-five bus. I resign myself to hoofing it home and head back down the steps. He meets me halfway.

"I'm missing the bus for this, so I hope it's good," I say.

He looks around, puts his head down a bit, and mumbles to himself, "Man, this is weird."

"Dude," I say. "I have a half-hour walk ahead of me and it's freezing balls outside. Spill it, already."

He sighs and pulls out a piece of paper from his back

pocket—the same piece of paper that his friends were passing around in the woodshop, I think.

"I didn't make this, okay," he says. "I want you to know that. But it's being passed around and I thought you should know about it. I think it's from that cheerleader bitch's Facebook or something."

I reach out and grab it from him. I start to open it.

"Wait!" he says.

I stop, look at him.

"Uh, I mean, maybe you should wait until you get home? You might not want me standing here. We don't know each other that well and—"

"What the hell is it?" I say. "Me naked or on the toilet or something?"

"No!" he says. "Well, I mean, not *totally* naked or anything. It's just kind of..."

I wrestle it open.

My stomach drops.

The picture is a close-up of me in my bra, pulling on my cheerleading vest. It's a little blurry but the hair is unmistakable. It's me, all right. And holy shit, my boobs are huge. I can't believe how massive my boobs look on camera.

I look at Corey. His eyes look sorry. I open my mouth to say something, but then I turn and run up the steps and down the hallway.

"It's not that bad!" he yells. "You can't even see anything. Really!"

I blow past the vice principal, Mr. Davis, and he yells at me, too.

"You! With the red curls! Slow it down!"

I peel around a corner and head for the girls' restroom. I hide out until I'm sure the school is mostly empty. Then I run all the way home. My brother and mom are in the kitchen; as I pass by them, I tell my mom I have homework, and then I dash to my room, slam the door shut, and lock it. I fire up my laptop and go to Starsha's Facebook page.

On her status, she has directed everyone to her new blog, gingerbitch.com, the header of which is the picture of me in my bra with a little black edit box covering my eyes. As if that is supposed to disguise me somehow. I must have been getting changed in a locker room at an away football game. She and her minions must have taken it with a phone then laughed all winter about Ginger Bitch Murphy's double-D rack. There is also a picture of my bent-over butt during a cheerleading pyramid. Swell.

But what really hurts, what really cuts deep, are the other pictures. There are pictures of me in elementary school when I still had all the baby fat. Me doing embarrassing kid stuff. In one, I'm wearing an ugly grass-stained polka-dot bikini that's a few sizes too small. I'm rocketing headfirst down a Slip 'N Slide during a field day on the last day of school. Then there's another one of me making an obnoxious face and wearing a SpongeBob shirt. It's been cropped to cut out everyone else in the picture, but I know who is standing next to me—Kirsten. It was at her tenth birthday party, the year I decided to have a go at straightening my own hair because I hated how curly it was. I ironed it with my mom's flat iron and burned it so badly that she had to practically shave it off. I looked like a fat, kinky-headed boy.

I slam my laptop shut, race back down the stairs, grab my coat, and head out the door. My mom chases after me, holding a spaghetti strainer.

"Where you going? Dinner's almost ready!"

"Library! Big paper!"

"Eat first, and then I'll drive you."

"It's only four blocks! McFatty's is right there, I'll grab a Big Mac!"

Then I run the nine blocks to Kirsten's house and bang on her door.

I'm seriously going to strangle her.

Kirsten opens the door. She gives me this look like *Whatdoyouwant?*

"You bitch! How could you do that to me?" I say. "Those were pictures we took in grade school! I thought you were my friend!"

Her brows wrinkle up in confusion. "Wha—"

"Don't play dumb—at least have the spine to admit it! The picture of me at your birthday party after I'd scorched myself bald!"

"What are you talking about?" and her voice is getting louder now. Oh, she's good. She looks and sounds genuinely perplexed.

"The website, dumbass, gingerbitch.com! Like you don't know."

Her faces blanches. "What?"

I mock her, "*What?* Please, the one Starsha put up to make fun of me!"

She takes a deep breath and steps closer to me.

"Look, I may be pissed at you," she says, "but *that* I would never do. I'm not the only person in Lakewood with a camera, you know. My mom made me invite every girl in the class to that party. Like thirty girls or something. I don't know where the pictures came from, but they didn't come from me. And frankly, I resent the implication. Although I do understand it. See, you're in deep shit with me right now, so you're turning things around in your head to make me look like the bad guy. You were the one who tied this friendship to the tracks and walked off with some frat boy you just met. You! So when I said I don't need any more of your bullshit drama, I meant it!"

She steps back inside and slams the door.

My throat catches and the tears start trying to push their way out. Because this is yet another thing that he has taken from me. If the ski trip hadn't happened, I'd be hanging with my besties, hating on my enemies, and pretty much loving life. My peace, my virginity, my friends, cheerleading, and now my pride; he's taken it all. And with everything he takes, the Fairy Tale Lie unravels a little more. And I need it. I need the Fairy Tale Lie.

I fight back the tears by taking off running. I run the streets of Lakewood and let the biting wind and gritty slush harden me from the outside in. As I run, my face and ears ignite with a cold burn. My muscles ache, like my legs are still figuring out how to run. But after a while, the strangest, most astonishing thing starts happening—the worries, the heartache, they just start falling away, just dropping out of my mind and onto the pavement. The ski trip, Dax, Kirsten, the website...*plop, plop, plop.* It's like magic. I run and wonder about it. I wonder about how speed and fatigue, wet and cold can act like a spell, how they can affect the body and the mind, how pain can feel good sometimes. And running in January is painful, trust me. But I focus in on it, to keep everything else from getting back in. The cold burn that started in my face and hands spreads to my feet and legs. It stays in my extremities a long time but I keep up with it by running my engine at full speed.

I run until I'm colder and more solid and unyielding than I've ever felt in my life. And I don't care that it hurts. I don't care that I want to scream from the pain, because I think it might be worth it, this terrible, shredding pain. Because at some point, the numbness will come—it must come. And maybe if I do this long enough, and do this often enough, the numbness will stay and I will no longer be Sid Murphy, helpless ragdoll, sleeping toy. I will be Sid Murphy, human glacier, suit of armor forged from ice.

⌒

It's Monday morning and I am in luck. It snowed twelve inches overnight and shows no signs of stopping. So, lucky me, snow day. Even luckier, I'm home alone. Liam spent the weekend with his dad and stayed an extra night. My mom went to work at her job because the concept of "adult snow day" only exists in warm, tropical locales like Cincinnati and Dayton.

I spend the whole day shoveling. First the driveway, then the sidewalk, then the neighbor's porch. Every two hours, the snow is back. The menial nature of the job is a relief from having to think too much, and I enjoy the backbreaking pain of it. I look over at Mr. Snowblower three doors down and stifle the urge to yell "Hey, pussaaay! That all ya got?"

I start to get woozy around noon and realize that I haven't eaten. The hunger strike has to end. I go inside and stuff my face with anything I can get my hands on. Dried cereal, Pop-Tarts, a whole stack of bologna. It's like I haven't eaten in weeks. Wait, that's right, I haven't really eaten in weeks. And suddenly I'm so freakin' hungry, I can't cram it in fast enough. Who knew cold SpaghettiOs right out of the can could taste so heavenly? When my belly is stretched to capacity, I stumble to my room and lie down to enjoy it. I close my eyes, and at first it's kind of awesome, like I'm floating in a warm, quiet ocean. But about five minutes into the groggy haze, the room starts spinning. My stomach cramps up and my mouth goes all watery and metallic-tasting. I run to the bathroom and…

…blagggh…out it all comes.

After a few minutes, when the heaving stops, I get up and rinse my mouth with mouthwash. I splash my face with cold water and look in the mirror. My eyes are bloodshot, but I feel so much better that it kind of weirds me out a little. I shake it off and go back outside to give Mother Nature another ass-kicking. I shovel fast and hard and try to push the images of food vomit out of my brain. I shovel and shovel and pretend like the whole thing never even happened.

It's eleven p.m. and I've been lying here for over an hour. I went to bed right after dinner, exhausted from shoveling all day. Now I've woken up and there is no hope of getting back to sleep anytime soon.

Also, I'm starving.

It's like my body is catching up with itself after the weeks of not-eating since the ski trip. Like someone stuck cardiac paddles to a really lazy tapeworm that's been living in the folds of my stomach: *Clear! Zzzzzz! Now eat!*

I go into the kitchen and eat the leftover pizza from dinner—three slices of pepperoni with anchovies—along with a shit-ton of other stuff. I start getting that crampy, drunk feeling again. I sit at the table and feel disgusted with myself.

I glance over at the sink.

God, it would be so easy. Just lean over the sink, take your finger and—

But I don't want to go there. I'm not turning into some walking, talking, bingeing, puking, made-for-TV train wreck. I get up and head back to my room.

I try to read. No luck. I go online and force my fingers, eyes, and brain to just check my e-mail. I force my fingers NOT to perform Google acts of horror and not to go on torture expeditions at gingerbitch.com.

I have a message that Corey Livingston has requested my friendship. I go to Facebook and accept him, but before I can begin a proper stalking of his profile, he pops up into my chat screen.

Hey, Sid. Good news.

Hey, Corey. Oh?

That website was taken down.

I shrink Facebook and immediately race to gingerbitch .com. Instead of me in my bra, there's only a blank screen that says, *The site you are looking for was not found.* I'm relieved, of course. I mean, Jesus, who wouldn't be. But then I start wondering how it is that Corey knows the website is down, unless he went trolling the Internet in search of cheap Sid Murphy thrills. I write him back.

How did u know it was down if u werent on the site? Going 2 gawk or something?

NO!

Long pause.

Then he writes: **I know b/c I'm the one who contacted the server and made them take it down. Thx a lot, Sid.** And he's pasted a copy of the letter.

Attention Blogpal, I am writing because I am the father of the girl in the pictures on gingerbitch.com (see link). She's a minor and if you don't shut that blog down immediately, I'm going to call the authorities and then sue you for every last penny you've got. Signed, Ivan A. Kegman, Attorney-at-Law.

And I feel like a total jerk now.

Sorry. I didnt mean 2 say that.

U were upset. Its ok.

Thx. I really appreciate that u did that.

No prob. Then he writes, **But dont think Ive forgotten the dr pepper incedent. Ur still totally screwed on that one.**

Gotcha. Bring it.

Then we both just sit and stare at our screens. I mean, that's what I do. He could be sewing curtains over there for all I know.

Finally, he writes: **Well. Its late and ur prob tired. Ill let u go.**

I pause and try to think of something funny to say. But everything I come up with sounds stupid so I just write: **Thx again. Really.**

No prob. Cya at AV Irish.

I write, **Cya Corey**, then I pause, backspace, and leave it at **Cya.**

Then I click myself offline so he won't know I'm still on Facebook. His user name drops offline, too, and I wonder if he really left, or just fake-left, like me. I look back over our exchange, reading it a few times through. I resist the urge to cut and paste the lines into my BEST IMS OF ALL TIME file, something I often do when I have a really memorable or funny exchange with someone. If we'd chatted about something other than Starsha's horrid website with pictures of my enormous half-naked breasts on it, I would have saved it. But I don't want to remember why Corey and I were chatting, just that we were. So I click out, shut it down, and head to the living room to watch late-night TV shows in hopes they'll make me sleepy. And on my way through the house, I try not to think about how Corey Livingston is not stupid at all. I try not to think about how he was smart enough to write that fake letter, something I was too stupid to think up when I carry a 3.7. I try not to think about how Corey Livingston only misspelled one word during the whole chat—*incident*—and how that's better than most guys, even with spell-check.

~

I go to the living room, where my mom is sacked out on the couch. I look at her, all relaxed and dreamy. She's probably dancing through a meadow with pink butterflies or floating in a gondola with a hot guy feeding her grapes. Doing whatever it is she does when that second layer of Ambien kicks in.

The TV is running, so I sit down on the love seat and pick up where my mom left off. *Iron Chef America* is just starting on Food Network. I settle in to watch our local Cleveland boy, Michael Symon, take a Parisian-trained charlatan to the Kitchen Stadium woodshed. I usually get kind of pumped up watching this show, especially when Iron Mike is swinging the spatula, but my enthusiasm takes a nosedive when, sadly, the mystery ingredient is revealed.

Okra. Bleck.

All those anchovies go darting around my stomach like they're fighting in a bucket.

I flip up one channel—QVC—Southwest Treasures. Joy. I watch Mary Beth do her chipper best to sell me the most god-awful turquoise nugget necklace ever crafted. Yep, this is it. This should bore me right through the Sandman's front door.

And an hour later, it's two o'clock in the morning and I'm still bright-eyed and bushy-tailed. All that pizza-anchovy-swill is still slopping around inside me. I turn off the TV and pull the blanket up around my mom. Then I grab my tennis shoes and coat and sneak out the back door.

I'll run it out of me, this sick, gross feeling. I won't puke it out. I'll run it out.

I mean, running is good for you, right?

The snow has finally ceased and it's a bit warmer than it was a few days ago, but I bring a hat and gloves anyway. The running-until-frozen-solid thing worked great on Friday after Kirsten and I had it out on her porch, but when I actually got home? Not so much. I was raw and wind-burned. I looked like I'd stuck my head and hands in the microwave. My mom was pissed when I came rolling in after dark, heaving and sweating, my face lit up like a jack-o'-lantern. She made me soak my hands in warm water and took the blow dryer to my face, then bitched me out for leaving my phone behind and not calling her for a ride. Thank god she didn't notice that I had no actual books or paper on me. I'll have to be more careful about running in bad weather; bundle up, buy some running pants or running tights—or whatever the hell it is runners wear.

Ronan peeks out of his door in the garage and stares at me as I leave the drive. I run around the neighborhood for about an hour, using the street because the sidewalks are knee-deep in snow. I cut down some side streets until I reach The Diner.

Shelley Keep It Green is not there, but another girl is working. She is sitting at the counter like a customer and is watching a *Seinfeld* rerun on a TV mounted in the corner. I keep going and pass Johnny Malloy's Irish Pub, where a drunk comes waddling out, yelling profanities to no one in particular. He nearly knocks me over, and then yells, "Watch where yer goin'!" I cross the street quickly and he yells again, "Ah, I was just joshin'! Don't be a-scared. Hey! Wanna go fer a drink?"

I run the whole way home. Ronan is still waiting for me in his pen. He rarely gets walked anymore because Mrs. O'Leary's knees are shot. Her nephew has to come over twice a week to clean his run and cusses like a truck driver the whole time.

I pet Ronan through the fence and tell him that next time, I will take him with me.

11

I am pure exhausted. I spend most nights with my eyes popped open like dinner plates, jogging the streets with a monstrous-looking dog loping alongside me. I keep pepper spray at the ready because I think Ronan would sooner lick his balls than bite someone, but he is good company and enjoys the late-night adventures. It feels good to run. Not that suicidal, ugly, no-hat-or-gloves type of running I did that one time, but just regular, head-up, well-clothed, bouncy type running that says, "Look at me! I'm a jogger! I heart jogging!"

It feels good, healthy. It's like this whiteout comes over me and strips everything away until all I can feel and see and hear is the running, my feet rhythmic on the pavement, the burn in my legs and lungs, the road ahead. Plus, the new running shoes I picked up at Geiger's are kind of cute. I don't mind occasionally looking down at them. They match my hat and gloves: navy with pink stripes.

My mother has no idea I run at night, sometimes for two and three hours at a time. If she knew, she'd freaking kill me because a) *What sane female jogs at night, Sid?*; b) *You have to get up for school, so get your ass in bed, already*; and c) *You already ran after dinner for two hours so just what in the hell is going on here, young lady?*

Ugh. I do. I run after dinner sometimes, too.

I know it sounds crazy—like what kind of nutcase runs four or five hours a day?—but it's not like I do it all the time. Just on days when I'm really anxious or stressed out. Anyhow, my mom would flip out if she knew about the night running.

Katherine, she's a sly one. Not a whole lot gets by her. Thankfully, she pops that Ambien at ten forty-five every night, so I just sit and wait for the sleep fairies to whisk her away, then out the door I go.

The downside to all this late-night exercise is that it doesn't bode well for daytime learning. I'm beat at school. I play catch-up with naps on the weekends when my mom is at open houses and Liam's at his dad's. And sometimes after school, before my mom gets home, I'll lay in Liam's bed with him and doze while he plays video games or watches cartoons. Mostly, that's all I do anymore—doze. Deep, uninterrupted, dreamy sleep used to be a must for me, but I don't like staying still and quiet for that long anymore. One, maybe two hours at a pop, several times, spread out over a twenty-four-hour period, works better now; because when I stay asleep for more than a couple hours or so, my mind gives in. My mind sinks deep down and starts dreaming. It turns into a very vulnerable place, a blank canvas where horror comes to fingerpaint and play. So, no thanks, you can keep the dreaming.

But it's starting to catch up to me. My grades are in the crapper. It's Thursday, I'm at school, and the minutes are creeping forward like paralyzed snails. I take my midterms and use my arm to prop myself up, but my head keeps rolling forward, jerking me awake. I'm on a narcoleptic-insomniatic roller coaster with no brakes. The up-and-moving moments between classes are only slightly more bearable. I walk like the living dead from class to class wearing sweatpants and sweatshirts.

On top of that, I feel like a jackass because I've avoided Corey all week. For the last couple of days, instead of going to the AV room last period, I've been going to the nurse's office carrying tall tales of migraines and PMS. But two days on the nurse's cot is about all you can get around here before they start talking doctor's notes. So I have no choice now—time to face the Ginger Bitch music.

I feel weird seeing him after what happened. I mean, what he did, writing that letter, it was really cool, and I should feel grateful and relieved to have a person in my life who would do that for me. But somehow, right now at least, the gratefulness and relief are being outweighed by feelings of utter humiliation. I might have been able to shake the mortification earlier if gingerbitch.com weren't still such hot gossip around here. Unfortunately, even though Corey put gingerbitch.com out of her misery, the stench of her rotting corpse lingers on. A couple guys made shitty comments to me yesterday at lunch, and it's pretty much sucked up my whole week. I'm usually fairly adept at shutting haters down, particularly if it's in defense of someone else, but when someone cracks off about my boobs or ass, especially right to my face, my sharp tongue tends to curl in on itself. The worst part? Bethany, my new BFF? She pretended she didn't hear the comments when I damn well know she did. She was standing right next to me when two sophomores looked at my chest and said: *I wonder if there's any melon back there? For some reason, I'm craving melon.* I grabbed a juice, threw fifty cents on Bethany's tray, and stepped out of line, headed to the table.

Back in the day, Kirsten would have dressed those guys down until they ran crying from the cafeteria holding onto their shrunken wieners. Even tiny little Paige wouldn't have stood by and done *nothing.* She would have thrown a spork or called them assholes or *something.*

Not Bethany. Newp. Bethany busied herself with intently studying salad toppings and just left me flapping in the breeze. When she finally made her way to the table, she immediately launched into an overblown tale about her sister's pregnant guinea pig getting lost in the couch for two days. It was obviously fiction, but everyone laughed, and so I pretended to buy it, too.

Ha, ha, ha, that's so funny, Bethany, ha, ha, ha. So on and so forth. Whatever, point is, gingerbitch.com and her big, brassiered breasts are still out there, lingering.

But…no more hiding out. Despite the fact that the Awkward is crawling up my insides like a fungus, I trudge forth.

Downstairs to the basement.

Headed for the AV room.

Gnah.

I stand outside the door, take a deep breath, and turn the knob. When I step inside, I stop in my tracks. The room is different. The table is pushed to the side to make room for a big flat-screen TV and two beat-up, mismatched recliners. The TV is propped up and anchored to a dolly using several strings of bungee cables. Corey's behind it, plugging it in or something.

"Hey, Sid. Welcome to our new home theater," he says from behind the screen.

I walk in and set my stuff on one of the beat-up chairs. I think he's hooking up a DVD player.

"How'd you get a TV that big down here? And furniture?"

"Simple," he says. "Mrs. Nicholson? Teaches freshman history or some shit? She went on maternity leave. The sub couldn't get the TV to work, so instead of telling him he's an idiot who can't work a simple remote, I told him the TV was busted and I needed to take it down for repairs. Then I snagged my friend TJ from one of his many study halls and had him help me roll it down here. The chairs are from one of those storage rooms down the hall. I jimmied the lock—drama club props or something. Wanna know the best part?"

"What?"

"Nicholson's out for the rest of the grading period. TV's all ours."

"Clever, clever," I say, laughing, and then sit down. For a Goodwill chair, it's not bad.

"So what are we watching?" I ask. "Soaps? *Judge Judy*?"

"Got it. Finally," he says to himself, and then pops up from behind the screen waving a DVD. "I thought we could broaden our horizons with a little community theater."

He says it in a snotty, professorial accent.

"Uh. Okay," I say.

So I guess we're watching some PBS crap. Well, at least we're not talking about gingerbitch.com and Siddy, Siddy's Big Fat Titties. . . .

He walks around to the DVD player and turns it on.

"You see, Ms. Murphy," he says, continuing on with the accent, "I'm a big supporter of the arts, so I thought a local production of *Peter Pan* would be just the thing. It was filmed in 1982 and was recently transferred to DVD, and it stars a young but dashing Albert C. Davis as that lovable rascal Peter."

Okay, now I'm thinking he might be high or something. Yes, he's definitely high. He and this TJ guy got high in the bathroom and stole a big-screen TV off the freshman sub and then they broke into a storage closet and stole Goodwill furniture off the drama club. Maybe Bethany was right about him.

He turns to me, sees me looking at him like he's nuts.

"Albert C. Davis?" he says.

Like I should know who or what he's talking about. I look at him blankly.

"Lakewood High's version of a third-world dictator? 'You! With the red curls! Slow it down!'"

"Oh!" I laugh. "Mr. Davis. Got it."

And so that's what we do for most of the period. In between running videos and equipment around, we laugh our asses off at Mr. Davis, age twenty, swinging from a ceiling in green tights to the tune of "You Can Fly! You Can Fly! You Can Fly!"

And because our recliners are right next to each other, I am able to zone in on something I haven't noticed before. The way Corey smells. I mean, I've picked up the aroma of cigarettes before—it's kind of a hard scent to miss—but I'm picking up something else now, something better. Doughnuts, maybe? I detect a definite Irish Spring, soapy thing going on, too. The blend of it all is rather intoxicating.

I try to ignore it and focus in on the TV. I laugh as Mr. Davis flits back and forth on the stage, jumping around on a poorly constructed pirate ship that is about to fall out from under him. I laugh and focus and try to ignore Corey's presence next to me and the smell of cigarettes, Irish Spring, and doughnuts.

I am dreaming of him. I'm dreaming that we're on the ski lift and he has his arm around me and is pulling me close and talking into my ear. I can't hear what he's saying; it's just whispered mumbling. Then I look ahead at the other side of the lift, the side with the empty returning chairs, and see Liam coming toward us. He's wearing his pajamas that look like a baseball outfit. He sees me and pushes his safety bar up and then slowly stands in the seat holding his arms out from his sides for balance.

"Look, Sid! No hands!" he yells.

I start to scream for him to sit down, to put his bar down and hang on, but something cold and slippery slides over my mouth and I'm unable to move it away—my limbs, my whole body is paralyzed. Frozen stiff, I sit with this snake of a man next to me and watch helplessly as Liam starts to fall, starts to plummet to the ground.

My eyes roll back in my head and my eyelids fly open. My heart is pounding and I'm soaked in a frightened sweat. I slip out of my bed and across the hall to Liam's room to sit on the edge of his race car bed and carefully, quietly, lay my head to his back. I want to wake him up. I want to fold him up in my lap and hug him tightly into me. But I just sit and listen to his heartbeat and breathing until my own heartbeat and breathing settle down again. When I'm calm and the nightmare seems far enough away, I get up and tiptoe out of his room and head downstairs. Out the back window, I can see Ronan staring at the back of the house. He is outside in his run, sitting attentively at the gate waiting for me. He is used to our routine by now.

Tonight, we have to run all the way to the twenty-four-hour pharmacy on Hilliard. It's kind of far, but it's the only place where I can get what I need at this hour. I get Ronan out of his pen and he makes no noise—no barking or jumping. He knows to be quiet and slip into his leash. We sneak around the house and down the driveway. He waits until we're down the street to start huffing and puffing and butting my legs with his head, the way dogs do when they're excited to see you and want petting or a treat. I stop walking and give him his due. I scratch behind his ears and give him the hamburger I didn't eat at dinner. Then we are off and running. We cut down a side street and onto Detroit. Everything is dark—all the bakeries, gift shops, and galleries are closed. The only places open are The Diner and Malloy's. I stop in front of the window at The Diner and jog in place so I can look inside. It's empty except for one man who hangs over a cup of coffee in a booth, and the night waitress is manning her post in front of the TV, watching that show where paparazzi stalkers hunt celebrities around the clock. They lurk in bushes or outside nightclubs and then report to base command with their photographic kill shots. Ugh, I would never see Shelley Keep It Green watching something like this. She's Discovery Channel or Nat Geo all the way.

Ronan snorts, letting me know he's had enough of this waitress and her dumb TV show, too. We take off, finding a steady, even pace for about half an hour. At this time of night, it's green lights the whole way down Detroit, where the pharmacy sits at the Hilliard intersection.

I don't want to leave Ronan outside, so I poke my head in the door to ask the cashier if I can bring him in. My night vision has kicked in, and the brightness of the store assaults my eyes.

"Can I bring my dog in? I'm afraid someone will steal him or he'll get spooked and run off."

She looks him up and down.

"I dunno, he's kind of big," she says.

"If he takes a crap, I'll clean it up, I swear. Besides, there's nobody here and I'll only be a sec."

She looks at me, still uneasy, but nods.

"Just tie him up by the door and make it quick."

"Thanks."

I walk over to the racks and candy machines by the door to look for a way to hitch him up. Easy listening music is playing overhead, Christopher Cross, waxing "poetic" about the inner serenity he has found through the pastime of "Sailing." I tell Ronan to stay and I loop his leash around the leg of the free circulars rack. I freeze when I see my mother's face staring back at me from *Homes Magazine*. That unsold Tudor on Lighthouse Road made the cover this issue, and her picture is in the corner of it. I get a stab of shame; it's like she is watching me and going, "Tsk, tsk, tsk," for what I'm about to do. I turn the magazine over so the cover isn't showing.

I walk quickly toward the pharmacy counter, where all the scandalous items are kept in plain view. The pharmacy window is shut and has a PHARMACIST ON BREAK, RING BELL FOR ASSISTANCE sign, with a big arrow pointing toward a makeshift doorbell.

I look over the shelves: packages of condoms, tubes of lubricants, cans of feminine spray.

And pregnancy tests.

Yes, I am late. Very, very late.

I scan the choices. So many different kinds—ones with little urine cups, ones with sticks to pee on, ones with blue lines, ones with pink dots. And then there are the simpleton ones that scream out PREGNANT or NOT PREGNANT in the little results window. I guess these tests are for the truly rattled, for the petrified basket cases who can't even bear to decode directions. I look at the prices, shocked at how expensive they are. A piece of plastic that you take a whiz on, stare at for three minutes, then toss out costs twenty dollars? I only have fifteen. There's a cheaper test, a generic store brand that costs twelve, but its spot on the shelf is empty and has an OUT OF STOCK sign in place of it.

I need one of these tests.

I stand deliberating for a minute and contemplate shoplifting. It's a small store. I look up at the round mirror at the end of the aisle that reflects back toward the cashier. She's at her counter. I can see Ronan, too. He's standing at attention, poker straight and looking in the direction where he had last seen me.

Shoplifting?

I don't even know how to go about it.

Do I shove it in my pocket? Slide it up my sleeve? Do I divert attention, take the heat off by buying something else?

I am suddenly terrified. I have never deliberately stolen a single thing in my life. When it comes to anything even remotely resembling thievery, I start to sweat and wear the guilt like a thrift-store wedding gown. I even feel guilty when I get free drink refills at Taco Bell. In fact, one time when I was about eleven, I accidentally walked out of a store holding a pack of gum in my hand. Kirsten, Paige, and I were at Everything's A Dollar buying candy and junk food for a sleepover. I'd meant to put the gum in our little shopping basket but was so engrossed in conversation while shopping that I just clean walked out with the gum in hand. About twenty minutes later, when we'd walked almost the whole way back to Paige's house, I realized I was holding a sweaty, melted pack of Bubblicious in my fist and made them walk all the way back in the roasting July heat so I could pay for it. Kirsten and Paige tried the whole way to talk me out of returning it.

You didn't mean to steal it, so it doesn't count, especially if you don't actually open and chew it.

Just throw it away at my house.

We can stop by the playground and pass it out to some little kids or something. That way it's like charity.

I felt like God was watching and some giant cosmic hammer would swing down and flatten me if I didn't pay for it. When we got into the parking lot, I had it all planned. Paige would stand outside with our bags and Kirsten and I would do a loop-de-loo around the store, walk up to the counter, and casually pay for the gum. No big deal. But when we got to the door, I was so afraid that I leaned halfway inside, chucked my ill-gotten gain toward the candy rack, and yelled, "Run!" We took off as though our very lives depended on it, convinced that the candy police were hot on our tails. One of our bags split open and we lost half our legitimate purchases somewhere between Everything's A Dollar and Paige's front porch.

"Can I help you find something?" a voice says behind me. I jerk around and the clerk is staring at me.

"Uh, uh..." I stammer. She looks down at what's in my hand.

"Ohhhh," she says. She's a college-age girl who looks like she doesn't actually go to college. She has stringy blond hair and long artificial nails, and she reeks of a sickly sweet, dessert-type perfume.

"Uh, I have to go. My dog is waiting."

I try to put the box back on the shelf, but my hands are shaking so badly that I knock off about ten other boxes. I squat down and start to pick them up. The reality of my situation sets in. No—it floods in. A voice says: *No one will blame you, your mom will understand, she will pay for a trip to the clinic.* And another voice argues: *But you couldn't live with having done that . . . ever . . . because he or she would still have been part of you . . . half from you . . .*

The store is getting very small and I am trying to grab boxes, wobbling around, toppling over, and grabbing the shelf to balance myself.

"Hey, calm down. It's okay," the cashier says, kneeling down to help me. "I've had several scares myself. Chances are good that you're not."

"I only have fifteen dollars," I say, looking at her and trying to choke back a nervous breakdown. "You're out of the store brand. I don't have enough. . . ."

She looks up at the empty space on the shelf. She reaches up and grabs the box next to it. The one that tells you in plain English if you're pregnant or not pregnant. The one that costs twenty dollars. She hands it to me.

"We have a replacement policy. If we're out of the store brand, you get the lowest priced brand name instead."

A wave of relief washes over me.

"Really?"

"No," she says, shrugging, "not really." Then she adds with an awkward laugh, "But we should!"

I smile a nervous smile and we both stand up. I pull my money out of my pocket and hand it to her all wadded up. My hands are still shaking. I look at her as she is smoothing out the bills. I memorize her face. Underneath her smudged black eyeliner there is a kindness, and I wonder if she knows Shelley Keep It Green. She will be the Drugstore Madonna to me now.

We walk to the counter and she rings me up. She hands me my change and I drop it in the little plastic box that is sitting on the counter with a little girl's picture pasted on it. I give the dollar and nine cents to Mia Peeples, age four, of Dogwood Lane, who needs help paying for an operation.

Then I thank the cashier and go to retrieve Ronan. As I open the door to leave, I stop halfway through it and look at my Drugstore Madonna, who is leafing through a magazine, and a need wells up inside me. Before I can stop it from coming out, the need spills quietly out of my mouth.

"I didn't want to."

She looks up from her magazine.

"He took it," I say. "He stole it from me."

I can feel my face getting hot, my eyes burning.

Her eyes are hurting and I am regretful now. I am sorry that I have handed her, uninvited, a piece of what I carry.

"I'm so sorry," she says.

"Me, too," I say with a trembling chin.

I confess these things to the Drugstore Madonna because I don't know her and she doesn't know me and I will never come into this store again. Ever. But I don't feel better having done it. The burden is actually heavier now.

"Thanks," I say, then turn and walk out the door.

I look down at Ronan. My mind says one thing: Run. Like he has heard me speak out loud, Ronan takes off and we run, as fast as we can, into the cold, starless night, the February air drying my face a little more with each step.

13

There is a God: NOT PREGNANT. I can only assume that stress, heavy exercise, and rapid weight loss have thrown my period off. I've lost sixteen pounds in five weeks, mostly off of my ample chest and plentiful thighs. But the badonkadonk junk? Still in the trunk. My ass is as big as it ever was.

So basically, none of my clothes hang right anymore. My mother has noticed my slimmer face and figure and keeps asking me if I'm sick. *No, I'm not sick,* I tell her. *I am going out for track and watching my weight. Jeez, shut up about it already.*

My mom has not sold a house in over a month. It is February, and while "lookers" are numerous, "buyers" are not. While we are not necessarily hurting to pay bills, I don't want to ask for money for new clothes. So I need a job if I want to buy them. I have filled out job applications at a pet supply store, Starbucks, and The Diner. I can walk and jog to all of these places. I figure it's not just for the clothes money, but it will be a good way to keep busy after school and on weekends. *Downtime* is no longer in my vocabulary.

So far, none of the places have called. Probably because my applications are so pitifully void of anything other than my name and address. There is always McDonald's; they're *always* hiring. Especially work virgins—they love to break in doe-eyed work virgins. If you're sixteen and have a pulse, you've got a job. But I'm not that desperate yet. I'll dip into my babysitting/ birthday money before I go that sad route. Besides, there's no point in buying clothes yet. I've still got nine pounds to lose. I figure by the time I fill out applications, then interview, then start working and finally get a paycheck, I will be at my desired goal weight and I can go shopping for new jeans and bras. I'm shooting for a C cup—a size I haven't seen since sixth grade.

I choose a pair of sweatpants, a black tee, and a hoodie before heading out the door. I run to school now. I load up on the deodorant, wash my face, and fix my hair in the locker room before anyone gets there. Only the janitors are there, and they don't seem to mind as long as I clean up after myself.

On my way out the door, I notice that the newspaper is sitting at Mrs. O'Leary's door, still wrapped in orange plastic. It doesn't seem right; Mrs. O'Leary never forgets her paper. She rises at four thirty sharp and has the paper completely read—cover to cover, coupons clipped, crossword done—and neatly folded at our door by seven for my mother to peruse over her morning coffee. She always sets the funnies on top with little notes written to Liam and me in the margins. All Mrs. O'Leary asks is that we take all the papers to the recycling headquarters once a month along with her glass and plastic.

I knock on her door but she doesn't answer. I peek in her front window and see that her television is on, set to mute with captions running because she has trouble hearing it now. Her door is locked, so I go around the house, pull back some overgrown shrubs, and peek into a side window. My heart drops into my stomach. She's in the hallway outside her bedroom, lying facedown on the floor.

I run back toward the front of the house. I trip coming up the porch steps and bang my shin really hard. I scramble inside and run through the house to find my mother. She's in the shower.

"Mrs. O'Leary! Mom! Help! It's locked! She's on the floor!"

My mom jerks back the shower curtain, sopping wet, the shower still running; grabs her robe; and runs to the junk drawer where she keeps a spare key to Mrs. O'Leary's half of our house.

⁓

Massive heart attack. The funeral was small—just her nephew, his family, a few scattered people from her bridge club, the priest, and us. I wanted to bring Ronan, but the priest wouldn't allow him in the church and the nephew didn't care enough to protest. Poor Ronan has howled nonstop for days. His howls of grief can be heard around the clock, far and wide, throughout the greater Cleveland area. My mom finally broke down and has been letting him inside at night.

We are watching *America's Got Talent*; I'm rooting for the black, dreadlocked guy from West Virginia who sings Sinatra. I love an underdog. A commercial comes on, so I get up to bring Ronan in for the night. When I get to the door, I see that a van is pulling up. Mrs. O'Leary's nephew is backing a van up to the garage like it's a moving truck. He gets out and heads over to the dog-run gate holding a leash.

My mom and I run out and ask him what he's doing.

"Getting rid of your problem. Thanks for keeping an eye on him, feeding him and whatnot."

"Where are you taking him?" I ask.

"The pound. My wife is allergic and I don't have time to take him to a wolfhound rescue. The nearest one is in Canada, and I can't take a day off work to drive him all the way to Toronto."

I freak. And I mean completely out. A beautiful specimen of a dog like Ronan? Unneutered? Sitting in the pound? He'll be snapped up by the first piece of breeder trash to come along. He'll be half-starved and sitting in his own crap in a week while the bloodsucking puppy mill owner sits back making a fortune off puppies. Ronan—my guardian angel—an unloved, shit-covered, flea-bitten puppy maker? Hell, no.

"Yeah, you're not taking him to the pound," I say. "Unbelievable. I mean, your aunt loved this dog. So he's staying right here. This is my dog now."

I snatch the leash from him before he tries to wrangle Ronan up into the van.

My mother, who has been fairly adamant about the fish-only rule, just looks at me like I have become possessed. I throw her a daggered look that says, *Mother or not, I will scratch your eyeballs out if you mess with me on this.* The nephew looks at my mom.

"Fine," she says. "But I'm paying the vet bills with your college money."

The nephew shrugs, climbs into his van, and slips quietly out the drive, happy to have his problem solved. My fears abated, I kneel down, hug Ronan close, and think, *This is my dog now.*

14

It is the middle of March, the grading period is almost over, and my grades are a disgrace. Three Cs. My mother, thankfully, is not a grade Nazi, so she will probably just tell me to do better next time, which I will.

I have a hat on, but my hair spills down behind me in frozen little coils. I took a shower before bed, so it was still damp when Ronan and I woke to go running. The weather is starting to break, but the snow is still piled up in places in dirty, half-melted clumps. Streetlamps light us up, every hundred feet or so, as we pad quietly down a deserted Lake Road, the park entrance just ahead.

I am deep in thought, tuned into the feel of my body, thumping along and enjoying the ease of my slimmer frame. I am thinking about how many calories I am burning, trying to do the calculations in my head, when an old white pickup truck passes us, slams on its brakes, and then pulls into the park entrance, blocking us from going forward. Ronan lets out a growl, bares his teeth, and leans forward, stretching his leash. This is the first time I have seen him act like anything other than a complete teddy bear. I turn to run us the other way and can hear the driver's side window being lowered behind me. I fumble for the pepper spray that I keep in my pocket.

"Murphy?" a voice says.

I turn around and recognize the face. It is the Living Stoner, a cigarette dangling from his lips. My Spidey senses, which were at five-alarm panic, quell, sending a warmish chill of relief up my spine, down my arm, through the leash, and into Ronan, who relaxes immediately. I breathe out and walk closer to the truck. I am sure I look frightful: sweating, breathing heavily, and sporting a red nose.

But it's not like I care or anything.

"Hey, Corey," I say, tilting my head back because he is so high up. He doesn't look at me. He can't take his eyes off Ronan. He takes the cigarette between his thumb and forefinger and blows a stream of smoke away from us, out the side of his mouth and into the cab of his truck.

"What the hell kinda dog is that?" he says, still looking at Ronan.

Ronan looks longingly over at a cluster of trees. I release his leash to the full extent and let him sniff his way over.

"He's the banana snow-cone making kind."

On cue, Ronan raises his leg and prepares to let loose on a

mound of remnant snow that has piled up against the trunk of an enormous tree.

"Oh, look," I say. "He's about to make a fresh batch. Want one?"

"Ha, ha. You're a riot," the Living Stoner says and stamps out his cigarette in the ashtray.

When Ronan finishes, he walks over, rears up, plants both paws in the window and drags a huge meaty tongue across the Living Stoner's face.

"Agh!" he says, pulling back and wiping the saliva with his sleeve.

Ronan settles back down beside me and looks up the street, completely bored and done with the both of us.

"Good boy," I say.

"No, really, what kind of dog is it? So I know never to adopt one." Corey wipes at his face some more.

"An Irish wolfhound."

"Damn, you really are hardcore Irish, aren't you?"

"That's right. Even got the dog to prove it."

He grins and then asks, "So what are you and your *horse* doing? Jogging at, like"—he looks over at his interior clock—"four thirty in the morning?"

"Couldn't sleep," I say.

"Well, I'd tell you it wasn't really safe for a girl to be night-jogging but I think you'll be okay with your wolfhound next to you. And I don't sleep well, either. I work at the bakery on Fifth. DiRusso's."

"A baker, huh?" I say. *So that's why he always smells like doughnuts.*

"You tell anyone and I'll kick your ass," he says. "And your little dog's, too." He points a finger at Ronan, who looks backward and snorts defiantly before yawning. The word "bakery" has stuck in my head now. My stomach responds with a growl.

"So you make doughnuts and stuff?" I ask.

"Yeah. Doughnuts, strudels, cakes, pies. I make a wicked almond macaroon tart; I'll bring some for AV tomorrow. A parting celebration, if you will. You can taste my *wares*." He adds a slight flourish to that last word.

I ready Ronan's leash. "Sounds good. And don't worry, I won't tell anyone. Your secret's safe with me, doughboy. We're all guilty of something, right?"

"Ain't it true," he says as he puts his truck in reverse. "Be careful. Wear white next time. That dark coat's gonna get ya steamrolled."

He gives me a quick wave and his taillights disappear down the road. I watch as he turns down a side street and out of sight.

Corey Livingston is a baker. That's why he smells like cinnamon and doughnuts.

Ronan and I turn toward home. I'm looking forward to AV time in a way I haven't before and am sad that it's our last day tomorrow. I've barely spoken two sentences to Corey all grading period, if you can believe that. After that day when we watched Mr. Davis make a fool of himself as Peter Pan, Corey brought in a DVD box set of *Deadwood*, an HBO Western that got canceled a few years back. I groaned internally when he first presented the idea of watching it because, as a rule, I don't do Westerns, but after one episode I was hooked. We only got through the first season, but he said I could borrow the rest. It was nice of him to do that—to bring that TV in and the recliners and the DVDs. Half of me wonders if he went through all that hassle so he wouldn't have to sit there feeling awkward about the gingerbitch.com fiasco, thinking up small talk day after day. The other half wonders if he did it so *I* wouldn't have to feel awkward and sit there thinking up small talk day after day.

All I know is, I've learned more about Corey Livingston in the last five minutes than I have in eight whole weeks. I think he's okay. As a friend, I mean. Any guy who knows how to make an almond macaroon tart can't be all bad.

⁓

As I head to the AV room, my heartbeat is doing the quickstep. He returned the TV yesterday, and the other, smaller TVs are all loaned out or busted. We'll have no buffer in the room, no reason to sit, stare, and not talk to each other. I decide that I'll eat one pastry or doughnut or whatever he brings and then make like I'm going to retrieve borrowed videos. Or maybe I'll clean it up in there—organize shelves or dust or something. Busy, busy, no time for chitchat, last day, need to look like we're working in case an authority figure drops in.

I open the door and there he is. Pastries are sitting on the table, a professional display on a tray, with two napkins on either side. He has already cut me a piece of something that looks like a nut roll.

"Hey, Corey."

"Hey, Sid."

"Looks good. You make all this yourself?"

I'm trying so hard to be casual that I think I may be coming off phony. Aloof. Cold, even. My brain seizes up then starts pumping out random insanity. Relax. Think casual. Comfortable. Prewashed. Old blue jeans. Relaxed-fit Murphy, that's me.

"Yep, bright and early," he says. "The nut kolache is the best, but…"

I watch his lips moving and he doesn't seem to notice that I'm about to reach up, unzip myself from the skull down, jump out of my skin, and yell, *Surprise! There's a crazy person in here!*

"…I kind of screwed up the crust on the tart, though, I was in a hurry. Usually, I don't eat this stuff, but I skipped lunch, so…" his voice trails off.

I sit down and pick up my nut roll. The silence thickens. The awk-werd is palpable. It's as if, by talking outside school for five minutes, by revealing tiny details about our outer lives, him being a truck-driving baker and me being a wolfhound-owning night jogger, both of us being insomniacs, we have crossed a threshold, walked through a portal that has made us real people to each other. We are no longer Former Cheerleader Turned Gingerbitch Slut and Drug Dealer Turned AV Shop Rat. Now, we are Sid and Corey, official human beings, guests at a farewell pastry party, breaking bread, and In This Together Now. We are two people who actually have some things in common and could possibly even be (gak!) friends.

If I stuff my face, I can't talk. So that's what I do—I stuff my face. Not literally, I mean, but I do eat a cannoli, an almond tart, and a cheese danish without much stopping. It's surprisingly tasty. For real. My nerves will not, however, allow me to relish his wares the way they so richly deserve to be relished, and all I can muster is a smiling nod of approval and a pathetic thumbs-up.

When there is nothing left to eat, when we have demolished the whole damn tray, I slap the table and say, "Well, I'm gonna go collect videos from all the classes that haven't returned them. Thanks for the pastries. They were really good. Nice almond filling," and then I break my neck getting out the door.

I plug in my iPod, select Fiona Apple's *Extraordinary Machine*, and get down to business. I move from classroom to classroom, collecting videos and accompanying booklets on flower reproduction, the migratory patterns of Canadian geese, AIDS in Africa, the inner workings of the circulatory system—you name it. I burn through every song on the album, and when I have an entire stack of videos and pamphlets that reach to my chin, I head back down to the AV room with at least fifteen minutes to spare. I turn the corner at the end of the hall just as the music starts up from the beginning. I'm trying to toddle everything without spilling and have only a little farther to go. Maybe I can organize them extra slowly and burn another ten minutes. Then make an excuse to run to the bathroom and burn, oh, say, another—

I get a shove in my back and the entire load explodes down the hall like a deck of cards.

I whip around, jerking out my earbuds, to find Starsha and Amber standing in front of me, laughing their asses off. Starsha spotted me at my last stop, when I was collecting a long-overdue video on the invention of the microchip. The teacher was standing right there, so all we could do was cast malignant stares at each other, but it seems they have followed me all the way down here. I'm not sure how she managed to pluck Amber from her class so quickly, but she's like royalty around here, so I'm not surprised. No teachers or hall monitors question Her Highness when she decides to go traveling during the day.

I look down the hall at the mess.

"I'd have thought you'd be more coordinated," Starsha says. "All those times I went diving off that pyramid, and you never once dropped me."

She's right. I used to imagine taking a big step backward at just the right moment so I could watch her splat like a wet frog right in front of me, but I never had the nerve or true desire to actually go through with it. I may be vicious, but I'm not evil. Nope, I caught that bitch's bony ass every single time. And all it bought me was gingerbitch.com and a clusterfuck of videos to clean up. Well, cheerleading is history and times have changed. And I'm feeling a little nostalgic for the Sid/Starsha kindergarten days. Starsha's eyes widen as I lunge at her. Her face twists up as I go straight for her hair.

Hair-pulling.

Cliché? Probably.

Amateurish? Totally.

I never said I was a kung fu *Kill Bill* cage fighter. But I'm not afraid of a good, old-fashioned cat fight. Especially with Starsha, whom, while it's been quite a while—over a decade, really— I've scuffled with plenty.

It takes me a second to gain my footing, but with two handfuls tightly in my grip, Starsha goes down to her knees, just like old times. The sights and sounds are so familiar—her yelping, my snarling—it's like we're back in the play kitchen fighting over who gets to crack the plastic Easter egg into the pink frying pan. Amber jumps on my back and starts yelping, too. During the yanking and slinging and yelling, one of Starsha's hoop earrings gets ripped out, and she lets out a screech that echoes down the hall. Still, the whole thing is over in about five seconds when someone comes rushing up to pull us apart. It's Corey; he peels Amber off my back like she's a flea and yells at me to let go of Starsha's hair.

"Not. Before. I claw her eyeballs out!"

He puts two big hands over my wrists and squeezes my fists open. Starsha jumps up and runs over to huddle with Amber, who is hunkered against the wall. He holds me back from jumping at them.

"Let go!" I seethe at him.

Starsha, realizing the fight is now over, begins to examine her injuries. She starts pulling the loose hairs from her head, and they drift in little tufts to her designer riding boots.

"Get the hell out of here before a teacher or somebody comes," he says to them. "You want to be suspended?"

He turns to me and says through gritted teeth, "Calm the fuck *down*."

I struggle to loosen myself from his grasp; I need to get some more of that hair. This shit is long overdue. When someone else comes hustling around the corner, Corey releases me, and we all four stand at attention like, *What? Wha'd-we-do? What?*

"What's going on here? I heard screaming!" Coach Letty says, looking to Starsha and Amber for an explanation, obviously not caring what might come out of either mine or Corey's mouths. Starsha throws me a look of death, and I can see her mind working. I can see her queen-bee cheerleading legacy flashing before her eyes. *What to do. What to do. There weren't enough witnesses to claim an all-out attack, there's no blood or visible bruising...*

Corey pipes up. "The two of us banged into the two of them coming around the corner and all the DVDs went flying. Sid slipped and fell. It just surprised us, is all. I was helping her up. Right, Sid?" And he stares me into agreement. I nod my head to the coach.

Coach turns to Starsha, who is looking at me with her eyes squeezed into vengeful slits. She says nothing for a few moments, just stands and weighs her options, like whether or not she should risk her chances at future prom queen by getting into a catfight with Ginger Bitch Murphy.

"Yeah, that's right," she says, putting a hand on her hip and looking around at nothing in particular. "We were all just walking so fast and talking so much that we hit each other head-on." Then she bends over dramatically and picks up the DVD nearest her from the floor. She smiles fakely and holds it up. It's a documentary on cannibalism.

"Oh look," she says, "this is exactly what we were sent down here to get. What a co-inky-dink. Well, gotta run."

She looks at me, cocks her head, and says, sickeningly sweet, "*TTFN, Siddy,*" before turning and walking back down the hall, swaying her hips slowly from side to side. She looks back at Corey and smiles as Amber skitters two steps behind her like a good little handmaiden. Coach turns to face Corey and me.

I clench my fists as Starsha turns around to mock me behind Letty's back. Walking backward down the hall now, she mouths, *Fuck you, Ginger Bitch*, before rounding the corner and stepping out of sight.

The gym teacher eyes Corey and me suspiciously before throwing up her hands.

"Well, clean this mess up and get back to class," she says, and walks into the sad little faculty-only exercise room. My brain is on fire as we pick up the spilled DVDs. When both of our hands are full and they are all picked up, my feet stomp down the hall. I am fuming.

I could have taken them both easily, if only I'd had more time. It would be worth another suspension just to black one thickly mascaraed eye or bust one overly glossed lip. When I get into the AV room, I sling my DVDs onto the floor and kick a chair over before planting my rear end on the table, arms crossed. Corey closes the door with his foot and starts filing his portion of the DVDs on the shelves.

I am still furious. I have been minding my own damn business all grading period—why can't she just leave me alone?!

After a minute or so, Corey finally speaks.

"Jeez, the ski trip, AV duty... fighting? What's next, Killer? Bomb threats? Arson?" He chortles as if this is funny.

I look over at him smiling smugly. He thinks I'm a snotty fallen cheerleader who's finally gotten one of those things he's had his whole rotten life: a bona fide reputation. I can't believe I sat and ate all those pastries with him. All that fat and calories, and for what? So he'll like me? Screw him.

"How about drug dealing?" I snap. "I could do that. Grow a container garden of weed in my basement? You could teach me the ropes—which seeds to plant, proper lighting techniques?"

He smarts visibly, his eyes wounded. He grabs his backpack, slumping past me as the bell rings.

"You think you know everything about me, but you don't know shit. See ya 'round, Sid."

He slams the door on his way out.

I am stung with guilt; he was just throwing a joke out to lighten me up after saving my ass. I am left alone in the AV room, arms crossed like a brat, the lights buzzing overhead.

15

The days are getting longer. It's five o'clock on Saturday and I'm at the park, resting with Ronan after a good run. The sun is still fairly high in the sky and the temperature is a tolerable fifty degrees. While it feels warm in comparison to last week, some overzealous, cabin-fevered fools are actually wearing shorts, running along the bike path pretending not to be freezing their half-nekkid asses off. I am sitting on a bench swing with Ronan at my feet. Ronan looks out at the water, the wind blowing his fringe back, his tongue flapping as he pants. I pull his travel bowl out of my backpack and give him some bottled water to drink. We ran six miles today and we'll run another one and a half on our way home.

Ronan laps the water up and then looks back toward the lake.

I wonder if deep down inside somewhere, he knows instinctually about the Irish Sea and where his ancestors came from. Does he know that he is a war dog by nature? That is, before domestication bred the scrap out of him? I remember the way he bared his teeth at Corey when he pulled up his truck a couple nights ago when we were jogging. I am sure, if provoked, he could shred someone. But right now, he is happy to sit with me, sniffing the watery air and spying far-off gulls diving for fish.

I don't know Ronan's birthday, so I decide to make it St. Patrick's Day, which is tomorrow. Besides my mom and brother, he is my one true companion. I decide that I will ask my mom if we can go to the parade tomorrow, all four of us, meaning Ronan, too. Yes, I will do something fun and positive with the people I love. It will be a new day. A rebirth. A turning of the proverbial inner leaf.

All this fresh air and goodwill should generate some relief from the guilt I feel for having bawled Corey out, but it doesn't. I still feel like a total jerk.

"Let's go, Ro," I say, getting up from the bench.

My dog and I head toward home.

It's five a.m. I went to bed at eight and woke up at four. Eight magnificent hours of sleep, uninterrupted by nightmares or restless leg syndrome. I swiped one of my mom's sleep aids and slept right through the guilt of having done it. The proverbial inner leaf is starting to curl around the edges already.

But now I am on a mission—a guilt-eradicating mission. I left Ronan at home, where he is surely pouting at the window. I am walking to The Diner on Clifton. Their special Patty's Day breakfast menu is already on the board, served midnight until noon.

I scan the choices. There is the Leprechaun's De-Light for the waist-conscious: warm soda bread and low-fat jam served with unsweetened Irish Breakfast tea. Sounds good, but not what I'm looking for. There's the Patty's Day Porridge for the more traditional diner: thick Irish oatmeal served with brown sugar, Irish butter, heavy cream, and blueberries on the side. Better, but not really practical as a to-go item. And for the true believers, there is the Irish Rib-Sticker Morning Feast: two eggs any style, served with warm boxty toast, bangers and hash, back rashers, and a simply mouthwatering side of blood pudding.

Thanks, I'll pass.

Last on the menu is the Cottage Staple, and bull's-eye, just what I need:

Beef and cabbage.

All day long.

On a plate.

Or in a bun.

Shelley Keep It Green is working. The revelry starts early in this neck of the woods, and the place is already full of merry, drunken auto workers fresh off the night shift. I order three corned beef and cabbage sandwiches to go and stand in the foyer, salivating at the smells wafting from the kitchen.

"So you're starting early, eh?" Shelley Keep It Green says as she hands me my bag.

"Aye," I say with a fake Irish brogue.

She smiles.

"Fiona, right? You give up veganism for Patty's Day?"

Ah, jeez, she remembers me. I'm ordering corned beef after claiming to be a skateboarding vegan. I could say it's for a friend? That I've got a Guinness-soaked tofu platter waiting back home?

"Um, yeah, about that—my name is actually, um—Cassidy. Sid for short. All that stuff about being a vegan and everything, well, I—I made it up. I'm not a vegan. Or a skateboarder. I wasn't in school that day and just needed somewhere to hang for a while. I'm sorry I lied. That was a weird thing to do."

Then I laugh nervously and add a hopeful joke: "I don't even know what carbon footprint really even means."

She rolls her eyes and rings my order up.

"Yeah, I kind of figured you were full of it, being that you were wearing leather gloves that day. Eighteen dollars."

I hand her a twenty. She pulls out two bucks from the register drawer.

"Keep it. And thanks for going along with my insanity. I needed it that day."

"Sure, no problem. But, don't lie to me again," she says, wagging her finger.

"I won't," I say, smiling.

"So, where you headed so early in the morning?"

"To see a friend. Well, to try and see a friend. If he'll see me, that is. We had this sort of fight and I'm going to grovel." I hold up the to-go bag and add, "Bribery."

"Ah, yes. Food—gets 'em every time. But it's kind of early for corned beef. You sure he wouldn't like something sweeter, like a pastry or something?"

"Oh, no. No pastries. Anything but pastries. Real food only. He works at DiRusso's."

"Then the corned beef'll do it. It's not Slyman's, but it's pretty good."

"Thanks. Have a happy St. Pat's."

"You, too. And good luck with the bribery."

I give her a quick wave and then head out of The Diner. The bakery is four blocks away and it's freezing out. I walk fast so the sandwiches won't get cold. I did an earlier pass of the bakery to make sure he was working. His truck was parked around back by the trash bin.

I stop to collect myself on the side of the florist shop next door. I don't want to be breathing heavily when I go in. I smooth my hair, which is extra loaded down with product so I don't look like the the Bride O'Frankenstein when I start up with the groveling. I calmly walk over to the bakery and step inside.

The jingly bell on the door rings, and an old Italian man comes teetering out from the back. He has on a bright green apron with iron-on letters that spell out KISS PASQUALE! TODAY, HE IS IRISH! It's not a cushy sit-down bakery like Panera, but a small, "real" type of bakery where it's all made to go; a friendly enough atmosphere, but with a "Get your food and get out. Go home to your families, people. Next!" sort of vibe.

"'Eppy St. Patrick's Day to you, Miss. You look-a Irish beauty with your pretty hair. What I get for you today? We gotta nice-ah scone and a fresh-ah soda bread. Today we Irish, too. Heh, heh."

The old man's eyes twinkle and I see why Corey works here. It's so laid back, like The Diner—no stuffy dress codes or stupid policies on proper ways to greet customers. And there's real music on—I can hear The Strokes playing in the back.

"Um, I'm here to see Corey," I say.

The old man's eyes widen with intrigue and genuine surprise.

"Corey? You here for Corey?"

I nod.

He steps in closer, leaning across the counter while lowering his voice. "He's a good boy. You date him? He no tell me nothing hardly, 'less I, how you say, push it out of him."

Then his voice goes higher and he waves his hand around and whines.

"Leave the boy alone, Patsy! Stop be so nosy! My wife tells me this. But Corey, he like son. So...you girlfriend?"

His eyebrows wiggle up and down.

"Uh, no. We're just classmates. Is he here?" I smile nervously, glancing at the swinging door to the kitchen. The old man looks disappointed that I have no juicy scoop for him.

"Ah, well. You too pretty for him. He needs haircut, he look like sissy punk, like Shaggy from the Scooby-Doo with that long hair.

"Coreeeey!" he hollers and waddles out from behind the counter, over to the front door, where he grabs his coat from the coat tree and steps outside. He lights a cigar and leans his back against the front window to smoke.

After a minute, Corey comes out, wearing a white apron over several T-shirts, whistling and wiping his hands on a towel. He looks at me, cuts the whistle, and stops dead in his tracks. He continues wiping his hands, slower this time, and then slings the rag over his shoulder. His head cocks back coolly, his arms cross defensively.

"Hey," he says.

"Hey," I say.

He has flour on his cheek.

Suddenly, I feel completely stupid and exposed, standing like an idiot with a big greasy bag of corned beef at five in the morning. Who eats corned beef at this hour? What the hell was I thinking?

I open my mouth to speak but nothing lucid comes to mind.

"What? You want pastries or something?" he says coldly. "Or did you come to chew me out some more?"

I slump and breathe out. Then I take a breath and just let it rip. I don't look at him when I speak, I look anywhere, everywhere, and say really fast...

"I'm sorry. It...I...it was a really crap thing for me to do, to tear into you like that, especially after you stepped up like you did, I could have been suspended, expelled maybe, and I had no right to treat you that way. Totally ungrateful and major tool behavior. God, and after you wrote that letter and got the website shut down? I feel really bad, like a big jerk, I'm just a...I'm just..."

Then I force myself to look at his face and say it more slowly.

"I am really sorry."

He looks at me, arms still crossed, face stoic, saying nothing.

"I brought you corned beef," I say timidly. My shoulders crunch up, and I hold the bag up, wiggling it like a moron.

His arms uncross as he saunters out from behind the counter, pinning me in place with a dirty eyeball stare, like I'm up to no good and he's coming over to get to the bottom of my bullshit. I lower the bag and my eyes widen as he comes to a slow stop about a two feet directly in front of me. He towers over me, his hands are now on his hips, and he is giving me a steady, unwavering stink-eye.

Damn, he's big.

After a second or two, he calmly reaches out and takes the bag from my grasp. He brings it up and cups one big hand underneath it and rolls the top of it open with the other hand. Still eyeballing me, he spreads the top apart with his floury fingers. He peeks down inside, just a quick downcast of the eyes, before resuming his glare. Then his eyes soften a little.

"Fine," he says, sighing. "Let's eat. There's a table in the back."

"So I hear this high-pitched shrieking sound, like an actual cat fight, and I look out and you're wrestling around with Barbie and Skipper, cussing like I don't know what."

"I was cussing? I don't remember any cussing," I say through a mouthful of food. God, I'm so freaking hungry. I can only imagine how much fat and calories I'm inhaling right now, but man, is it good.

"Oh, you were cussing, all right. You called her a . . . what was it again?"

Corey holds his sandwich and looks up contemplatively.

"Oh, yeah, I know. 'A dirty dishrag skank.'" He enunciates each word with precision. "Yeah, you were telling her she was going to be...and how did you phrase it? 'Balder than Elmer fucking Fudd' when you were done with her."

He takes a big bite of sandwich.

"Fiction! I did not say that," I say, choking a little on my food and slapping the table before pointing a finger at him. "Bullshit-fiction, never happened."

"Did, too. Ask her," he says matter-of-factly, mumbling through a mouthful of corned beef.

"But I don't remember it. I mean, I remember being angry and some kind of words coming out of my mouth, but I don't remember what they were. And I've never called anyone a dirty dishrag skank in my life. What does that even mean?"

He laughs. "Then you had a rage-induced blackout, because you totally said it."

I take another bite, swallow, and then lean in with curiosity. "Can you really black out from rage?"

"Sure," he says. "Rage can do strange things to the mind. Rage can make you forget things. It happened to me once when I was about eight. An entire ten minutes erased from my life."

"What happened? Was it a fight?"

"Yeah. Well, not a physical fight—a verbal one."

"Tell me."

"You don't want to hear this story. Trust me."

"Okay, now you *have* to tell me."

"Not while you're eating."

"I have the stomach of a billy goat."

"All right," he says, shrugging. "You asked for it. You're gettin' it."

Popping the last of his sandwich in his mouth, he leans back in his chair, like he's going to need to get comfortable for a while.

"So I had this cat who'd just had kittens. My mom and I, we were living in this little house in Brookpark, right before we moved here, and next door was this crackhead with a kid. I think the kid's name was Andrew or Andy or something. Anyway, he was like four and couldn't speak because his mom was a junkie and didn't pay attention to him at all. She would just set him outside at dawn and bring him in at sunset. He'd stand in the yard and grunt at cars like he was a dog or something. Weird. Anyhow, my mom and I started to feel sorry for him, so we would invite him over, feed him—we took him for ice cream once—and let him play with the kittens. He got to where he started just walking in our house without knocking and he'd just be *standing* there in your bedroom when you came out of the shower. Freaky. Anyhow, we kept trying to explain to him that he couldn't do that...that he had to knock first. But he wasn't getting it. One day he came inside while my mom was napping and I was at school. He came in and..."

Corey stops. His face goes solemn and slightly stunned. I can tell from his expression that this story just shifted gears. It is being mentally refiled in his memory bank, switched from the *Oh Man, Check It Out, This One Time* shelf to the *Ugh, I'd Almost Forgotten That Shitty Story* shelf.

"What happened?" I ask.

He looks at his hands and says more delicately, "He took the kittens out on the patio and doused them with a bottle of lighter fluid that was sitting by the grill."

I jerk a little. I was expecting a twist, but not something that bad.

"So...he cooked them alive?" I say, feeling a little queasy.

"No, he didn't light a match or anything. He...he didn't know what he was doing. He was just playing. He thought the lighter fluid was like a squirt gun or something."

"So he poisoned them?"

"Yeah. I came home from school and smelled gas so I woke my mom up. The cat was running around the house like a maniac, panting, and jumping, and freaking out. I picked her up and smelled the lighter fluid on her. My mom ran over to the cat box and the kittens were gone. The mother cat had carried them back in, one by one, and hid them all behind the fridge. She was sick from trying to lick the lighter fluid off them. We washed them all up really well. But one of them died later that day; he'd gotten the worst of it. The other four were okay in the end. We had to take the mom to the vet to get charcoal put in her stomach. She was fine after about a week."

"That's awful," I say. "What happened to the crackhead and the kid? And how did you know it was him if you were at school?"

"Our back door was still open, and we knew who'd done it. He was in love with those kittens. My mom called the police and they found the kid in his closet, covered in cat scratches. We thought Crackey would get in some kind of trouble but they didn't do shit to her. 'It's just cats and the kid's fine,' they said. After the police left, I freaked. I went over and started screaming at her and the kid, calling her everything in the book. I told her that my cat was a better mother than she was. That we were lucky he didn't burn our house down and lucky we didn't have a baby at our house. That her son would have killed a baby if he'd had the chance. The kid was crying. His doped-up mom was crying. My mom had to drag me off their porch kicking and screaming. All the neighbors were on their lawns watching. That's what the kid two houses down told me, anyway. I don't remember it. I don't remember anything past watching the police pull down the street."

"That is a terrible story. I'm so sorry that happened to you. And those poor cats."

I look at him hard. I want him to know that I mean it. Then I look down and grimace at my food. I fold up the rest of my sandwich in the wrapper.

"Told ya," he says.

"Yep, you sure the hell did."

He rocks back in his chair a little.

"I still feel bad for yelling at the kid, though, even if I don't remember doing it. He didn't know any better."

"You were eight. You were a kid, too."

"Yeah, well, I guess the point I was making is that rage can do strange things to the mind. That, and don't bathe cats in lighter fluid."

He says this kind of joking, taking a halfhearted stab at humor.

"Yeah, I guess so," I say, going along with his feeble attempt to glean some sort of moral from this grim tale. He wraps the sandwich papers into a big ball and tosses them into the trash can that is sitting about ten feet away.

"Two points," he whispers to himself.

Then we sit listening to a car commercial on the radio, trying to digest our corned beef, cabbage, and revulsion. I think about his words: *Rage can do strange things to the mind. Rage can make you forget things.*

"You cold?" Corey asks.

"Huh?"

"You just shivered like you were cold or something. I can get your jacket from the front."

"No, I'm fine. I just... um, was thinking about those kittens."

I look around, not knowing what to say. As if sensing the need for a mood enhancer, Corey jumps up and heads toward the radio over on a shelf.

"Let's listen to something upbeat," he says. "And I'll show you how to make pizzelle and clothespin cookies."

"What?"

"You know. Um, pizzelle. It's an Italian wedding cookie."

I know what they are. When my mom was married to Vince, we made them every holiday with an old-fashioned iron brought over from Italy by his grandfather. The cookies would come out looking like a snowflake. But I let Corey continue to describe them. I am speechless that he knows how to make these things, and he looks cute talking about it.

"You know, they look like lacy waffle wafer thingies. And

clothespin cookies, they're, uh, those little cream-filled spirals you see on cookie tables at weddings and stuff."

He realizes how ridiculous he sounds, sighs, and rolls his eyes.

"I have to make three dozen of each before I leave; they're for a baby shower order."

And then this towering hulk of a person, this enigma that I thought I knew to be a complete stone-bag loser, is up and moving, talking about lacy waffle wafer thingies and little cream-filled spirals. And he is putting on The Beatles.

My personal audio-kryptonite.

Fack!

My heart melts upon contact with George, Paul, John, and Ringo. We have every Beatles CD ever made at home. And all the old vinyl records. And the 8-tracks and cassettes. My mom's mom loved them, then she passed it down to my mom, who loves them and passed it on to Liam and me, who love them. The Beatles are like honorary Murphy family members. I recognize the album cover from across the room.

Rubber Soul. Double fack!

I should go. I've been here way too long. I don't even know why I'm still here. I said I was sorry, he accepted my apology, we broke bread, and now I should go. I start to make an excuse to leave, but "Drive My Car" comes on, and he says, "Go wash your hands and pull up that hair, Irish. You're helping. Corned beef or not, you still owe me. Plus, I still haven't gotten you back for the Dr Pepper. I'll let you work it off in trade."

We spend the next hour making cookies and goofing around.

While the pizzelle are fairly quickly made with a big, industrial-size pizzelle iron that cracks off six at a time, the clothespins are more tricky. His clothespins are wound flawlessly and come out looking like perfect "little cream-filled spirals." The ones I make look like lumpy, crooked, falling-apart Play-Doh. The song "Michelle" comes on while I am rolling my sorry pat of dough out for another batch of clothespin rejects.

"Ahhh. This is my song," I say. "My mom picked my middle name after this song."

"What about your first name?" he asks.

"Cassidy? It's Irish. For curly-haired. Go figure, right?"

I say this in a tone thick with self-loathing while pointing a doughy finger at the mop of bright red ringlets piled on the top of my head. Surely they sit in a tangled explosion, glowing like the Fourth of July.

Corey cocks his head and studies my hair with a serious look on his face.

"Curly-haired, hmmm. Nope. Not really seeing it."

He grins sideways.

I roll my eyes, then concentrate keenly on my dough.

"I always wished she would have picked the first name Lucy. From 'Lucy in the Sky with Diamonds.' I used to dance to it in my room when I was little. I'd turn off all the lights and spin around in circles until I was dizzy and then lie down and look up at my ceiling. I had all these glow-in-the-dark sticker stars. They'd swirl and spin and I'd think, *Wheeee!* I thought I was high."

Corey laughs.

I look at him laughing and it occurs to me that I've never shared this story with anyone until now. I go back to my dough.

"Anyhow, she was afraid that with the hair, people would assume it was because of Lucille Ball. I should be thankful, though, that she didn't go with what my dad wanted—Tallulah—Irish for *prosperous lady*. And thank god she gave me *her* last name; otherwise I'd be stuck with O'Tooley. Can you imagine?"

"Ta-*lloooo*-lah O'Tooley," Corey crows, trying it out. Then he laughs and says, "Ah, no. That's Irish for playground ass-kicking."

"Eh-yah," I agree. "Douchebag tries to name me freakin' Tallulah O'Tooley and then takes off before I'm even born."

"No shit. Me, too." Corey says, pausing to look at me for a second before resuming the dough-rolling.

"Well. Mine stuck around until I was four," he says. "Waited until I got good and attached to him and then flew the coop with a stripper. I saw him once when I was thirteen, for like an hour. He has two kids and lives in Mississippi or Missouri, or one of those M states, I dunno."

We both look at each other and I feel a connection being made. A connection through abandonment. It's something that none of my friends could ever understand, because even though they've got crazy divorced parents or miserable married parents, they've still got two.

"Well, at least your dad didn't pick your name out of *Auto-Trader*," he says, cutting his flattened dough into long strips. "Mine picked my middle name after a car."

"No. What is it?"

"I'll never tell."

"Nissan? Corey Nissan Livingston?"

"Ha, ha," he says dryly.

"Corey Corvette!" I blurt, absolutely sure I have the right answer.

"Nope."

"Corey Mercedes Livingston. Corey Porsche Livingston."

"What? No. Jeez, those are girl names. Forget it, Cassidy Sid Lucy Ta-*llooooo*-lah Michelle My Bell whatever your name is, ain't gonna happen."

"Oh, come on. I told you mine," I say flicking flour at him.

He flicks some back and says, "Tallooooolah O'Tooley…"

And now we are in a flour war.

Mr. DiRusso walks back and catches us horseplaying.

"Hey, you waste good flour!"

"There's a sandwich for you on the table," Corey says to him, nailing me in the head with a big blob of dough.

"Okay, truce," I say, holding up my hands with my face half-turned away. Corey gives me his infamous dirty eyeball and we both put down our weapons.

"Okay. I'll let it go for now," I say, picking dough out of my hair and tossing it in the trash can. "Besides, I have other ways of getting my information."

"You wish. I'm a man of mystery. You'll never find out squat if I don't tell you myself."

"You'll see," I say, nodding and threatening him, when really I don't have the slightest clue as to what I'm even saying at this point. Mr. DiRusso walks over to the table and sits down. He picks up the remaining sandwich and starts eating.

"Why you still here?" he says to me with his mouth full. "You no date Shaggy but you stay and do his work? Play tootsie with my flour? Sure. I no pay you though. I only afford one worker."

"She's my indentured servant for the day, Mr. D," Corey says as he winds some dough onto a little baking rod. He looks at me, smiling, and adds, "Payback for being a big bee-yatch."

"Nice! You hear how he talks to me?" I say to Mr. D. "I'd never date a guy who treats me so poorly."

"Good for you. He's a bum."

Then things go quiet for second. A nervous glance passes between Corey and me. Were we just flirting?

Mr. D smacks his lips.

"Bee-yatch," he says. "What is this bee-yatch?"

I hold back a laugh but Corey starts howling.

Mr. D. looks confused and says, "What? What I say funny?"

My laughter has been held prisoner for months. It has been pinched and folded, squeezed and shoved deep down into myself, but at this moment, it escapes from me with a thunder. The Incomparable Sid Murphy Cackling Guffaw has returned in all its obnoxious glory. And for the first time in so long, I let it fill the room.

~

When we're done, I am on top of the world. We say our good-byes and I am sent home with a box of one dozen damaged, but still tasty, clothespin cookies to share with my family. The sun is shining and it's rather pleasant out, so I carry my coat over my arm. I'm practically skipping down the sidewalk as I approach Malloy's Pub. A lot of people are standing around outside, coming in and out of the place, and I can hear fiddle music when the door swings open and shut. A group of guys standing against the building notice me as I approach the corner where the pub sits. They're in their late twenties, early thirties maybe, and their lecherous whistles and gawking send my high-flying mood diving straight into the dirt. I can't cross the street until the light changes, so I'm stuck listening to the catcalls. They're smoking cigarettes and cigars and pipes and god knows what else, and judging from the way the one guy is hanging on the other, they are all completely drunk.

"Hey, sunshine. How's it going?" a guy in a black peacoat says, handing his pipe to his friend. He breaks off from the herd and walks up to me. "Come inside for a little. It's hoppin' in there. I'll buy you breakfast and a Bloody Mary."

He thinks I'm older. Ugh. Still, his hands are in his pockets and he's wearing an Irish derby and rocking back on his heels. Even though he's glassy-eyed drunk, he looks fairly harmless up close.

"I'm sixteen," I say and force a smile. Then I pull out my uncharged phone and pretend to dial a number as I wait for the light to change.

"Whoa, sorry," he says, pulling his hands from his coat and holding up his exposed palms. "You look older's all. I ain't looking for jail time."

He starts to turn away, then pauses, smiles sideways at me.

"Sixteen, huh? You sure?"

"I think I would know my own age," I say, trying to look occupied and distracted with my uncharged phone and box of cookies. I listen to my phone not ringing and wait anxiously for the invisible person on the other end to pick up. I watch the traffic light and tap, tap, tap my foot. Busy, busy me, no time for chitchat.

As the light changes, I start to cross. Peacoat heads back to his crew and one of them gets vulgar. It was bound to go there. It always does when drunken men gather uselessly on street corners.

"Shake those humps, baby! Magically delicious!"

The group busts up laughing. I look back to make sure they aren't following me and see Peacoat shove a short, chubby guy in the shoulder. Chubby defends himself—"Sixteen? No way! She had tits for days, man! Didn't you see 'em?"—and they all laugh.

I head down the sidewalk feeling gross. I put my jacket on while awkwardly maneuvering my box of cookies. They've ruined everything. Still, I try to rekindle the good feelings I had two minutes ago. I say to myself, *Corey Livingston is a cute baker. C-U-T-E, cute. He bakes waffle-wafer thingies and looks cute doing it.* But as I walk home, block after block, the Corey shine refuses to resurface. The butterflies that were floating around in my stomach when I left the bakery have grown thoroughly frenzied, flailing around like hornets in a jar. The brightness of the sun has gone from pleasant to glaring.

I dig down and really concentrate on Corey and the bakery and the fun we had together, but the images that keep popping in my head are of drunken assholes and dead kittens or images of a young Corey standing on a lawn, yelling and crying his eyes out. While he never said he cried, my brain adds that part because, well, he was eight years old when it happened, so of course he was crying. Then I think of his words again: *Rage can do strange things to the mind. Rage can make you forget things.*

And before I know it, my mind is back at that night. And then the morning after. And I start thinking maybe I wasn't drugged after all. I start thinking maybe my brain is choosing to forget all those hours I can't account for, that maybe it was consensual and things went bad afterward. There was a lover's quarrel, or his girlfriend walked in on us, or I saw his driver's license and realized he was like twenty-five or something, and there was drama—a verbal confrontation.

I walk faster as I try this new scenario on for size. I run the words and ideas over in my head and try to smash and squeeze the puzzle pieces together. Consensual Sex interlocks with Ski Trip Guy interlocks with Girlfriend Scene interlocks with Rage Amnesia.

I stop walking and stand, holding my box of cookies, staring at nothing. I consider this churning, spinning, misshapen picture puzzle that I have forced together in hopes that some kind of lightning bolt will hit it and it will somehow gel together, forming a crystalline portrait of truth, and I will finally see what really happened to me. My subconscious will jump up and down with relief and scream from the rooftops of my mind: *That's it! There it is! It's been there all this time!*

But this doesn't happen. All I get is a dark, spinning whirlpool of images that makes a hissing sound. And a creep of flesh up my leg, up my thigh.

No. Rage Amnesia is not it at all. As much as I'd like to

believe that I'd unleashed some superhuman fury within myself that resulted in amnesia, I know this is wishful thinking. There was no confrontation or rage coming out of me that night; the only thing I did that night was lay there while it happened, my mind and soul drifting in the void, my body laid out like a gift.

The thought of this makes me start to tremble. I start walking again, faster this time. I look down and realize that my shaking hand is holding a cookie. I have reached into the box at some point without knowing it. I go ahead and eat it, and then another, thinking, *Just two. I can run later.* The fear and paranoia are growing and the need to run is niggling at me, relentless, like an itch that needs to be scratched. The ringing in my ears is getting louder. The Truth is calling. So I eat a few more cookies, trying to block it out with the crunching in my mouth. I'm so full and I've eaten too much already today, but I can't stop. I turn into an alleyway and cram the remaining cookies in as fast as I can because I need to get rid of them so I can lose the box and run. I can't stop myself. I start sobbing as I eat them. I eat them until every single one is gone. I get dizzy as I look into the empty box. I feel disgusting and dirty. I tense up and try to fight it back down but am seized with an uncontrollable urge. The Urge comes to life. It takes form and crawls up my body, sinking its monstrous hooks into my gut. It leans into my face and with a screaming whisper, it tells me: *Get rid of it.*

Get.

Rid.

Of.

It.

Before I can stop myself, my finger goes down my throat. Far down. And it takes a second, but with persistence, everything comes out in wracking heaves. All my beautifully imperfect cookies are now on the pavement where they are mixed into this grotesque and runny cookie-and-corned-beef-and-cabbage omelet.

I cough and drop the box next to it.

I lean against the building, crying. But the tears are not because I feel bad; they're falling because I feel good. And the Truth is so, so still now.

But the ecstasy is short-lived.

When I feel the sick in my mouth, feel the bits and pieces of the food that didn't make it out, I start to feel guilty. I spit the acrid remnants out and then look up at the wedge of sky, so clear and blue, peeking out between the rooftops, and I wonder what is wrong with me.

As I lean with my back against the building wiping my eyes and mouth, an elderly couple walks arm in arm by the opening of the alley. They look over at me and wave. I wave back, smiling, as if to signal, *Everything is fine here, there's nothing to see, so move along.*

When they pass, I stand up straight and step over the mess. Then I start running. I run for over three hours.

⌒

As I shlump up the sidewalk, I see my street sign up ahead and a whimper of gratitude escapes my lips. I am exhausted and weak. I lost my zing way the hell down on Lake Avenue, almost into Rocky River, the next town over, and have been dragging myself home for almost an hour. My house, my bed, my pillow, have floated in my field of vision like a mirage. I seriously thought I would never get here.

Right as I turn down my street, my mom's car pulls up, and Liam's in the backseat. She stops and rolls down her window.

"I bought you a phone for a reason, Sid. Please keep it on. I have an open house for a ranch on Belle Street. I have to fill in last minute. Janet's having gall bladder trouble. Vince is meeting us there to take Liam down to the parade. He said you and Kirsten could join them if you want."

Then her eyes plead for forgiveness. "You're not mad that I can't go, are you?"

"Oh, no. God, no," I say. Then it hits me what she just said. *Kirsten.*

"Wait, what? Did you just say Kirsten?"

"Yeah, she's at the house. Have you two been fighting or something? When she showed up at the door, I realized how long it's been since she's been over. Anyhow, she could use a parade, she's not looking so hot."

"So she's at the house?"

"Uh-huh. Anyhow, I gotta run, so call Vince if you want him to pick you guys up for the parade."

"Yeah, okay," I say and then lean in to give her a kiss, thankful that I don't have to go to the parade after all. She pulls away and I think, *Holy crap. Kirsten is at my house right now.*

17

I walk down the street and think about how three minutes from now I will be face-to-face with Kirsten Lee Vanderhoff, former BFF, who dumped me two months ago. I mean, I flub one time and I'm cast out like the devil? And after all those times, all those years, that I was there for her. Countless nights that she'd slept over because her parents were drunk and fighting. She'd spoon in next to me in bed and look up at my sticker stars and wish out loud that she could live at my house, wish out loud that we could be sisters. Then she dumps me flat because of one lousy mistake?

I concentrate hard and summon up images of protection— imaginary plates of armor sliding up and over my heart, rusted barbed wire wrapping itself around me. I lock out all warm, fuzzy thoughts and feelings of Kirsten Lee Vanderhoff, Public Enemy Number One.

Then I think of Public Enemy Number Two and wonder where she is right now. I wonder why Kirsten isn't at *her* house looking "not so hot." Paige Daniels with her Harry Potter–loving, closet-gamer, half-Bible-beater, half-elf self, scampering around school like a chipmunk, all the time maneuvering so we'd never be caught on the same side of the hallway. That little squirm. She took the simple act of ignoring someone and elevated it to an art form.

I see Kirsten's clownmobile in my driveway and I walk up my yard. She's sitting on my porch. She looks at me and I give her my best *Whatdoyouwant?* face. She says nothing but I can tell from her eyes that she's been crying. This makes my insides start to thaw and crackle for a moment, but then I think: *Good. Cry, then.* I march past her up the steps. I go inside and almost, *almost* find the strength to shut the main door and lock it but at the last second, I can't do it. I let the storm door bang shut, but the main door hangs open.

As I walk toward the kitchen, I can hear her creeping inside behind me. I kick off my shoes and dump my coat on the floor. Leaning on the door of the fridge, I down half a carton of orange juice without getting a glass. Kirsten settles into a seat at the kitchen table. I don't offer her anything. I put the juice back, slam the fridge shut, wipe my mouth with my sleeve, then turn to her.

"What? What do you want?" I say.

Her eyes slink back into her skull. She shifts, tries to get comfortable in her seat.

"I came to tell you"—she says, pausing, and her voice is like splinters, dry and cracked, like she's been crying for days—"I came to tell you that I get it. I get why you did it."

"Did what?" I say, and I'm trying to stay solid, trying not to yield, but it's getting harder by the second, what with her face and voice looking and sounding as pathetic as they do.

"Why you ran off with that guy," she says. "Why you ditched everyone and everything and took a chance. I get it now."

I say nothing. I don't know what she's talking about. And as much as I'm dying to know what she's talking about, I don't want her to *know* that I'm dying to know what she's talking about. She picks her purse up from the table and walks to the sliding door that leads to the back patio. She pulls out a pack of cigarettes, slides the door open, and looks at me before stepping outside.

"Follow me, Sid? Please?"

She reminds me of a sad, beaten-down puppy that just wants to be picked up. Ugh, I hate her. I step over to the door and she is sitting on a wrought iron chair with her knees up. There are no cushions—we put those away in the fall—so I know it's probably cold and uncomfortable. Still, the sun is out. It's crisp and bright, and even though it's still technically winter, you can sense that the world is about to melt. I walk out, grab the chair across from her, and sit down.

"You know Patrick Callahan? Pat?" she says, lighting her cigarette, looking out into the yard at nothing, her voice getting far away. She doesn't wait for me to answer. She knows I know who she's talking about.

"We started seeing each other right after the ski trip. For real seeing each other, not just a hookup like at his graduation party. He came home from OU one weekend for the annual Callahan Manly Man Meal at Bucca di Beppo." And she uses air quotes on that last part, her cigarette flickering up and down between her fingers. "To celebrate all those XY chromosomes his Catholic daddy's been pumping out over the years."

She takes a long drag. Deep, like she invented smoking or something. I want to say: *Smoking, Kirsten? How very melodramatic.* But I don't. I just continue staring a hole through her.

"Paige and I were there with Lindsey Rourke and Julianne Bell. You should have seen it—every Callahan boy and man crammed into that big V.I.P. booth."

She laughs a tiny laugh. I don't join in because all I'm thinking is how she just said, *You should have seen it,* and how I want to yell, *Well, no! I shouldn't have seen it! I couldn't have seen it, because you freaking dumped me, remember?*

"Anyhow, he called me later that night and we went out the next night. Then the next weekend. And then the one after that. We finally did it on the fourth weekend, seventh date. He got us a hotel—flowers, wine, Jacuzzi—the works. Then about two weeks ago, the phone calls started dropping off and he didn't come home to see me. Said he had to study."

She takes another long drag off the cigarette.

"So in my infinite wisdom, and against everyone's advice, I decided to drive down to OU Friday night and surprise him."

She makes a self-loathing snicker-snort.

"Oh, he was surprised, all right. Real fucking surprised." She turns to me in disbelief. "He's had a girlfriend down there the whole time. Some bitch named Tierney from Nantucket. She's on a music scholarship. A flautist."

She chortles with more self-disgust and says, "He tells me he loves me, sleeps with me knowing he was my first, and then one month later, tells me he's made a mistake and that he's really in love with Tierney the flautist from Nantucket. And he actually said it like that, with a straight face, like he's been saying Tierney-the-Flautist-from-Nantucket his whole goddamn life or something."

She takes a final puff of her cigarette, blows out a long stream, and says, "God, I'm so stupid," then leans down to crush out the butt on the concrete.

I still haven't spoken yet. I don't know what to say. I mean, I'm not glad she's hurting. I'm not. She was a technical virgin and that was a shit thing for Pat to do, but it's a little hard to feel sorry for her at the moment when...well...there's myself to think about. I was getting to the point where I was almost forgetting what her voice sounded like, what her face looked like up close. I was getting to the point where I was almost done mourning the lost friendship with her and Paige, and now she's back— and I can only assume that Paige isn't far behind.

"Anyhow," she says, looking at me hard, "point is, I came here to tell you that I get it now. How it feels to want someone. To want them to want you back. And how you'll do just about anything to get them to want you back. I knew it was a bad idea to go to OU, but I went anyway, because I wanted Pat, and I didn't care that I was ditching out on plans I'd made with Paige or that my parents might find out and take the car or that I might get down there and not like what I found. Nope, I just went out and bought a pink nighty from Victoria's Secret, hopped in the clownmobile, and headed south. I thought, 'If he just sees me in the nighty, he'll want me again.'"

The wind picks up and she wraps her arms around her knees, tucking into herself tightly.

"So I came here to say that I'm sorry I judged you so harshly. The punishment didn't fit the crime."

Then she looks down and starts to rock a bit, resting her trembling chin on her knees. "I'm sorry, Sid," she says. "I want my friend back. I need my best friend back."

And her eyes are filling up now, spilling over.

I get up and walk to the sliding door; I can't stand looking at her anymore. Part of me wants to reach out and slide open the door and go inside, leave her out here to freeze. But a bigger part of me pauses, looks at my reflection in the glass and feels the rusted barbed wire falling slack at my feet and the armor cracking wide open. I wish so much I could muster the resolve to scream, *Get Out! Go Home!* but my heart betrays me and blurts out what I'm really feeling.

"You really hurt me, Kirsten. I needed you, too. Back then. God, you have no idea how much I needed you. And you really, really hurt me, you and Paige."

Then I reach out to slide open the door, but before I can get it even partway open, she's out of her chair and rushing over, putting her hand out to stop me.

"Wait. Please," she says. She leans her head on the cold glass, puts her hands back in her pockets. She looks at me sideways and is right up in my face when she really starts crying. I refuse to look at her full-on; I look into my house instead, but I can see her in my peripheral, right there, inches from my face, sobbing.

"I'm sorry, Sid. Please. I really am. I just want things to go back to the way they were. Can we try? Please?"

She's all-out bawling now, which makes the iceberg that was my heart melt and flood upward, choking me in my throat. Then it just happens—I start crying, too, my head leaned forward on the glass. She wraps her arms around me and I can't stop myself, I hug her back. And we both bawl. We say we're sorry over and over and after a while, when we're both cried out, we go inside. We make peanut butter and jelly on RITZ crackers and then call Paige to come over, too.

Paige and I get our sobbing and apologies out over the phone, so when she arrives at my house, she just throws her arms around me on the front porch. I hug her back and realize how much I've actually missed this little garden gnome. I forgot how truly tiny she is.

"So how did you convince Judge and Delores to let us be friends again?" I ask as we walk into the house.

"You don't want to know." Paige smirks as we head for my bedroom.

"What? Did you sneak out? Are you on the lam?" Kirsten says.

"No," Paige says, laughing. "I'm here with parental blessings." And her face grows even smirkier.

"I used their Puritanism against them," she says. "I read the story of Mary Magdalene to them out loud at the dinner table. Told them how they need to practice what they preach. *Forgive.*"

I scour my dusty brain for long-lost catechism lessons on Mary Magdalene.

"Wait a second," I say. "You got them to let us be friends again by comparing me to a prostitute? Your parents think I'm the equivalent of a hooker?"

It's almost funny, somehow. I can't believe they think that little of me.

She bends down and fishes through her backpack like she's looking for something specific.

"Actually, you're worse than a hooker," she says. "You're a *Catholic* hooker. But, don't worry. I'm here to save you from your heathen ways."

"Oh, no," Kirsten says. "If you pull out a Bible I'm gonna cry. I'm gonna leave."

Paige looks up at us, grinning, then jumps up from the floor, shoving DVDs in our faces and growling, "*Rahrrr! Out Demons! I compel you!*"

I look at the DVDs. *The Exorcist*, one and two.

I grab one out of her hand and bonk her on the forehead with it. Then we head into my bedroom to eat junk food and watch Linda Blair's rotting head spin. And it's just like old times again.

It's a Saturday, the first week of April, and I need new clothes. Nothing, and I mean nothing, fits now. Kirsten and Paige wanted me to wait so we could all go together and make it an official "back together" event, but this is something I want to do alone. I don't want anyone looking at me, complimenting me, commenting on me, asking how I lost so much weight in such a short time. I'd rather just slip in, buy a few things, and then slip out.

I take the bus to the mall and head directly to the juniors' section at Macy's. I start to browse, frustration growing with each item I pick up. Spring clothes are on sale, but everything seems so skimpy. I hold a few tops up to myself and eventually put every one back. I decide I can do without tops. It's the pants that

I can't live without. I walk over to the jeans racks and everything is so low-cut and hip-huggingly revealing. The zippers are like two inches long on some of them. Another girl about my age is browsing, too. She has on a hot pink, super-tiny baby tee with a cartoon on it. She picks up a pair of jeans and heads toward the fitting room, her lacy red thong popping out the top of her pants. I shudder and keep browsing. I finally find some jeans that, while still low-rise, are not *super* low-rise, or, god forbid, super-*extra* low-rise—pube-grazers, yuck.

I glance over toward the misses' section, where the more conservative, mom-style jeans are sold. It's pleated, plain-pocket, nine-inch-zipper town over there. I'll try on the low-rise pair and see how they fit before I go that depressing route.

The dressing room is cold and my booth is already packed with piles and piles of jeans from other customers. I take my sweats off and pull on the jeans. I am expecting them to be snug but am surprised when they slide up effortlessly. A little *too* effortlessly. I button and zip them and then turn to look in the mirror; they're way too big. It must be a forgiving cut. Designers do that. They cut everything bigger and put smaller sizes on them so people will think they're skinnier than they really are and buy more clothes.

I look around in the piles of jeans strewn around the fitting room until I find another pair, a size smaller. I try them on, but this time, they're even more loose. I try on four more pairs. The last pair fits perfectly, and it's three sizes smaller than my old, pre–ski trip jeans. I look into the mirror with astonishment.

"Three sizes," I whisper to myself, turning around to look at my butt. While it's still big, it's not *huge* big, like it was. A grin spreads across my face. I get dressed and go back out to the main floor, where I blow every babysitting dime I've made in the last six months on new clothes.

⁓

When I get home, my mom has dinner all ready and waiting so I'm forced to sit and eat meatloaf, mashed potatoes, and yams. I look at the food and think about how yams are just orange potatoes, so I'm stuck eating two mountains of starchy overblown carbs, one drenched in a small pond of gravy, the other in a sludge of cinnamon butter. I eat it, though, because my mom is watching every move I make, every spoonful that goes onto my plate, and every forkful that goes into my mouth, all the while trying to look like she's not. I scoop out big portions like *Lah-dee-dee, lah-dee-dah, looks good, Ma! Yum!* and play my part in our ridiculous little dinner theater. When I'm done, she asks if Liam and I would like dessert, because, well, wouldn't you just know it, she has an apple pie and even bought real whipped cream to go with it, which is sooooo much better than the fake stuff, hooray!

I want to say, *Dessert, huh? So, tell me Ma, when did the notion of a Murphy dessert go from Chips Ahoy with milk to baking entire fruit pies in the oven? Relax, Katherine, I ate the fucking yams.*

I don't say any of this. I keep my best game face on and smile through dinner like it is Thanksgiving Day and I am just one hungry-ass pilgrim come to feast with the Indians.

Finally, after we do the dishes, she takes off for a few hours to get her hair cut. She's decided to cut it shorter, into a bob, so that clients will take her more seriously. I try to talk her out of it, but she says, "Sid, I haven't sold a house in two months. I'm pulling out all the stops here."

So I am stuck babysitting again. I shouldn't say stuck, because I don't mind. Liam's in his room playing the Wii that his grandma got him for Easter. I open my bedroom window. The sun is shining, the birds are singing, and the trees are budding. I take a deep breath of springtime air and think about how nice it will be to run in this weather. As soon as Katherine gets back, I'll take off, and that monstrosity of a meal will be nothing more than a distant memory. Those starchy yam carbs that are currently riding a river of gravy straight toward my ass—they won't know what hit 'em. I put on some music and get down to the business of cleaning out my closet. I'm going to make it into a sparkling, shiny showcase for my new clothes.

I put on an old song that I love called "Downtown" by Petula Clark. It's perky and upbeat and has that happy, girly feel that goes along with my happy, girly mood. Even Petula's name sounds perky and girly. I start pulling all my old jeans and tops off the hangers, throwing them into a pile on my bed. I start bobbing my head, dancing a little, and singing along. Quietly and to myself because my scratchy voice is a stark contrast to Petula's pure, angelic one, and I'd rather hear her than me.

After a few minutes, I am really getting into the spirit of the song, my voice is getting louder, and both the closet cleanout and the singing are reaching an animated pitch. Ronan decides he's had enough estrogen and gets up and goes into my brother's room. The pile of clothes on my bed is growing bigger and bigger and the song is coming up on its big soaring chorus.

Out of nowhere the merriment comes to a screeching halt. In the back of my closet, stuffed behind a ton of junk, I see something bright green peeking out. It's the coat that I wore on the ski trip, the one I borrowed from Kirsten because I didn't have any gear of my own. The mere glimpse of it slams into me like a bus and knocks me on my ass.

I pull it out and stare at it hanging limp in my hands. The lift ticket is still attached to the front of it. Then my stomach slides down into my feet as I pull the coat off the hanger. The music is blaring and has gone from girly and chipper to a shrieking sort of mockery.

I never even noticed the lift ticket when I put the coat in my closet all those months ago. As I look at it, really look at it, I feel dizzy and I have to sit on my bed to keep from falling over. The print blurs in and out of focus as I make sense of what it says: SNOW RIDGE SKI LODGE GROUP DISCOUNTED LIFT PASS. C. MURPHY. LHS SKI CLUB, CLEVELAND, OHIO.

As Petula sings, I reach a clammy, trembling hand into the pocket of the coat and pull out the receipt that he had written on.

CLEVELAND ROCKS!!!

I start to see fuzzy blackness and flitting little dots of light. "Seeing stars," I guess it's called. I've never seen stars before, and

I've always wondered what "seeing stars" looks like and now I know.

The music is even louder now. Petula is really belting out her anthem, really giving it all she's got, and I clench my teeth because this primal sort of anger and fear is building up inside of me, a panicked fury that is burning me up from the inside out. I stand up and stagger a bit. I take off my shoe and throw it at the radio to stop the singing but I miss and it just bounces on the floor. I walk over, and with a swooping hand, swat the radio off my dresser; it rattles over the side and is lodged between my dresser and nightstand. I jerk at the cord until it comes unplugged and the music stops. None of this helps because the music is replaced with the ringing hiss of the Truth. I sit back on my bed, put my head between my knees, and breathe deeply so I don't pass out. I put my hands to my ears to try and stop the ringing hiss and I am shaking badly now and my stomach is swimming with greasy meatloaf, gravy, and yams. The Urge is tadpoling around inside it, feeding off it and growing bigger and bigger. The Truth ridicules me, in a singsong voice from inside my own heart....*I took a course on shedding accents. I can pinpoint where you live by the way you talk. Blah, blah, blabbity-blah. God, you are so stupid. Cleveland rocks? Ha! You had it plastered on the front of you the whole time!*

I cross my arms snugly over my chest. Hot tears spill down my cheeks. I wipe them away and try not to listen to the voices inside me, but the Truth, it just gets angrier....

You are a fat, stupid slut, Sid Murphy. Your chest and ass are still huge. God, you're begging for it, walking around with that disgusting shit bouncing around. Three sizes? Come on! You can do better than that . . .

"No," I whisper.

But the Truth is stronger than I am. And as I get up and stumble toward the bathroom, I know what I need to make it quiet. The Urge swims around inside me, so happy to be called upon.

I close the bathroom door behind me and turn on the water.

I run the water loud and flush repeatedly so Liam won't hear.

19

Corey and I are friends now and I don't care what anyone thinks about it. He is the only person at school who was truly nice to me during those winter months when I had no real friends, and I haven't forgotten it. It means a lot to me now. In fact, he means a lot to me now. As a friend, I mean.

I go to the bakery sometimes in the early mornings to visit him. I get up at four thirty, run for an hour, and then stop in and hang out with him and Mr. DiRusso until six. Mr. DiRusso always reminds me that "he no pay me" whenever I so much as pick up a spatula or look at a measuring cup, but he sends me home with loot every time—a six-pack of doughnuts, a few scones, a cinnamon raisin loaf. I've been good about not eating them, though. It's like a contest I have with myself. If I can make it home without opening the box, I win. I give the prize to my mom and Liam for breakfast, telling my mom that I ate already. Then I run up to get a shower before school.

Today, I am getting a ride to school from Corey. Kirsten's car is in the shop and I was going to jog there, but I lost my mind temporarily and asked Corey for a ride. I think the dieting is going to my brain. He got this surprised look on his face, and at first I thought it was a bad surprised. I thought maybe I'd overstepped somehow. A flush began to creep up my neck and I immediately went into recovery mode, looking around at everything in the bakery except his face. The ovens, the marble slab kneading table, the cooling racks, babbling like a fool.

"It's okay, I mean, my mom can take me. You're probably in a hurry anyway. It's like right on her way to work and—"

He interrupted, saying, "No, that's not—I mean, yes. I can give you a ride. For sure. Your friend, too."

So I knew that the look had been a good surprised look. But still, I had to turn away because the flush kept creeping and I'm sure I was full-on blushing at that point. Tragic, I know. All I could manage was a quick "okay cool, see ya then" before bolting toward the front of the store, walking Mach ten.

It wasn't until I was already out the door and onto the street that I realized I had never even given him my address. I almost kept walking but turned around to go back and tell him where I live. As soon as I turned around, he was already hanging out the door, calling my name and waving me down. "It's seven seventy-five Berry Blossom, off Clifton!" I yelled to him.

"What about your friend?" he asked.

"I'll call her and ask if she needs a ride. Thanks again!"

He threw me a nod and I turned and raced for home. I didn't bother calling Kirsten. I'm not ready for Corey and my friends, or Corey and my family, for that matter, to be in the same spaces together. I can see it now: everyone over-talking, sizing one another up, being careful and polite, all the while searching for defects and shortfalls to pick apart later. So I'll be keeping things and people in my life separated for now. It's easier to manage things that way.

I'm getting ready for him to pick me up and I'm so nervous and the nervousness is making me sweaty. I'm used to seeing Corey in certain settings, the bakery mostly. Sometimes we see each other with our respective friends at lunchtime. We wave or nod to each other from across Burger King or Taco Bell. He goes back to talking to his group of friends, detention-type kids who make *woo-hoo* noises, and I can always hear the words *cheerleader* or *smart girl* or *redhead* thrown in somewhere. Corey will shrug and say something that I can't make out from across the room, but I know it's probably something like, "Shut your hole, Carzetti," or "Eat your burger, Olshansky. Idiots." I just go back to picking at my fries and talking to Paige and Kirsten or whomever we may be sitting with from school, mostly smart kids who are scared to death of the stoner crowd and don't say anything to me about Corey for fear of getting an earful.

We rarely see each other in school, though. He doesn't take the same sort of classes I do, so he's always in a different section of the building. He's more an auto shop, woodshop, remedial math type student, while I'm more honors and college prep. I asked him once why he doesn't take cooking since he's so good at that sort of thing, and he immediately stopped kneading the big mound of dough he was working on and looked at me with a face that said, *Are you high?*

"Because I'd get my ass pounded, Sid. Jeez."

"Oh. Yeah. Sorry," I said, chuckling.

Duh. I'd just gotten so used to him wearing an apron and being a baker that I'd lost my mind, I guess.

God, I'm really nervous. Did I say that already? I'm nervous because even though I know it's just a ride to school and we are totally just friends, it feels like he's picking me up for a date or something. And I've never been inside his truck before. It feels like a step toward something. A leap, in fact.

I know I'm being ridiculous. We're just friends and I'm acting like a freak.

I've picked out a billion different outfits and my room looks like a Laundromat blew up—there are clothes everywhere. I can't figure out what to wear. I mean, all he ever really sees me in is sweats with no makeup and that's been fine, safe for me actually, so why should I care now? I should just put on my usual sweats and be done with it.

But I don't want to; I want to look nice when he picks me up.

I haven't worn the clothes I bought yet. I went to put them on one day, but chickened out. I have been getting by with just sweats, and also wearing belts and long baggy shirts to cover up the shlumpiness of my old pants. I was going to return everything this weekend. After I came out of the bathroom that day when I flipped out from finding the ski jacket, I shoved all the clothes back in the bag and stuffed it under my bed. Then I immediately took the coat to Kirsten's house so I wouldn't have to look at it anymore. I ripped the lift ticket and receipt into tiny pieces and flushed them down the toilet, and I haven't had the Urge since. I haven't done you-know-what for a week now. I think that the "taking back, ripping up, and flushing away" ritual might have cured me of it. I'm just watching what I eat now and running a lot, which is fine.

I finally bite the bullet, removing the tags from a pair of jeans and then sliding them on. I decide to wear this cute turquoise baby doll top that has little daisies around the neck. I go to the bathroom and pull out the makeup bag that has sat untouched under the sink since the ski trip. I put on a little makeup, and even though it's very minimalist, I still feel like a hooker. I have to force my hand away from the wet washcloth on the sink. A voice is creeping into my head, saying, *Wipe your face. You look like an overeager tramp,* so I grab my hair stuff and go to my room. I sit on my bed and try not to look at the mirror as I towel-dry my hair.

⌒

Ronan is on the front lawn while I stand fidgeting on my front porch, my backpack at my feet. I cross my arms. Then I uncross them. I look down at my shoes, a pair of peep-toe pumps that have been collecting dust since last fall.

I try to think about nice things—birds, blossoms, summertime, the smell of Irish Spring and doughnuts—but all I can think about is how massive my boobs must look in this top and how big my butt feels in these jeans. I'm wearing one of my mom's bras because my bra cups have started to wrinkle in all the wrong places. But her C-cup is still too small and cuts into my sides. I'm glad, though, in a way, that my bras don't fit right anymore, because it means my boobs are shrinking.

"Come on Ronan! Get it done already!" I yell.

Ronan yawns, looks away from me, and continues milling around, looking for a nice spot to take care of business. It's a week into May and unusually warm out, like seventy-five degrees, and it's only seven thirty in the morning. I know that no one else will be wearing a jacket, so I have to force myself not to put a coat on. I adjust my neckline so there is no sign of cleavage. Then I continue to fidget, getting more and more nervous. I turn around and look at my reflection in the glass storm door to Mrs. O'Leary's half of the house. I turn my back-side and look at my jeans. Yep, the ass is still—

—I look away. I look at the FOR RENT sign in the window and am stung with sadness. I can't even look at a newspaper any-more without thinking of her. We still haven't been able to find a suitable renter for her apartment, and we are fast going broke. My mom has dropped all the premium channels on our cable and switched gas companies to get a better deal. The cereals Liam likes have been replaced with imposter brands, and we're eating a lot of pasta these days. Well, Mom and Liam are, any-way. I try to dodge dinner whenever possible and tell myself that I'm helping out with the grocery bill.

I look down at myself again and think of my mom and feel

guilty about the clothes I bought. I had no right to go and blow all my money like that. I should have bought something for the family. That's it. I'm going back inside. I'm putting the tags back on these jeans and returning them. It's for my mom, not because I feel naked in them.

Just as I reach for the doorknob, Corey's truck pulls into my driveway. He beeps and throws up a wave. Ronan barks and runs to greet him. Corey lowers his window and pets Ronan's head, then Ronan runs back toward the house. I let Ronan inside, lock up, and then head to the truck.

"Hey," Corey says. He leans over to the passenger side to open the door for me.

"Hey," I say, tossing my backpack into the backseat.

"So, does your friend—"

"No. She already has a ride."

"Cool. Watch your step, it's high."

I step up into the truck and slam the squeaky door. We get going and at first there is this longish silence and I'm relieved when Corey speaks first.

"Has your dog gotten bigger since I saw him last? He looks bigger."

"Nope, he's the same," I say. Then I add, "Maybe he just looks bigger in the daytime."

Corey nods. "Yeah, maybe."

And then another awkward silence. I scour my brain, but I am truly at a loss for conversation starters. I'm never this tongue-tied at the bakery. One, because whenever there's a break in conversation, I can busy myself with asking about bakery things or excuse myself to go to the bathroom, or Mr. DiRusso will walk by and say something. Two, because I know I have an escape hatch if I need it. I can just make up an excuse and leave altogether, and any awkwardness is ended gracefully with a *Gotta get going! See ya, Corey! Later, Mr. D.*

But I am always praying for another invitation on my way out, one that thankfully always comes. Corey will say something like, *Hey, come by Tuesday if you want, we're making rum cake for some old lady card club. We'll tie one on before school,* and then Mr. DiRusso will smack him in the back of the head, and we'll all laugh. I'll walk out swearing to myself that I will not go to the bakery on Tuesday, that Corey is just being nice, that I'm being a parasite and he doesn't really want me there, but I always end up back, walking in all nervous, trying to play it off like the bakery is just on my running route, no big deal. After a few minutes, I relax and my words flow freely because I always know that if things get weird, I can just take off like I have an errand or some last-minute homework.

Right now, we are trapped together for the next ten minutes and there is no bathroom to excuse myself to, no Mr. D to take the edge off, and no rum cake to joke about. There is absolutely nowhere to run. What there is, however, is a radio, and I'm relieved when Corey turns it on.

It's set to the local classic rock station. A commercial ends and "Born To Be Wild" starts up. I know the song from the *Jock Rock* tape my mom used to play when we'd go to the beach.

"Is this okay?" Corey asks. "I can change it. Or I've got some CDs in the backseat?"

"No, this is fine. I like Steppenwolf."

And I say this like "Born To Be Wild" isn't the only Steppenwolf song that I know. I say this like I'm a big follower of all things Steppenwolf.

"Really?" he says, "Cool. 'Magic Carpet Ride' will be next. They usually play doubles."

Okay, then. "Magic Carpet Ride." So that's two songs I know. I guess I actually do like this band or person called Steppenwolf.

The music provides a comforting cloak for the awkwardness. For me, anyway. From the looks of things, Corey seems fine, cool as a cucumber, mellow yellow, just like always. I am hoping that they play the whole Steppenwolf album. I might make it to school without jumping out at a red light.

I relax into my seat, or try to look like it, anyway. I tap my fingers on my knees to the beat, move my lips to the words. I check out the inside of his truck while trying to appear unfazed. It's an older truck. And when I say older, what I really mean is ancient. It's an automotive relic. It's all dials, and I can barely see it from where I'm sitting, but the odometer reads over 100,000 miles. It's probably a million miles, and they just ran out of zeroes.

As I continue to survey the interior of Corey's truck, the nervous energy I feel starts dissipating, and a new feeling starts seeping into me. I don't know what it is yet, though. All I know is that the smell of Windex is evident and a new leather-scented air freshener is hanging from the rearview mirror. I know it's new because it's fairly strong and the plastic packaging is still partially wrapped around it. I also notice that the ashtray has been cleaned out, and I see no signs of old ashes on the dash-board or in crevices anywhere. So he's a clean person, he keeps a clean vehicle. So what? I tell myself this and try to push the feeling away. The feeling that I don't know what it is yet.

I look out the window, and that's when I see them. Drops of water. I look around me. There are drops of water collected into the outside edges of all the windows. It hasn't rained in days and the morning dew has already burned off from the warm weather, but the drops are there; little ones, vibrating together into bigger drops that slide downward like tears. In a few minutes, the breeze will have dried them all and they'll be gone. But right now, they are here. And the emotion that I'm feeling reveals itself to me: *Assurance*. Because I know that before he came to my house to pick me up, Corey Livingston stopped at the car wash and cleaned his truck out. Corey Livingston cares what I think of him. I try to push the feeling away, but it's growing. Fed by those tiny drops that are almost gone, the assurance is blooming.

Into hope.

I snap to it and tell myself that I'm reading into things.

"So you quit smoking?" I ask.

"How'd you know?"

"Clean ashtray. Plus, you don't really smell like it anymore. No offense."

"None taken. Perceptive. Yep. One month tomorrow."

"Good for you," I say and look out the window again. I'm usually full of wit and conversation at the bakery, but my mind is tripping over itself to find something to say.

"Not that smoking hasn't been replaced by another addiction," he says.

He pulls something out of the compartment of his door and holds it up, wiggling it at me. Nicotine gum. Okay, cool. We're still on smoking. I rally and try to think of something clever to say.

Smoking...

Cigarettes...

Cancer...

Lungs...

Got it!

"Ah, but think of your lungs," I say. "They're thanking you with every chew."

Not my best material, but not a complete sinker.

"True. But my wallet sure isn't thanking me. Stuff's pricey. I'd be better off going back to smoking."

"In the short term," I say, pointing a highly enlightened finger upwards. "But think about when you're sixty and paying cancer bills. Think about being shackled down to one of those oxygen tanks and sporting one of those weird mechanical voice box thingies. You don't want to be the old scary guy who talks like a robot and smokes from a hole in his neck."

He laughs.

"As usual, Sid, you paint a picture."

Bull's-eye.

He snaps a square piece of gum out of the pack and pops it in his mouth.

"What's it taste like?" I ask.

"It ain't Dubble Bubble, that's for sure."

I take the pack off the seat, snap out a piece, and pop it into my mouth. I bite down and it's pure awful. Like mint-flavored candle wax. My mouth is tingling, going numb.

"Agh…" I say and roll the window down to spit it out.

He laughs.

"Told ya."

"Yep. Dubble Bubble, it ain't."

When we get to school, he asks, "You need a ride home?"

I start to say something like, *Well, if you're not busy* or *As long as you don't mind,* but I force myself to say what I mean, say what I want. And it practically kills me to do it, but I cling to the scent of leather air freshener that is now embedded in my clothes and hair and I somehow manage to force the words out of my mouth. They are quiet, but they are there.

"Yeah. I do. Thanks."

"Sure. Meet me at the truck."

"Okay."

And then the day drags on at an excruciatingly slow pace. Sluggish hours are divided into minutes, minutes are broken down into seconds, and seconds split themselves into nanoseconds. The first half of the day is especially taxing. My calculus teacher's words are heavy and thick and make me feel like I'm wading through a tar pit.

I stare at the clock.

Three thirty-five is Mount Everest, and I am an ant with a boulder tied to its back.

I perk up for a minute during fourth-period health when I

overhear a girl who is dating one of the guys in Corey's group tell another girl that a bunch of them are going to Mr. Hero for lunch.

Then I remember that Kirsten has no car today.

And the clock groans to me from across the room.

20

Kirsten, Paige, and I are sitting in the courtyard eating lunch. Well, I mean, *they're* eating lunch. I'm more or less pushing around the leaves of a wilted side salad that I bought for a dollar. After the usual small talk concerning things like the pig slop being served in the cafeteria and Paige's inability to find a size four shoe that isn't made for kids, Kirsten finally asks the million-dollar question, the one I've been waiting for her to ask for ten minutes now.

"So how was your ride to school today?" she says and opens her carton of milk. She is trying to be casual but failing miserably.

"I'm here, right?" I say. Then I hold up my wrists and add, "Look, no rope burns, no duct tape residue."

"That's not what I *meant*," she says, feigning insult.

"Yeah, it is," Paige says, popping a Tater Tot into her mouth.

"It is not," Kirsten says. "I was just asking a question."

"Sure you were," I say, taking a bite of my salad.

"Well, is it so wrong to want to know a little more about him?" She pauses, then raises an eyebrow. "He is pretty good-looking, now that I've seen him up close. I passed him on my way to the bio lab yesterday. He was at the water fountain, so I got in line behind him, and when he turned around, I had myself a good long stare. He's actually hot, if you're into that sort of thing."

"I'm not *in*to anything. We're just friends."

"Yeah, right," Paige says, popping another Tot. "Your eyes are this psychedelic green color. They always do that when you're excited or nervous."

"What?" I say, looking around at anything but Paige.

She's right. My eyes do that. My mother says she can always tell when I am excited or nervous because my eyes go from light green to this bright, watery turquoise color.

I try to take the focus off myself and throw it back on them.

"I mean, why does it always have to be so...so scandalous all the time with you two? And what do you mean by 'if you're into that sort of thing'?"

"Please. Like you don't know," Paige says.

And I do know. I know exactly, but I want them to do the talking so I can focus on getting my eyes back to normal.

"Oh, you know all right. That whole long-haired, rebel-rocker stoner thing," Kirsten says.

"Okay, first of all, he's not a stoner."

They roll their eyes in unison.

"Well, he's not a rocker! And second of all, his hair is not that long. Have you seen the hair on Jake Rivers? He's like a freaking chick out there on the football field. That's how guys wear it now. Don't you two watch TV?"

I flash a snotty look at Paige.

"Oh, wait. I forgot. You don't. No cable."

"Nice," Paige says, narrowing her eyes.

I sigh; that was bitchy.

"Okay, I'm sorry. I didn't mean it. It just feels like you two are ganging up on me is all."

"Oh, relax, already," Kirsten says. "We're just curious about what you see in him. I mean, you're our friend and we tell you our stuff. I told you about my date with that guy from Westlake. Justin with the biceps?"

I glom onto the change of subject and run with it.

"Oh, yeah. Justin Biceps. How's that coming along?"

"Okay." She shrugs. "I'm going to his prom. He asked me last night."

"Don't act excited about it or anything," Paige says.

"I'm excited," Kirsten says.

Paige and I groan. She's still heartbroken about Pat. She tries not to show it, but it pretty much devastated her.

"No, really," she says, trying to sound convincing. "I've been looking at dresses online and everything."

She pauses, then adds, "I have to admit, though—I'm more excited about the idea of walking into the Callahan kegger with him, those biceps wrapped around me. Because if there's a God, and if He loves me, then Pat-piece-of-shit-Callahan will be home that weekend. Probably with what's-her-face."

"Tierney-the-flautist-from-Nantucket!" Paige and I shout in unison.

"Yeah, bite me. And don't think I've forgotten what we were originally talking about. We were talking about you and Corey Livingston. My point was, we tell each other our shit. I told you about Justin. And Paige, she tells you about her letters from Bible Benny."

"His name is Ben! For the millionth time!" Paige says.

Ben's a guy from Cincinnati whom Paige met at a teen retreat in Columbus. While they've only seen each other in the flesh a total of four times, they've been in a "relationship" for two years. He's homeschooled and writes her letters with real pen and paper. It's kind of sweet, actually. A bit strange, but still, kind of sweet.

"Ben. Fine, whatever," Kirsten says. "And also, the elven cowboy. What's his name again?"

"Trent," Paige growls. "His name . . . is Trent. And he's not an elven cowboy. He's a seventeen-year-old hottie from Dallas who just happens to play Warcraft."

I grin. "Yeah, I wonder what Bible Benny would say if he knew about your cozy late-night raids with Kickin' Your Ass from Texas."

That would be Trent's avatar name: KcknUrAssfromTX.

Kirsten and I laugh. Paige defends herself, as if she somehow needs to do this.

"It doesn't count as cheating because Mendelora and Kckn-UrAss aren't real. Just because we hack and slay jungle trolls online, that doesn't make us a couple."

"Yeah, so if you're not a couple," Kirsten says, "then why do you race home every day to chat him up on TeamSpeak and then scribble his name all over the inside of your physics folder?"

I try to grab her folder, the one that she's wallpapered end-to-end with "KcknUrAssfromTX" in shiny red hearts. Paige snatches it back and sits on it.

"Ha!" I scoff, pointing at her. "See, doesn't feel so good, does it? Having someone you like picked apart by your friends?"

"See, so you do like him!" Paige says, finishing off her Tots, all proud of herself, thinking she's won something.

And even though I'm a bit rattled that she's caught me red-handed, I say with all the condescension I can muster, "Yes, Paige. I do like Corey, as a *friend*. That's what friends do, they *like* each other."

Then we all sit and pout for a second.

"He is too a rocker," Kirsten finally says, smiling deviously. "I asked Stacey Kelly about him in history; she dates one of his friends. Turns out he used to play guitar before he got sent to juvie. She said his mom hocked it when he left. To pay for her drugs."

"Well, aren't you just full of information," I say. "A regular one-woman detective agency."

And I say this in a tone like I couldn't care less, but inside, I'm all over these little scraps, filing them away for later, for when I'm alone and able to obsess in peace.

"Yep," she says. "Stacey said the guitar was worth a lot of money, but his mom only ended up getting a hundred bucks for it. He tried to get it out of hock when he was released. Pawn broker wouldn't budge. Said he had to pay full price. Someone finally came along and snagged it."

"Oh, man," Paige says, her eyes going big and gloomy. "That's so sad."

"Put him on your prayer chain at church, Paige," I say.

"Hey, be nice now," she says, wagging a finger. "But seriously, if it's true, it's really sad. Who'd do that to a kid? I mean, no wonder he's a dealer."

The bell rings. I stand up and smooth out my jeans, adjust my shirt.

"Yep, a regular gangster, that Corey Livingston," I say. "Spends all his time running kilos around Lakewood. Well, in between the macaroon tarts and clothespin cookies, I mean." I point a finger upward. "Oh! And the daily eight hours of high school he has to attend." I squint and nod extra hard. "Those drug dealers...they're big on education."

"All right. We get it. You win," Kirsten says, shoving me playfully as we walk into the building. "We'll lay off. Right, Paige?"

Paige smiles. "Yeah, fine."

"He's redeemed!" I shout. "Praise the Lord!"

As I walk to my locker, my mind is reeling. Rumors or not, I now I have something to keep my mind occupied for the next three hours. I obsess over it all afternoon.

I want to be the first one there, and I hurry, but he has beaten me to the truck. The parking lot slants upward a little, and most of the vehicles have a bird's-eye view of the back doors of the school. Corey is leaning against the front of the truck, talking on his cell, and I feel self-conscious as I walk down the long, long walkway toward the long, long parking lot. As soon as I hit the blacktop, I stumble a little, slipping on a rogue piece of gravel, my ankle grinding painfully sideways.

"Fucking heels," I mutter to myself.

And the new shirt that I wore today?

Well, I tried to ignore the way it was making me feel.

I tried to get comfortable in it, because I know I look fine.

The logical, sane side of my brain knows that the shirt is fine and appropriate. Totally pretty and girly. And that is precisely why the psychotic side of my brain hates it and will never wear it again. The psychotic part of my brain ended up throwing on a button-up sweater after lunch. It's been shoved in the back of my locker since December and was thoroughly wrinkled. But it was just there, beckoning me to cover up my big insufferable boobs. At least it sort of matches my shoes.

I'm halfway to the truck and it's at least eighty-five degrees out, heavy and humid. I'm getting warm fast. The blacktop is sticky and the sun is beating down on the top of my head like the eye of Satan. Two weeks ago, there were snow flurries, swear to god.

"Fucking Ohio," I mutter to myself.

Corey is warm, too. Even from a distance I can tell. He is taking off his hoodie, sliding each arm out, switching the phone from hand to hand. Underneath is a plain white T-shirt. It slides up for a split second when he pulls the hoodie over his head. He has hair on his stomach; not disgusting, wolf-man amounts, but just-right amounts. A splendid torso, indeed.

He throws the hoodie over one shoulder and pulls his T-shirt down. This is the first time I've seen him without multiple layers, and his shape is nice. Not like sinewy, ripped-up gross or anything, just solid. Masculine. I look away, at anything but his torso—at the trees in the distance, a blue car in the back row. I scratch my face, tuck the uneven lock behind my ear, reposition my backpack.

I honestly don't know what to do with my limbs and body.

I feel like I'm on display. Like a fat, naked trailer-park skank shlumping down the catwalk after Gisele and Tyra just floated by. I approach the truck and force my best smile. The truck is already running. God, I hope the AC isn't busted.

"Gotta go. Yep, I'll get it. Mmhmm. Bye," he says and hangs up, shoving his cell in his pocket.

"Learn anything useful in there?" he asks.

"Nope, not a thing."

And then he leans off the truck and I realize he is walking around to my side. He's opening my door. I start to panic. *Oh, god, please don't let him wait next to the door until I get in and then shut it like a freaking limo driver or prom date or something…*

He puts the key in, unlocks it, and then opens it a crack. I reach out for the door and take over. I pull back on it, and he looks at me and steps away to walk behind the truck and over to his side. Whew! Okay, the Open-and-Crack is fine. Totally not necessary, but not tragic date behavior either. I can live with an Open-and-Crack.

I get in and slam the door shut. It's like an arctic deep freeze inside.

"Oh, yeah, that's what I'm talkin' about," he says, climbing in.

He tosses his hoodie into the backseat. I haven't seen his arms in short sleeves until now. He has arms in addition to a stomach. I look out my window. We get in line behind what appears to be the entire faculty and student body, crawling along like mechanical ants.

"You mind if I stop off at the store quick before I take you home?" he asks.

"No, not at all," I say, positioning the air vent so it blows directly onto my face. I close my eyes. "Man, that feels good."

"I left woodshop a few minutes early so I could get it nice and frosty for us," he says, but the only word I hear is "us."

I sit up straighter.

I need something to do.

"Can I look at your CDs?" I ask.

"Sure."

I reach into the backseat and grab his disc holder. I start leafing through them. The Rolling Stones. Green Day. The Clash. Iggy Pop. The Ramones. *Billie Holiday? Fiona Apple?* The Strokes. Red Hot Chili Peppers. The Who.

"Oh, here we go. This okay?" I say and hold up The Beatles' White Album.

"Sid, you don't have to ask. I'm not a radio hog," he says.

I put in the CD. Traffic starts to pick up. Out my window, right next to us, is Lindsey Rourke's Toyota Camry. I see Kirsten's blond head in the backseat. Our eyes meet, and she jumps from shock, then she turns toward the person next to her. Paige sticks her brunette head in the window, too. She is practically sitting on Kirsten's lap.

I look over to see if Corey sees them, but he is concentrating on traffic. I shoot them the stink-eye. Their window starts rolling down, so I turn away and position myself so Corey can't see out my window.

I also turn up the music. Loud. I blast "Back in the USSR" until the windows are shaking and try to think of something distracting to say.

"So what are you making in woodshop?" I yell.

We've moved ahead a car length and I can see in the side mirror that Kirsten is yelling my name and hanging halfway out the back window of Lindsey's car, waving her arms.

"What?" he yells back.

"I said, what are you making in woodshop?!"

He turns the music down and says, "I'm not a radio hog but I'm not looking to go deaf either."

Then he sees the girls. Kirsten is leaned over the front seat beeping Lindsey's horn.

"Do you know those girls?" he asks, glancing back at them. "They look like they're trying to get your attention or something."

I look back. The jig is up. Kirsten is leaning out the car window, howling my name.

"Yeah," I sigh. "Unfortunately. They're my friends. So-called, anyway. They're trying to embarrass me, so that's why I turned up the radio so loud. So I wouldn't have to lay claim to such jackassery."

He looks back at them and grins. Then he slows the truck down so they can catch up and pull alongside us again. All four of them—Lindsey Rourke, Julianne Bell, Jackass Number One, and Jackass Number Two—are ogling like they are at a drive-through zoo.

I roll my window down.

"Hey, Sid! Hey, Corey!" Kirsten croons.

I turn around and glare at her. She is smiling and raising a single eyebrow, like *Ha! Got you now!*

I smile back at her and say, "Hey, Kirsten. How's it going?" but with my eyes, I'm saying, *I'm going to kill you, Kirsten Lee Vanderhoff. Dead Dead Dead.*

"Greaaaat," she says. "Hey, a bunch of us are going to Bearden's for peanut burgers. You guys wanna come?"

Her eyes are like big drops of glitter. She's so dead. The only question now is how she's gonna go. Strangulation? Baseball bat? Chain saw? I cock my head and smile at her all sugary sweet.

"Sorry, not today. Corey has this errand to run. But thanks for the invi—"

Corey leans past me and says, "Sounds great, Kirsten! We'll race ya there!" and hits the gas.

He makes a shrieking left through the green arrow at the main road. I can hear the girls squealing like toddlers as they peel off in the other direction.

"Don't worry, I won't hold you to it," Corey says, laughing. "Besides, it might cause a clique riot. A cheerleader and a shop rat dining out? Tongues will wag."

It makes me cringe to hear him say this. Does he think I don't want go because I don't want to be seen outside of school with him? Or is it the other way around—he doesn't want to go because he doesn't want to be seen outside of school with me? I'm not sure which one it is, but either way, it bums me out that he said it; that he just slapped labels on us and tossed us into opposing clique factions so easily.

"Ah, news flash, Corey," I say, "I'm not a cheerleader anymore. I was kicked off the squad, remember? But it means a lot to me that you still see me that way. Sid Murphy! Cheerleader! Because all cheerleaders are ditzy, popular, and fabulous in their own minds, right? All cheerleaders are future prom queens, their lives just one big ball of pom-pom sunshine."

"Sid, I was only joking. Relax," he says. And he seems genuinely taken by surprise.

"No. I won't. I won't relax," I say, my voice tightening up. "Because you said it. So on some level you must think it. So which is it? You don't want to go because you're too bad-boy cool to be seen out with some snotty, shallow cheerleader? Or because you think that *I* think I'm too high on the popularity pole to be seen out with a lowly shop rat?"

He interjects quickly, "I never said lowly. You said lowly. You added that. That's your word, not—"

"So that's it, then. You think that I think that you're plenty good enough to cart my fat ass to school, but not good enough to go eat a peanut burger with."

"Whoa! I never said that, I never said you have a—" he cuts himself off.

"Sid, really," he insists, starting over, glancing from me to the road. His eyes are really nervous now. "I don't think you think anything. I was just messing around because your friends were giving you a hard time. I don't even know why I said it. I didn't mean anything by it. I don't even like peanut burgers!"

"Well, sorry, buster, but you'll have to get the steak burger instead! Or a bacon cheese dog or a damn milkshake or something. Because you're going. *We're* going. After that comment, we're going to freaking Bearden's."

And my voice cracks a little and my eyes start to burn, so I turn toward the window and blink.

"Oh, man," he says.

He reaches over and touches my shoulder. Besides that time he played referee with Starsha, it's the first time he has ever made physical contact with my body. I jerk a little because I wasn't expecting it, and he draws his hand back. I can still feel its weight after he pulls it away, and I'm sorry that I did that— jerked away from him, I mean. It makes me look paranoid or überpissed, and I'm not. I think I'm just...I think...

Fack.

Who the hell am I kidding? I know what I think. I totally know. And the truth is, I think I really, really like Corey Livingston. So there you have it. Sid Murphy likes Corey Livingston.

And not just as a friend. She likes-him-likes-him. Ugh, I do and now I'm afraid he doesn't like me back. I'm afraid that because I was a stupid cheerleader or I have a big butt or I'm too mouthy and obnoxious or I'm every other thing under the sun that someone might find repulsive in a girlfriend, he doesn't like me back.

Jesus, and even if he doesn't think *any* of these things, I've gone and blown it all sky-high anyway by being a lunatic. I look into the side mirror. My lunatic eyes are about to pop out of my lunatic skull—they're all witchy and bewildered. I look like a bona fide nut job. I'm the hysterical female in every romantic comedy I've ever watched and hated. I'm the female who is always spouting off at the mouth, the one who always takes things the wrong way and ends up crying.

No. I will not be that girl. I won't.

Aaaaaannnnd now he's pulling the truck over to the side of the road, and in true lunatic fashion, I actually do start crying. Restrained, but enough to where I can't turn around now. He puts it in park and we sit in silence for a few seconds. This is too much. Too much for a simple ride. I'm hitchhiking to school from now on.

Finally, after what seems like forever, he speaks. Softly.

"I'm sorry. Please, Sid, don't cry."

"I'm not crying!" I bark, and my words are immediately followed by one of those involuntary double sucks of crying breath.

"Okay. Okay. You're not crying," he says.

I squeeze my eyes and pray really, really hard for something epic to unfold in the next two seconds—an earthquake fissure or a Lake Erie tidal wave, anything to take the heat off the fact that I just started crying in front of Corey Livingston for no apparent reason.

I open my eyes. Nothing. Just me and Corey, sitting in the truck on the side of the road contemplating Sid Murphy's lunacy. I think about how at some point in the very near future, I'm going to have to turn and look at his face and he will know. I squeeze my eyes shut again and two swollen tears roll down my cheeks. The cards that I keep pressed tightly to my chest at all times, that I keep hidden under a shroud of sarcasm and tough-girl bullshit, have in one instant spread themselves out onto the table, wide and plain for him to see. He will know that I care for him now.

"Just run your errand," I say. "Then take me home."

He says nothing, just pulls off the side of the road and merges into traffic. We drive for a while in silence until he pulls into the pharmacy parking lot, the one where the Drugstore Madonna works. *Greaaaat.*

He puts the truck in park.

"You coming in?" he asks. I look out my window, turned away still. I shake the back of my head no; I still can't look at him.

"Need anything?"

I don't answer. He pauses for a long while.

"I'll leave the keys so you can run the air and radio."

I nod, my head still turned away. I sigh with relief when he steps out of the truck. I fast-forward the White Album and listen to the song "I'm So Tired" and feel, to my very core, every single word of it. The mortification drains out of me.

I am so incredibly tired.

As I chew on my thumbnail and listen to John Lennon lamenting his woes and telling me, through a song, exactly how it is that I feel, I look down at a mess of french fries in the empty parking spot next to the truck. Some litterbug dumped them out of his car. The song "Blackbird" comes on next, and at the very moment that it does, a bird flies down to snatch up a fry. Not a blackbird, but a sparrow. I roll down my window and watch it fly off to a nest in the huge neon sign above the pharmacy entrance. The nest is tucked into the hole that forms the number four in the *Open 24 Hours* part. I press repeat and listen to "Blackbird" three times while I watch my own bird flitting back and forth, going from her number four home to the pile of spilled, mashed fries. Every so often, she perches on the tip of the number four and sings her little sparrow heart out, like she is in the middle of a fairy-tale garden. She is happy and making a life out of what she's been given. I listen to the song and watch my little bird.

After a while, Corey comes walking out, swinging a thin, white plastic bag. He reaches in and grabs something small from it before he tosses the bag into the truck bed. He climbs in, clutching something in his hand. I force myself to look at him. I need to smooth things over. I'll blame my mental collapse on PMS.

Yes, PMS.

Cliché? Maybe.

Low down? Totally.

I never said it was a good idea, but it's the only one I can think of. What other card do I have to play? Plus, guys don't know what to do when you play the PMS card. I've seen my mother do it a million times with Vince, and it always leaves him scratching his head.

"Hey, listen…" I say.

He interrupts me.

"I got you a present."

My eyebrows lift.

"Close your eyes and open your hand."

I hesitate but then close my eyes and hold out my hand. He presses something inside my palm. I open my eyes and look.

It's a single piece of Dubble Bubble.

A smile slides out of me.

"Now. How about that peanut burger?" he says, starting the truck and putting it in reverse.

"I'm buying," I say, sitting up straight and popping in my gum.

"Yeah, that's not gonna happen," he says.

I just shake my head and roll my eyes. I don't argue. I'm done arguing, for today anyway. I look one last time at my sparrow sitting on the tip of her number four nest, still singing like she's the luckiest, happiest bird ever hatched. Corey presses repeat on the CD player and we listen to "Blackbird" from the beginning.

⌒

"Ah, you didn't tell us he was funny, Sid. What gives?" Kirsten says on the phone later that night.

"I know, isn't he?"

No use denying it any longer—my infatuation with Corey Livingston is out there skipping through the butterfly fields. The girls thought we weren't coming to Bearden's because we took off in the other direction and then took so long getting there. The four of them were sitting huddled at a table, completely engrossed in whatever four jackass girls talk about when the fifth jackass isn't there. Corey walked over and snuck up on them, making them scream. I thought Paige was going to wet herself when he poked his head in between her and Kirsten at the table and said loudly, "Soooooo... how are your peanut burgers, ladies? Everything satisfactory?"

"I think you might be on to something," Kirsten says to me now. "I'm paying more attention to who's coming out of the woodshop from now on."

"We're just friends, Kirsten."

"Not for long. I saw the way he was looking at you when you were walking to the bathroom. His eyes never left your ass."

"Because he probably can't believe how damn big it is."

"Your ass is not fat, Sid. It's *joo-say!*"

"Whatever."

"Has he made a move yet?"

"What? No!"

"One week. I give it one week."

"Well, your car's fixed so I don't think so. Unless he actually asks me out, there's really no—"

"Oh, didn't I tell you? When you were in the bathroom, I

told Corey my car is kaput. He'll be picking you up for the rest of the year."

"What?!"

"'Bye."

Click.

I dial her back but she won't answer. She is on the line with Paige for sure.

I text her: **pick up bitch!**

She texts me back: **make me uberbitch!**

Im going 2 kill U

SM + CL = <3 <3 <3. TTFN!

After a few moments of shock, I feel glad.

21

It is the third Sunday of May, and Liam's seventh birthday is today. I'm in charge of retrieving the balloons and cake and organizing the games for the afternoon. I have commissioned a top secret banana-flavored Spider-Man cake from Corey and plan to pick it up after I get the balloons from the grocery store. My mother doesn't know anything about Corey, so she suggested I get a cake from the grocery store bakery. I've tasted their cakes, and they're like eating a kitchen sponge dipped in Crisco. I've seen Corey's work, and he's really quite good. He showed me how to make a rose out of icing once and then swore me to secrecy. If his friends in woodshop ever saw him decorating a cake, they would murder him cold.

I'm still waiting on my balloons. I'm running short on

time, and the Slowest Salesgirl in the Free World is only half done with the order ahead of mine...an all-white, three-dozen-balloon wedding bouquet. I call the bakery and tell Mr. DiRusso that I'll be a little late picking up the cake. About two minutes later, my phone rings. It's my mom.

"Balloons-R-Us," I groan, watching Balloon Lady and her sloth-like progression.

"Hey, Sid. Don't worry about picking up the cake," Mom says. "The bakery called, they're going to deliver it. Isn't that nice? Free of charge."

And my brain goes: *Wheh?*

"Wait a second. Who's delivering it?" I say.

"The bakery."

"But *who* from the bakery?"

"I don't know, some teenage boy who works there. Why? Is that a prob—"

"I gotta go, I'll be right home. Just, don't...I mean, I gotta go!"

I hang up and hurry up to the counter.

"Hey, let me give you a hand," I say to the balloon girl. "There are two tanks and I can make my own balloons."

She eyes me suspiciously. "No, that's not a good idea. This is complicated and you don't know how."

I slide behind the counter and grab a handful of blue balloons from the blue bin.

"Wait, you can't do that," she says. "You don't work here. You can't—I'm gonna get in trouble."

I pull one of the balloons around the helium spout and press it down; it fills up, stretching the rubber.

"Hey!" she says, and her white balloon slips from its nozzle. It farts and flies around in a big circle and then plops to the ground. I pull off my filled blue balloon, tie the end off, and wrap some red ribbon around the knot.

"Stop that!" she says.

I stare her down, cut the string, and loop it around the wire ribbon holder. The balloon floats up and I start on my next one. I lean in while making another balloon and give her my most threatening glare, really working my Medusa eyes at her.

"Listen," I say, "there are about twenty-five people waiting at my house for a dozen balloons and a cake that I have *yet* to pick up. The only trouble you're gonna have is if you try to stop me. I've watched you blow up exactly twenty-six balloons already. I think I can handle it."

She snatches another balloon from the white bin and huffs at me.

When I'm done and paid up, I hightail it out of the grocery store with my gaggle of blue balloons waving about madly. I stuff them into the backseat of my mom's car and peel out of the parking lot. When I arrive home, Corey's truck is parked on the curb, but there are no other cars on the street or in the driveway.

That woman has done it again.

She has told me twelve o'clock when the party doesn't really start until one.

She's done this to me my whole life—setting clocks fifteen minutes fast, having me standing outside for the bus twenty minutes earlier than necessary. She doesn't trust me to be punctual, which I almost always am, thank you very much. In usual circumstances anyway. But I guess in this one instance, her annoying little motherly habit has paid off, because I'm five minutes late. Score one for Katherine.

I look at Corey's truck and then at my front door. Corey Livingston is inside my house. He is inside the place where I live. *Fack.*

I wrestle the balloons out of the car and one pops in my face, making me shriek, while another slides out of the bunch and escapes altogether. There are ten kids, so I'm still good.

I clamber up the steps and into the house, releasing the balloons into the living room. I hurry through the house, past the kitchen where the table is dressed up with the cake displayed in the middle of it. A genuine likeness of Spider-Man doing his web-slinging pose is emblazoned on it with blue and red icing. *Happy 7th Birthday, Liam!* is written underneath. The guy really is a culinary artiste.

I look around, but the house is empty. I look out the kitchen window and see them. Corey is up in our maple tree, hanging a Spider-Man piñata for my mother. She is standing below him, chatting and smiling up a storm. A swell of anxiety starts in my toes and works its way up through my legs, gut, and neck, where it ultimately plants itself into a flaming blush on my face.

I head to the bathroom and sit on the edge of the bathtub to obsess.

What are they talking about out there, and why am I freaking out about it? Who cares if Corey helps out with my brother's birthday party? He's just being nice. But knowing both my mother and Corey, they've chatted each other up and she now knows he's a friend from school. And what's worse, he is right up her alley. Unlike most moms, Katherine likes the long, moppy hair on guys and has always been a sucker for brown eyes. By now, she's probably invited him to stay and has visions of prom dresses in her head. The worlds that I keep carefully separated into manageable little circles are converging, and I don't like it. Compartmentalization, that's how I roll. First Bearden's with the girls, now this. I have the Corey-Bakery-Truck circle. I have the Mom-Liam-Ronan circle. I have the Kirsten-Paige-School cir—

And then my mind pulls a fast one. It sneaks up behind me and asks: *What about the eating disorder–ski trip circle?* I push the question away and tell myself I don't have an eating disorder. I don't have an eating disorder because I've only done that Urge thing a few times. My mind counters, *You've done it seventeen times. And add a P. You mean PURGE. It's called bulimia. B-U-L—*

—and now my circles are revolting on me.

They are overlapping into a Venn Diagram Apocalypse.

I want my separate circles back.

I can manage separate circles; a life of overlapping circles calls attention. People—my mom, Kirsten, Paige, Corey—might start noticing something's wrong if they're all thrown together into one big circle. And I guess by saying this, I've up and admitted that there is, indeed, something wrong with me.

Enough.

This is nonsense.

I get up and splash cold water on my face. I wet my fingers and paste the uneven lock—the missing ski-trip lock, the *stolen* lock—behind my ear before I walk out of the bathroom and down to the backyard.

No problem. There is no problem. No problem here at all.

~

"Sid!" My mom beams when I step outside.

She walks over and stands next to me with her face positively aglow. We watch Corey dangling Spider-Man by a rope. He waves to me, I wave back. Ronan barks at me from his pen and then settles back down to work on his treat. He has been sequestered because Vince's mother, who has never even laid eyes on Ronan, is afraid of him.

"Is this too high?" Corey yells to us from the tree branch.

"About a foot lower!" Mom yells back to him, looking up and shielding her eyes from the sun.

She mumbles to me through a big smile, "You've been holding out on me, young lady."

"So it would seem," I mumble back, looking at Corey, shielding my eyes and smiling too.

I give Corey a thumbs-up and he ties off the rope.

"Rides to school. Early morning trysts. I thought we were closer than this, Sid."

"You did not just say the word tryst."

"Tryst, rendezvous. Whatever you want to call it."

"You're cut off, Mom. Really. No more bodice rippers."

"They're called historical romance novels, Sid."

"Bodice ripper, historical romance novel. Whatever you want to call it. The point would be that you've read one too many. We're just friends."

Corey climbs down out of the tree and brushes his shorts off before heading toward us. He is getting tanner by the second and smiling from ear to ear. I think his teeth could blind someone. The only phrase that I can conjure up is the one that is written all over my mom's face:

Man candy.

"Friends. Righhhht..." she says, before stepping inside.

Liam runs up behind Corey and tries to jump on his back just as Corey reaches me. Corey bends down a little and hooks his arms underneath Liam's legs, hoisting him up. Our eyes lock. Corey is studying my reaction.

"I like Corey!" Liam says. "He showed me a trick!"

"Oh, yeah? What trick is that?" I say, turning my eyes to Liam.

Liam leaps down and pulls out a pack of miniature playing cards from his back pocket. They are supposed to be part of the loot bags, but he's already busted into his.

"Cut 'em, then pick a card," he says.

I cut the deck and pick a card, holding it so neither of them can see what it is—the two of hearts, of course.

"Now slide it back in," Liam says.

I slide it back in and Liam reshuffles the deck. He flips through them and then plucks out a card—the two of hearts.

"Hey, that's pretty good. How'd you do that?" I ask, looking from Liam to Corey.

Corey grins and nods to Liam.

"You wish, loser," Liam says, and takes off running.

Yes, young Liam's studies are coming along nicely. With Corey's help, we may make a smart-ass out of him yet.

"Well played," I say to Corey.

We both smirk with pride as Liam runs toward the house. People are starting to arrive. We stand in the yard for a second. I look up at Spider-Man, dangling.

"Well, I'd introduce you, but I can see that my mom's skipped the formalities."

"Should I leave?" he asks, looking at me with a grin, knowing full well I wouldn't dare let him.

"No, but you're helping with the games. We've got Hang-Spider-Man-From-A-Tree-And-Bludgeon-Him-With-A-Stick-Until-Candy-Falls-Out-His-Butt Game. We've got Break-Your-Face-Sack-Race. A wet T-shirt contest disguised as a water balloon toss, annnd..."

I squint, trying to remember the list I'd made.

"...Pass the Orange."

"Pass the Orange?"

"You know, put it under your chin and pass it to the person next to you without dropping it or using your hands."

"You playin'?"

"I have to. None of these kids know a single thing about games. Unless, of course, it involves a big-screen TV and a hand controller."

As if driving my point home, Liam and a few of his class-mates come tearing out the back door, across the patio, and onto the lawn. One blond kid wearing a designer polo shirt and swim trunks stops cold, looks around at the yard, and whines, "No pool? Aw, man!"

Another kid grumbles and kicks up dirt, saying, "You don't even have a trampoline." Liam looks over at me, his little face twisted into a panic. Corey crosses his arms and glares at the brats.

"I'm in," he says. "The little fuckers won't know what hit 'em."

At four, when the parents come to pick up Liam's classmates, they are all hanging on Liam and Corey like sunburned, Gymboree-clad barnacles. Corey organized a Capture the Flag squirt gun war that lasted for two hours.

And Liam is a rock star.

~

I sit on my bed and think of Mr. Hero.

No, not Corey. The fast-food joint.

After the party, my stomach and heart and every last nerve ending were lit up like a nuclear bomb Christmas tree. When Corey pulled out of my driveway, I felt like I might blast off into space or explode into a million stars. I was so dizzy with happi-ness and freaked out by how great I felt that I immediately threw on my sweats and went running. I needed to burn the slap-happy-stupid out of me. I was running down Detroit, and that's when I saw him. Mr. Hero. He was just there, beckoning to me with his neon sign and heavenly vapors.

I should never have brought money with me.

But I had to fill a prescription for my mom's sleep aids, and there was nearly twenty bucks left over, and all I'd eaten all day was a thin slice of Spider-Man cake, which was so good, but hardly a meal. I couldn't decide what I wanted; it was between the Hot Buttered Cheesesteak and the Romanburger. I got up to the counter and stood there forever. The cashier and the people behind me were growing impatient, so I just ordered both. Since it was cheaper in the long run to get the value meal, I got the drink and large Potato Waffer fries too. And it wasn't even a diet—I got a real Pepsi. Oh, and a slice of cheesecake.

Now I'm home, lying on my bed like a disgusting, sweaty pig. I turn on my laptop and google a website called FastFoodKills .com and calculate the calorie damage.

Hot Buttered Cheesesteak: 669 calories.

Romanburger: 860 calories.

Potato Waffer Fries: 428 calories.

Large Pepsi: 280 calories.

Cheesecake: 280 calories.

For a grand total of 2,517 calories.

WTF?!

I can't believe it. All that from one damn meal? Ugh. And even though I ran six miles afterward, I know that the majority of the calories are still there, booking a one-way trip to my ass.

I get up and head to the bathroom. I mean, the food has been swirling around in my stomach for almost two hours. So it's not like I'm starving myself; I'm just trimming off some of the excess. I walk into the bathroom and I promise myself it will only be this one last time.

It's Friday night of the last weekend before the last week
of school. None of the seniors have classes next week, so the
partying starts tonight. The Callahans are kicking the graduation season off with their usual kegger. Only this time, they've
rented two giant hot tubs rolled in on flatbeds.

We head out of my house, Kirsten hanging on to Justin
Biceps. Paige can't come because her mom found a copy of
Macbeth stuffed under her mattress and flipped out, so they're
at a prayer intervention with some wackjob minister at their
new church. They left their old church because the youth
group held an Easter egg hunt for the younger kids last month
and Paige's mom decided that because there are no Easter egg

hunts or magic rabbits in the Bible, the High Hopes First Assemblage of God must be dabbling in paganism. Their new minister isn't even a real minister; he bought his license online and holds services in an out-of-business hair salon that rents by the month. Paige's English teacher even called Mrs. Daniels to tell her that Paige was reading *Macbeth* for a term paper and that the play is actually considered to be a text of Christian allegory. It didn't matter. When Paige's mom pulled out that book and read the first line—*Thunder and lightning. Enter three* WITCHES.—that was it. God help her if they ever find out about her Warcraft account.

So no Paige, which makes me the third wheel tonight.

The Callahans live about six blocks from my house, so we walk it. I keep about five feet ahead of the lovebirds so as to keep their constant kissing and tender glances out of my direct line of sight. I love Kirsten, but when she gets a boyfriend, it can be nauseating for the first few months. I don't blame her, I guess. He's good-looking if you like the military thing—hair buzzed off, shirt tucked in, all squared away nice and neat. Plus, he seems really sweet and genuinely interested in Kirsten, so I'm trying my best to be happy for her, even if, deep down, I'm pretty jealous about the whole thing. She's had like five or six real boyfriends in her life, and I've never even been on a real date, just awkward pairings glued together by Kirsten. Some friend of whomever she's dating and I will tag along to the Berea Fair or the Metroparks. It never works out. Either he's too short or I'm too fat or he's too boring or I'm too bossy. Whatever the case, we both end up miserable thirty seconds into the date.

It's a nice night—not too hot, not too cold—and I'm looking forward to this party. Mostly because everyone—geeks, jocks, burnouts, goths—will be there, including Corey and his friends. The Callahan kegger knows no prejudice. We turn onto Magnolia and the road is lined bumper-to-bumper with cars and their front yard looks like it's been turned into a parking lot. People are filtering down the street and we join the crowd that is headed toward the loud music. When we get to the backyard, the first two people I see are Starsha and Amber, splashing around in string bikinis on top of the Rub-A-Dub Hot Tubz flatbed.

"Figures," I say.

Kirsten holds on a little tighter to her man.

"Skanks," she mutters.

The line to the keg is about twenty deep and looped around the patio. It's a nice yard, pretty big by Lakewood standards, and completely enclosed with a privacy fence. The place is filled end-to-end with kids from school, and there's a small bonfire going near the back with people sitting around it in lawn chairs. About five or six beat-up picnic tables are placed around the lawn, and music is being blasted out a third-story window, which is really just an attic converted into a bedroom.

Pat's bedroom.

Or *the lair*, as Kirsten now calls it. It's where she and Pat first hooked up last year, and where they spent most of their time before he broke up with her.

I scan the crowd for Corey, but don't see him or his friends anywhere. Tate Andrews and Hunter Brady stumble past us, shirtless, their swim trunks dripping wet. They cut to the head of the line, completely ignoring Celinda Monroe and Natalee Flowers, who are patiently waiting their turn along with everyone else. Tate fills his cup and turns around a little too quickly, slopping beer foam down the front of Natalee's shirt. She jumps back and starts wiping at her chest. Tate doesn't even apologize; he just stumbles away laughing. I grab a red cup and get in line.

"Babe, would you get us a plate of something?" Kirsten says, looking up at Justin. "I didn't eat dinner and I'm starving. I'll get your beer for you."

"Sure, babe," he says and then leans down to kiss her good-bye, like he's heading off to hunt for wild boar and not just walking over to the Callahan garage for some cheese cubes and crackers. Bleck. I make a quick promise to myself never to call anyone "babe" or send them to fetch me cheese cubes. As soon as Justin's out of earshot, Kirsten leans in.

"Far southwest corner. He's over there. With *her*. Don't point."

I scan the yard. The crowd is getting bigger by the second.

"Southwest corner? I'm not a park ranger, Kirsten. You mean by the hot tubs?"

"No. By the fire. Sitting on the picnic table."

I see him, Pat Callahan, all cozied up to some brunette in a pleated skirt. She's wearing a headband and an argyle sweater. It's not quite summer yet, but still, she's dressed like she's headed to the library in November.

"Please," I say, trying to assure Kirsten of her physical superiority. "Who wears that to a keg party? Snotty sorority chicks, that's who."

A group of freshmen get in line behind us, all wide-eyed and nervous, clutching their cups like someone might snatch them away. The line moves forward a smidge.

"Still, she's gorgeous," Kirsten says. "And don't say she isn't, because she is." Then she gets teary and says, "Shit. I was really hoping she'd be hideous."

I look toward the open garage and see the top of Justin's head. He's talking to a couple of hockey players and, I'm sure, loading up on multicolored cheese cubes. He'll be heading back in a second, and Kirsten looks like she's about to burst into tears. I look over at Pat and his preppy East Coast girlfriend.

"Yeah, she's pretty. So he'd best enjoy himself tonight, because they'll be broken up in a week."

"What? How do you know?"

"Because she's from Nantucket. You know who lives on Nantucket? Rich people. And now that Tierney-the-Flautist-from-Nantucket has seen her boyfriend's house and met his family, in all their rolling-hot-tub glory, she'll run for the hills, or the seashore, or the vineyard, or wherever it is that girls from Nantucket run to when they figure out they're dating a broke-ass jock from Ohio."

I take a deep breath and then a sip from my cup, forgetting that it's still empty and I've been standing in this keg line for like two days. I look over at Kirsten, who's staring at me all starry-eyed, her mouth half-open like she's in a trance.

"What? Wha'd I say?"

Her face breaks apart into a big smile. She grabs me around the neck and squeezes just as Justin walks up. She whispers, "I love you, man," and gives me a quick kiss on the cheek, and then turns to wrap herself up in Justin's free arm.

"Go grab us some chairs or a bench somewhere," I say. "I'll get the beers."

Because I know they're going to start making out now. Kirsten hands me the cups. They walk over to a half-empty picnic table and start making out, feeding each other cheese cubes.

When I'm finally on deck, ready to get us all a frosty cupload, some short guy in front of me says, "Sweet, just made it!" and turns around with his three-quarters of a cup of beer. He looks up at me.

"Sorry, Red. Killed it," he says and walks away.

I step up, pump the keg, and groan when it pisses bubbles into my cup. I hear someone yell, "Beer Run! Back in twenty!"

I grab three cans of no-name cola swimming in a half-melted storage bin of ice. I head over to sit with the lovebirds. Thankfully, on my way over to them, I spy my old lunch buddies, Bethany and Emma. I hang out with them for a while as they discuss the fact that Starsha's new Canadian boyfriend just showed up and Tate's freaking out about it. This is mildly interesting news to me. Still, my eyes prowl the faces and shirts that walk past, scrutinizing the various classmates coming and going, sharply on the lookout for Corey or one of his crew.

Then I see him, or what I think might be the top of his head—a tall guy with shaggy brown hair heading toward the house. I break away from Bethany and Emma to go talk to him. I push my way hurriedly through the fray, excusing myself over and over, trying not to spill my can of flat, store-brand cola. I see TJ, one of Corey's friends, and ask him if Corey's here.

"He went to use the bathroom, I think," he says, pointing toward the house.

I open the back door, which leads into a closed-in porch. I ditch the pop in a trash can and walk inside the house, which is crawling with kids from school. I circle the main floor—kitchen, dining room, living room, foyer—but I don't see Corey. Now I'm back in the smallest, most crowded kitchen ever, trying to make my way around to the dining room again, when someone cups their hands over my eyes. Reaching up to feel them, I can tell the hands are big and kind of rough, and the guy feels tall. I whip around with a smile on my face.

It's not Corey.

It's Tate.

Ugh.

He has a towel wrapped around his waist, still no shirt, and his muscled chest is right in front of me, inches away, standing all ripped-up and proud of itself. *Cringe.* I turn to make my getaway.

"Sid, wait up. Hey, where you goin'?" he says. But it's all slurry, like *Where-er-ye-goin?* "Hey, come back. I need to talk to—"

—hurrying, hurrying, pushing my way through the crowd. The closed-in porch is now packed with kids, and the easiest way out is down the basement steps. It's a walk-out basement, if

I remember correctly, so I'll just shoot out the basement door and into the backyard.

"Sid! Siddy! Hey...wait up!"

I get to the basement, but the damp rec room, or what used to be a rec room, is now some kind of storage area. The door leading out the back is blocked with boxes and furniture and a fully decorated Christmas tree. I turn to run back up the steps but Tate is coming down the stairs, piss drunk with his shirt off.

"Siddeeee...why you running? I just want to talk to ya."

He comes around the steps and looks to his left, switches on a brighter light.

"Tate, what do you want? Honestly."

"What? I just want to—"

"I mean, you and me...we're not friends. At all. So what are you doing?"

"I just want you to come swimming in the hot tub with me."

"Sorry. No bathing suit," I say and try to walk past him. He puts out his arm and leans to the right, blocking me.

"Move," I say.

"God, what's your problem, anyway? Just come outside and hang with me for a while."

I cross my arms and stare at him firmly.

"Look, Tate. I don't know what kind of ridiculous games you and Starsha are playing with each other. I don't know if you're dating or broken up or friends-with-benefits or swingers or what. But I do know one thing—trying to cuddle up with Sid Murphy is not going to help your cause. She thinks I'm a fat ginger-

bitch pig and she will never touch you again if you come anywhere near me. You're better off trying to get on Amber or
Cameron or one of the other—"

"Are you that stupid? Really?" he says.

I blink at him.

"I mean, come on. Starsha's so goddamn jealous of you it
keeps her up at night."

"You're mental," I say, moving to the left so I can squeeze
past him.

He leans the other way, blocking me again. "She's jealous,"
he says. "Trust me, she's always been jealous of you. And it's
not because of your hair or your height or your awesome
fucking tits. It's because you don't give a shit what Starsha Lexington thinks or wants. You never have and never will. It's
because she doesn't impress you. She doesn't scare the shit out
of you the way she does other girls." Then he snorts, his eyes all
glassy. "Or the way she scares guys for that matter. This one at
least."

I pause to see if he's done pontificating about Starsha, Her
Majesty.

"Well, that...that's nice to know, Tate," I say, nodding and
smiling tightly. "Now, can you move out of the way, please? My
friends are waiting for me."

"Just come up and hang out with me for a little bit. Please,"
he says, and his eyes are all desperate and pleading.

I sigh, envisioning myself on the arm of Tate Andrews.

Ew. No way. Not even for some good-time Starsha kicks.

"Sorry, Tate. I just don't think—"

"You really do think you're better than all of us, don't you?" And his face has gone from pleading and drunk to angry and drunk.

"It's not that, it's—"

"No, you do," he says, his voice getting louder. He moves forward, walking me backward into the rec room. I am starting to panic; my heart, which was already pounding like a jackhammer, is about to shoot up into my skull.

"Yeah. You think we're all a bunch of dumbass jocks and cheerleaders and Sid Murphy is so much better. You've lost all this weight and think you're hot shit now. I was too busy looking at Starsha to notice. But now I'm looking. I'm looking, Sid."

I back into a stack of boxes. The flitting dots of light, like the ones I saw when I found my ski coat, are back. Static hisses in my ears and the world is getting far away.

Then someone yells, "Hey!" from behind Tate's big body.

Tate backs away and Corey comes running up. He catches me right before I go down. I don't pass out, not all the way—I just kind of settle onto the ground and watch things spin.

"What the fuck, dude!" Corey says to Tate, reaching up and shoving Tate backward.

"I didn't do anything. I never touched her!" Tate says, growing instantly hysterical.

"Sid, are you okay? What's wrong?" Corey says.

But I can't answer him. I'm trying to hang on to myself but

the floor tiles are doing this jerky spinny thing and I feel like any second I'll be gone, floating in some dark, empty space.

"Go get her friend," Corey says, his voice gritted up. "Kirsten-something, she's blond."

And while I can still hear and see everything, I think my head is coming off for good this time. I think my head is rolling off my neck. It's headed right toward that Christmas tree that keeps moving back and forth.

Tate starts backpedaling. He realizes he's crossed a line.

"I'm sorry. I didn't...I would never—" he says.

"Go. Get. Her. *Friend!*" Corey yells.

Tate turns and runs up the stairs.

"Sid. You okay?" Corey asks, squatting down in front of me.

"Um..." I say, blinking hard. I put my hands on the sides of my head and for some reason this helps. And after a moment of looking at his face up close, I speak. And what comes out is...

"You have long lashes."

His eyebrows stitch together in confusion. He smiles a little. Then he gets focused.

"Listen, what happened? Tate's drunk off his ass. Did he do anything? I mean, did he—"

I shake my head no. Things have stopped moving now; my head is clearing.

"No, nothing like that. He's just—um—he's pissed Starsha's making a fool out of him again. I don't think—I mean—I don't think he's like that. I just want to go home."

Kirsten comes running down the steps with Justin and Tate. Tate stops at the bottom of the steps. He looks like he's about to cry.

"I'm sorry, Sid," he says, and his face is terror-stricken, ashamed. He runs back up the steps.

Kirsten puts her arm around me, and after a minute, I stand up. Then we go home.

23

It's Friday, the last day of school. The Diner on Clifton called last Saturday and I interviewed with Shelley Keep It Green. I start this coming Tuesday as a waitress. I can wear jeans and a T-shirt and any kind of apron I want so long as it's not plain; it has to be funny, cute, or funky.

I ordered three aprons over the Internet and am having them shipped second-day air. One says IRISH PRINCESS and has shamrocks all over it; another is vintage-looking with a delicate flower print and ruffles; and the third is black-and-white and says WHICH PART OF "IT'S NOT READY YET" DIDN'T YOU UNDERSTAND?

I climb in the truck and head off to school with Corey. We've discussed the incident at the party for the past week, and I'm really hoping he finally lets it go today. While he has tried to be delicate about it, all week the rides to and from school have consisted of Corey asking me if I'm okay, asking me if Tate has bothered me at school. He hasn't, by the way; Tate Andrews is officially scared to death of Sid Murphy. Whenever Tate spots me in the halls, he immediately takes off in the other direction. Corey thinks there's more to the story, but there isn't. Well, technically there is, but it's nothing Corey needs to concern himself with.

When I got home after the party, I was pretty wrecked. My mom was asleep, and Liam was at his dad's. This left me free to devour everything in the fridge, throw it all up, and go running. I ran for three hours. Then twice on Saturday and twice on Sunday. But I physically can't do it anymore. My legs were really hurting by Tuesday, so I'm back to normal running now. Just a couple hours at night.

Before Corey can even bring up the party or Tate, I flip on the radio and blurt out my good news.

"I got a job. Waitressing at The Diner on Clifton. I start next week."

"That's great," Corey says. "One of my summer jobs starts next week, too."

"Oh, yeah? You work two jobs in the summer?"

"Three. I work in the dry stacks building at the marina—that starts next week—then landscaping for this friend of my mom's. Then my regular hours at the bakery. The landscaping starts today, right after school."

"Busy, busy. How'd you get the job at the marina?"

"Mr. D has a boat. He got me in."

Suddenly, it occurs to me that I will have no reason whatsoever to see Corey anymore. School is over and we'll both be working. He doesn't even have my cell number. I guess I can still come by the bakery now and then.

"I'm really looking forward to the marina job," he tells me. "It's like this big private party all the time. Not stuck-up sailing and yachting types. Just average Joes with a powerboat or Jet Skis who treat the staff nice. Like friends. I went a few times last year with Mr. D and his wife. People hang around playing volleyball and bocce outside the Whiskey Island Club. I went out a few times on Mr. D's boat with him and his fishing buddies last year. Learned how to water-ski."

"Wow, that sounds nice. You'll have a great summer," I say, nodding and smiling.

But inside, I'm thinking, *I might not see you until September.* I get a knot in my throat and look out the window.

Long pause.

"There's this summer kick-off party tonight. It's at the club, but there's technically a restaurant section, so you don't have to be twenty-one. People bring their kids, too."

"Oh, that should be fun."

The knot is growing bigger, tighter. My throat aches.

Longer pause.

"You wanna go with me?" he says, and I jerk a little.

The knot breaks into pieces and slides down into my stomach. The butterflies gulp, gulp, gulp the pieces up. I think I'm flying.

"Sure!" I say, then internally wince at my overeager tone. I rein it in a bit. "I mean, I could meet you there if you want."

"I could just pick you up," he says. "Parking is kind of a bitch if you don't have a pass."

"Oh, okay, sure. Whatever's easiest."

"I have some lawns to do, but I should be done by six or seven. Say eight thirty?"

"I'll be ready."

And my heart goes: *Wheeeeee!*

———

Holy crap, what do I wear?

I try on sixty-five million outfits and end up calling in the reserves. Kirsten's car screams into my driveway. I look out my window; she and Paige are running from the car with armfuls of clothes. I can hear my mom opening the door for them and the three of them bouncing through the house, Liam and Ronan in tow—the whole revved-up gang is heading toward my room.

"Man, your hair rocks!" Paige tells my mom.

My mom crows shamelessly, "I know, doesn't it?"

My mom hated the soccer-mom bob and went back to the salon the next day and got this choppy, short-banged, frame-the-face deal with funky highlights. It looks killer. Her sales have picked up some.

"Sid has a date! With a total *stuh-uhhd*!" my mom sings as she comes into my room.

"Yippee!" Kirsten squeals.

I may have to knock all their heads together.

"What's a stud?" Liam asks as they all pile onto my bed.

"Stud is a word that old people use when they mean hot," I say, my head stuck in my closet.

My mom sticks her tongue out at me. I can see them all in my full-length mirror on the inside of the closet door. Kirsten and Paige are lying across the bed on their stomachs, their heads propped in their hands, kicking their feet back and forth like five-year-olds. My mom is sitting Indian-style with a pillow in her lap. Ronan is sitting on the floor letting Liam use his back as a long, hairy sliding board; over and over Liam slides down Ronan's back on his stomach.

Kirsten says to my mom, "At first I thought he was like this degenerate because of the whole juvie thing, but then I met him and—"

I freeze.

Kirsten and Paige freeze.

They both look at me through the mirror. Kirsten's head picks up from her hands, her jaw dropping.

Oops.

I busy myself hanging up clothes and hope my mom missed it. Nope—my mom's face blanches. She looks at me through the mirror, hangdog.

"Juvie?"

"He got caught doing graffiti when he was like twelve," I say, turning around quickly and waving my hand. "Stupid kid stuff. Ages ago."

My mom looks at Kirsten.

Her head goes back into her hands.

"Graffiti. For real," Paige says.

"O-kayyyy," my mom says.

Liam interrupts. "I'm hungry. Can we make popcorn?"

He is standing up and pulling at my mom's shirt now. She turns her attention to him. I whip around and mouth to Kirsten: *WTF?* She makes this nail-biter *Sorry!* face at me.

"In a little bit, hon," she answers Liam. "When Sid leaves, we'll watch the new SpongeBob and I'll make popcorn."

I close my closet door and turn around. I fish around in the clothes that Kirsten and Paige brought. I hold some tops up to myself. We all wince in unison. I may be smaller than I was six months ago, but still, these will never fit. I turn back to my own clothes and narrow it down to three long tops. I hold them all up.

"Which one?"

"Pink," Kirsten calls. "It shows off your phenom' rack."

Paige nods in agreement.

I pitch it behind me. My mom glares at them both and says, "Green. It shows off her beautiful eyes."

Kirsten sighs.

"Green it is," she says.

The blouse is long-sleeved and kind of a loose, billowy, tunic style, so that's good.

"Out," I say, jerking my head toward the door, pulling the shirt from its hanger.

"Liam, hide your eyes," my mom says, and neither she, Kirsten, nor Paige budge.

"I mean all of you," I say, waving toward the door.

"It's just us," my mom says.

I shoot her a look and she gets up from my bed, taking the girls with her.

"Fine, sheesh," she says.

I don't want my mom or the girls seeing me naked. They'll comment on my figure and then my mom will make me eat something. All the time she's watching, ambushing me with these big meals and telling me it's "family night" three and four times a week. Saying things like, *What did you eat today? Didn't you already run this morning?* I'm down quite a bit in weight, but for my height, I'm still at a number that's considered normal. So no worries. I still have more to lose before I'd be considered underweight. I'll stop before then. I just need to lose a bit more. My goal is to be a C cup. I know that's quite a drop from a double D, but I don't care. C cups are nice, normal-sized boobs. So it's all a nice, healthy goal.

When I put the top on, I spy a pair of leggings in Kirsten's pile of clothes. I look at the jeans I'm wearing. They look decent enough, so I probably shouldn't push it. Still, I want to see what the leggings look like. I pull them on and look in the mirror. I've never worn leggings in my life. I turn around and around, examining everything from various angles. The tunic-style blouse is really long and covers my butt thoroughly, and the leggings, well, I think they look pretty good.

And they'll look even better when I lose five more pounds.

I put on some makeup and a little perfume and look at the clock: eight fifteen. I emerge from my room to the nauseating smell of microwave popcorn.

When Corey's truck pulls in at twenty-five after, all of them are sitting on the couch, including Liam, squeezed in, shoulder-to-shoulder, one, two, three, four, with a big bowl of popcorn in the middle. Wide-eyed, looking at the door, they shove it in, crunching away. I scream at them in a whisper.

"Please don't act like you're at the damn movies watching the Sid and Corey show!"

"Oh, right," Kirsten says and gets up fast, turning on the TV and draping herself across the floor. Ronan sidles in beside her. My mom jumps onto the recliner and picks up one of her bodice rippers upside down.

"Mom!"

She looks at the front of it and flips it around. A sinewy, oiled-up guy in an unbuttoned pirate shirt is grasping the waist of a moaning pirate wench. *The Forbidden Sea*. She throws the book behind the chair and picks up a *Homes* magazine. Paige doesn't know what to do, so she just panics and runs to the kitchen. Liam stays right where he is, sitting up straighter, staring at me, and shoving popcorn in his mouth. I shoot him the stink-eye.

I open the door and Corey is standing in front of me, his hands in his pockets. He's wearing multiple layers, wrinkled, and I like it. I was hoping he wouldn't go all preppy on our first date or, god forbid, be holding out a bouquet of flowers.

Wait a minute. Did I just say date? Is this a date? Or is it just friends?

I think it's a date.

Christ, I'm sweating again. Fack.

Man, he's tanner than he was earlier today, rosy under the

eyes. I think his hair is picking up summer highlights. The landscaping is paying off. I feel very white. White and sweaty.

"Hi?" he says, looking at me funny, like he's trying to figure out what's going on with me.

It occurs to me that I've been standing here staring at him, sizing him up and down, like a starry-eyed assface, like he's some kind of Abercrombie & Fitch mannequin set down in my doorway for endless inspection. I haven't even greeted him. Jesus, I'm jacking this all up and he just got here. I snap out of myself.

"Hey," I say, waving him in. "I just have to get my bag."

I smile, turn around, and squeeze my eyes shut, trying to pull it together.

Corey steps inside. I walk over and get my purse from the end table. Yes, I'm carrying a purse tonight, which I never do. But as of right now, Sid Murphy is an official purse-carrier. Because no decent guy wants to date a pocket-stuffer. Plus, I have no pockets now that I'm a leggings-wearer.

"Hello, all," Corey says.

More awkwardness. Him nodding around the room, rocking on his heels, hands in his pockets, while the spectator idiots stare back at him, all smiling ear-to-ear.

"Hi, Corey!" Liam bellows. Then he jumps up from the couch, runs over, and hugs Corey's waist. Corey puts a hand on Liam's head.

"Hey, little man."

Liam looks up at Corey and asks, "Are you and Sid gonna get married?"

Every drop of blood in my body rushes to my face. My mom

barks out a laugh and Kirsten's face goes horror-stricken. I hear a faint whimper drift out from the kitchen.

"Jesus, Liam!" I say, peeling him off Corey's legs and pushing his smiling, gap-toothed face backward.

He laughs his evil little butt off and runs away, skipping and singing. "Sid and Corey, sittin' in a tree, k-i-s-s-i-n-g..."

He used to be sweet, and I have no one to blame but myself. I feel like dying. I grab Corey by the arm and pull him out the door.

"'Bye," I say, to no one in particular.

I stalk us down the steps and around the side of the house, where Corey is parked in the driveway. How can I recover from this? There is no way. Liam is a dead brat walking. I let go of Corey's arm and press my back against the house. My hand is over my eyes and I seriously can't breathe.

"That little shit. How red is my face? Is it bad?"

"It's starting to get dark out, but if I had to guess, I'd say you've passed red completely and moved on to a more purple hue."

"Great," I whisper, mortified, still holding my breath.

"Breathe, Sid. In. Out. In. Out." He's trying not to laugh.

He's standing right in front of me. I let out the air. I breathe some air in. I still can't look yet.

"Okay. Just give me a sec," I say, shaking out my hands and knees, my eyes still closed. "I just need all the blood to drain back into my legs before I can walk."

"Take your time," he says. Then he adds, "I mean, a bride needs her legs if she's gonna walk down the aisle without falling."

I burst out laughing and cover my face with both hands and turn away, pressing my face against the house.

"What?" he asks, laughing. "It's already all planned. A marina wedding. Everyone's waiting for us, and that little shit's ruined my surprise."

I laugh even harder, my shoulders shaking.

"Don't make me laugh. Can't you see I'm trying to die of embarrassment here?"

After a few seconds, I calm down and turn around to look up at him. Corey is right in front of me, smelling of Irish Spring and looking into my face.

"You have the most amazing laugh," he says, grinning.

"Don't you mean the loudest and most obnoxious?" I say, crossing my arms and looking around, still slightly embarrassed.

"No."

And more thoughtfully, he adds, "I mean...amazing."

He pauses to choose his words.

"It's like this light coming out of you. I could be in a crowd of thousands and know right where to find you."

I don't know how to respond. I think it's the loveliest thing anyone has ever said to me. I look up at him, stunned. Everything slows down. He reaches out and brushes my cheek with his knuckles.

"I know it's before the date has even started, but can I just do this now?"

My heart is beating so fast. My arms drop slowly to my sides. Oh, god, I think he means to kiss me. Yes. Yes, he does. But am I ready for this? I look at him standing in front of me, waiting for my answer. I've seen this boy almost every day for nearly six months now, but he doesn't just assume. He doesn't just take it. He has asked permission first.

He has asked *first*.

My eyes start to burn. I blink hard and nod yes.

Because, yes.

I am ready for this.

He cups the back of my neck with his hand and holds the other against my face, rubbing my cheek with his thumb. Slowly, he leans down and kisses me.

Soft, then deep.

I ooze against the house. I can feel his kiss in my whole body, like warm liquid pouring through me—gold, rich, and melting. After about a minute of what can only be described as sheer ecstasy, Corey rests his forehead against mine so we can both catch our breath. Then he takes my head into his hands and looks at me hard, like his heart is breaking.

"I have wanted to do that for so, so long."

I cannot speak. I can only nod yes and hope he knows what I mean. He kisses me more…

"…for months and months…"

"…when you sprayed me with Dr Pepper…"

"…at the bakery when you were holding that corned beef…"

"…and every single time I see you…"

I lean against the house and hold on to his wrists so I don't dissolve into a puddle. And I kiss him back. Over and over, I kiss him back.

24

I dig waitressing, maybe because I'm really good at it. The Diner on Clifton is awesome. I think I might skip college and work there forever. They have lots of interesting, happy clientele, and the staff is stellar and fun. I've picked up all of this catchy diner lingo, and I use it at every opportunity.

Adam and Eve on a raft! (Two poached eggs on toast.)

In the alley! (Serve it on the side.)

Kill it! (Cook it well done.)

Cremate it! (Burn it to a crisp.)

I especially like when people order two scrambled eggs. I get to yell, "Two eggs! Wreck 'em!" really loud.

I wear my hair in these big, obnoxious pigtails. The curls

look like showers of sparks coming out of both sides of my head, and customers love it; I get fat tips when I wear my hair like that.

It's hard sometimes being around all that food, though. I feel really proud of myself if I leave without eating anything. But I usually cave and grab a piece of bread or something small to hold me over. I'm human and cannot exist on air alone. I know this. I know I need to eat more. But still, even though I feel hungry and want to eat everything I see, a bigger part of me resists. Most of the time, anyway. Sometimes it gets away from me, the desire becomes overwhelming, and I stuff myself sick. Then, well…you know. But most of the time, I just try to stay strong and not eat too much. Besides, when I see her, my mom is always poised and ready with the grub, which I try my best to avoid. If she could tie me to a chair, jack open my mouth, and shovel it in, I think she would. She's getting harder and harder to fool.

Kirsten and Paige come by The Diner when I work sometimes. So do Corey and his landscaping buddies. They stop in if they're doing a house nearby. I'm allowed to talk and hang out with them as long as they're eating and I don't ignore my other customers.

But last week?

There was an incident.

I sat on Corey's knee between orders for a few minutes. He put his one arm around my waist while he ate with his other. He kissed the back of my neck a few times where my pigtails separate. Not gross, get-a-room type of kisses, just quick, sweet ones. I leaned back into him and was inhaling his yummy, boy-sweat-earthy-cut-grass smell while also getting a cheap, under-the-radar thrill from his unshaven razor stubble against my cheek. It's a departure from the way he usually smells and looks, but I like it just as much. I can't help it.

Anyhow, he bobbed his knee and hugged me tighter with his arm and said, "Man, your waist; it's like a wasp or something. Here, bite…" and he held up a forkful of potatoes. I ate it, but then he came back with another forkful, so I told him that I was full, that I'd eaten a ton in the back already. He didn't say anything. I felt awkward, and I think he felt awkward, too, because he just scraped his food around and looked at his plate. I pretended to be interested in his friends' comments on how weed killer's been linked to sterility, then I got up from his lap, relieved that one of my customers was waving me over for a coffee refill.

Corey loves kissing the back of my neck for some reason. It gives me a shiver—a good shiver. Before the ski trip, I used to pray for a shiver like that. I would nod and act happy when Kirsten and Paige would tell me their magic moment stories, but then I would feel miserable deep down. I thought I might never get a chance to feel that way about someone and to have someone like me back in that way. I thought no one would ever want me, looking the way I do.

And then, after the ski trip, I tried not to think about that stuff at all, because the thought of someone's hands on me made me ill. I don't feel that way with Corey, though. We've been seeing each other as boyfriend and girlfriend for a month now, and I love hugging him and holding his hand. That's all we've done though, that and a ton of kissing.

We make out in his truck, mostly, because it's usually the only place we can be alone. We park by the lake at night and put on music and kiss and talk for hours. About once a week, though, his hand will travel up my arm or down my side and he'll play with the hem of my shirt. He'll move his fingers underneath and up my stomach and that's when I tense up. My body says, *I'm not ready for that!* And right away, he will move his hand back up my arm to cup my neck or face, or his hand will find my fingers and slide them into his. I think I might be ready for more soon, but for right now, I'm just enjoying the kissing. I hope he is, too. I think he is.

I feel really comfortable with him and we talk about a lot of things. I'm still trying to guess his middle name. I've thought of every car I can come up with and still don't know it. He likes the game: *Corey Solstice? Corey Taurus? Corey Acura?* I thought about looking for the answer on the Internet, but that would take the fun out of it.

One thing we never really talk about, though, is his mom. He has a clever way of diverting the conversation whenever I mention the word *mom*. Also, he doesn't talk about his home or house or anything. One time I brought up the idea of coming over his house, and he tensed up, so I immediately changed the subject. I tried to look him up in the phone book and online, but he's unlisted. Kirsten says that she's pretty sure he lives somewhere over in Birdtown, which is an older section of southeast Lakewood. It's really charming, if you use your imagination. It's this tiny section of the city that was built up by Slavic immigrants back a hundred years ago or so. It's kind of run-down now, which is a shame, because you can see how beautiful it once was with all the churches and old three-story houses. Artists rent some of the empty factory buildings for work space. I think that alone makes Birdtown altogether beautiful. I want to tell him that he should be glad to live in such a place and that I would be thrilled to spend my time there, but I think it would make him feel uncomfortable if I said that.

Even though he won't talk about his mom or his home, he tells me other things, private things. He told me something one night that made me want to cry at first (I didn't, though; I didn't want to make him feel worse about it). He told me that he's dyslexic and not cut out for college. Instead, he wants to go to the Culinary Institute of America in New York to become a chef. That part made me smile. He'd be good at that. He's worried about the essay part of the application, so I told him I would help him with it, that I can write essays in my sleep.

Then, we talked once about *It*.

I asked him once if he'd ever done *It* and immediately wanted to slap my own face.

I prayed that he wouldn't ask me back, because I don't know the answer to that question. How does someone like me know the answer to that question? We were sitting on a bench swing at the lake; I was lying across the swing with my head in his lap, looking up at him, and we were swinging and talking. We were laughing about a movie we'd seen together, this romantic comedy. Not the eye-rolling, sappy, make-you-sick type romantic comedy, but the raunchy, hysterical kind with a fun, but sort of romantic, ending. There were sex jokes throughout the whole thing and, I don't know, we were laughing about it and the question just kind of slipped out of me: *Have you ever done it?* And then I froze immediately.

He grinned and looked away at the lake. I think I embarrassed him. He chewed on a fingernail and then looked down at me.

"I'm almost nineteen, Sid. I'm a guy." And he nodded his head yes.

I smiled awkwardly and then sat up. I'd figured as much. I knew what the answer was before I even asked it. He has a confident, unrushed way about him when we kiss and touch. He's in no hurry at all. If things start getting intense, he'll pull away for a breather, change the CD, take a sip of his drink, strike up a conversation. The anxious, groping, needy phase is over for him. He's been there, done that, and done it all the way, probably a lot. I don't know why I asked it—it just came out, and I didn't want to know more. To know who she was or who *they* were would hurt me. If they were girls at school that I would have to see in the flesh, it would be very painful.

He was right on the verge of asking me about my own experiences when I blurted, "You know what I'm in the mood for? A sin-a-chocolate eruption from Mitchell's." As if I would ever order such a calorie-laden monstrosity.

I jumped up and made a beeline for the truck, practically skipping, as though three scoops of dark chocolate ice cream swimming in a bowl of cinnamon hot fudge were foremost on my mind. I just didn't want him to see my face and know that I was hurting inside. I was terrified he would ask me back if I'd had sex. But what he did was come up behind me and put me in a kidding sort of headlock and say "Sin-a-chocolate eruption? Hey? You knocked up or something?" I laughed really loud. I think he was just so shocked or thrilled that I mentioned going for ice cream that it threw him off of asking me back. Or, more likely, he was just being sweet because he knew I was hurting inside.

⌒

"Sid, are you pregnant?" my mom says to me, holding my hands in hers.

"What?!"

"You know you can tell me anything, right?" My mom is looking at me with tears in her eyes.

"Why would you ask me that? No! I'm not pregnant. I've only kissed the guy. Good god, Mom."

"But you haven't had a period in two months. And you don't want to eat. I thought I heard you throwing up the other morning after breakfast."

"What? Balls! Get your hearing checked. I eat fine, and I have too had a period!"

Lie.

"Sid, I live here. I'm your mother. You have not had a period."

"I'm not pregnant, Mom. Shit!"

I get up and storm out of my room.

"I believe you," she says, chasing after me. "But still, I've made you an appointment with the doctor."

I stop, turn around, and look at her.

"What?"

"Sid, you've always been regular. I can set my watch by you. If you're not pregnant, then something else is wrong."

"I don't need a damn appointment with a doctor, Mom. I'm fine."

"It's on Tuesday."

"Well, tough. I have to work on Tuesday."

I continue storming through the house, with Katherine hot on my heels.

"No, you don't," she says. "I know your schedule. You're going. End of discussion."

I stalk out of the house and down the porch steps.

"Sid!" she calls after me.

"I'm just going around the block, Katherine!" I yell. "Don't worry. I'm not *running* away."

My tone is dripping with scorn as I throw up my hand. I can hear her going back into the house. I walk around for a while because I don't have my running shoes on and the shoes I'm wearing pinch my feet. I am fuming mad, because basically, well, I'm screwed. The baggy clothes and tops aren't going to cut it. They'll weigh me for sure. They always weigh you at the doctor. After a while, I go home, and when I'm sure my mom's busy with Liam, I weigh myself. I haven't weighed myself since I reached that goal I'd set a few weeks back. The scale makes this dinging sound when you step on it, so I run the water.

I'm below normal for my height. Shit.

I'll have to eat a lot between now and Tuesday.

Night comes, and I toss in bed for hours; I can't get to sleep because I'm so upset. Why does she have to be so nosy? I don't care that I'm considered underweight for a girl who's five-foot-nine. All I care about is the fact that my boobs and ass have finally shrunk to the point where I can tolerate owning them.

⁓

I am sitting in the doctor's office waiting room with my mother. I love my mom to death, but right now, at this moment, I really hate her.

"You don't need to go in with me. I'm almost seventeen. I'm too old to have my mommy in the room with me at the doctor's. So you need to stay out here, got it?"

"But Sid, I've always—"

"I will walk right out of here, I swear to god, Mom. Right out the door."

"Okay, fine. But I'm talking to Dr. Garritano when your exam is over."

The nurse calls me into the exam room. When the doctor comes in, they weigh me, measure me, and take my blood pressure, and then begin to ask me a ton of questions. I answer most of the questions, no problem, but when he gets to the question about whether I'm sexually active, I freeze.

"How you answer that question will stay between us, Cassidy," the doctor says.

I look over at the nurse. She nods a bit, trying to assure me that he's telling the truth.

The doctor doesn't look at me, he just scribbles what is surely nonsense on my chart.

My heart thumps. Because this is another chance that I have to tell.

God, I need to tell. I know I do. It is so inherently wrong, in so many god-awful ways, what happened to me. I look around the exam room, I look at the nurse and at the doctor. I think about my mother sitting out in the waiting room, flipping through a dog-eared copy of *Redbook*. She knows something is wrong, but she can't put her finger on it.

I open my mouth . . .

I try to say it . . .

I try to tell . . .

but I can't.

The doctor looks up from his chart. My mouth goes dry with thoughts of telling, and I can't do it. So I answer the doctor's question.

"Yes," I respond. "Not now, though. About six months ago."

And I hope like hell it will be left at that.

"Were you safe? Did you use protection?" he asks, looking at me dead-on this time.

No. I was not safe. No. I was not protected.

But that's not what I say. What I say is the lie.

"Yes. I am always safe."

After the exam, when my mom comes into the room, I am out of my napkin dress and fully clothed again. She asks the doctor, right in front of me, if I'm a healthy weight. He shows her on his growth chart where I fall. She is dying for it to be below the curve. But I fall right at the very low end of normal, just a hair above the little red line.

"Now get off my back already, Mom. God!" I say when we leave the office and head toward the car.

I turn on the radio so she won't try to talk to me.

I look out the window and am thankful that they weighed me before I took off my clothes for the pelvic exam, which, by the way, is sheer torture, and don't let anyone tell you any different. Anyhow, like I said, they weighed me before the exam. I have on multiple layers and put two crescent wrenches in the bottom pockets of my cargo pants before we left home. Clever, huh? Altogether, it added three extra pounds. I still gained the other five the hard way though, so I need to lose three pounds to be at my goal weight again.

I ate a lot to gain those five pounds in three days. And the Urge only broke me once. And it was brutal to cut out the running. I had nightmares every night. I felt guilty and good at the same time, all the time. It's hard to explain—it was like this roller coaster. To eat as much as I did and to keep it down made me feel good in one way, because, physically, it tasted and felt good to my body, but I'd feel guilty at the same time because I knew it was a lot of calories and I shouldn't be eating it. And also, I felt guilty because I knew I was only doing it because I had no choice. I had to do it or my mom might find out about me. But then I'd feel good because I knew it was only temporary. I knew I would be able to get rid of it again as soon as the appointment was over.

I felt like I was getting away with something.

I still do.

I don't know.

It makes no sense.

I don't even know what I'm saying now.

⌒

It's three days after my doctor's appointment when the nurse calls. I have no diseases, no HIV, no chlamydia, no gonorrhea, no syphilis, no nothing. These things have worried me for six months, and I'm glad I know for sure now. I'm glad my mom made me go, because now I know for sure. I can put it behind me for good. I don't remember it, and I can pretend it never happened. I have no worries now.

And I got my period today.

It's light, but it's there.

So I'm fine. Really.

25

I'm in the truck with Corey. He picked me up from work after the dinner shift. It's about nine o'clock, and we're headed back to my house to watch TV and hang out. He has a couple errands to run, so we hit the ATM drive-through first. He flips on the interior light and digs through his wallet for his card, and because I'm sitting right next to him, I'm able to sneak a quick peek at it. It's his mom's card, and her name is either Anne, Annie, or Anna Livingston. He takes a hefty sum of dough out of Anne/Annie/Anna's account—three hundred bucks.

I guess it's none of my business—we've only been dating about six weeks—but his evasiveness when it comes to the subject of his mother has my interest in the topic fully piqued. I hate that I'm nosy like this.

Then we head toward the pharmacy. Prescription drugs for Anne/Annie/Anna? I don't know. Kirsten did say she has a drug problem of some kind. I tell him I want to wait in the truck. He leaves me the keys and I listen to the radio while I wait. I don't want to go in, because I'm afraid I might run into the Drugstore Madonna. She might say something like, "Is this the son of a bitch who did it?" or "How'd that pregnancy test turn out?" In reality, I know she would never do that, but still, I'll just stay out here where she can't see me or even know I still exist.

Corey comes out of the store looking pissed about something. He's talking on his cell phone, but stops short of the truck. I crane my neck casually but still can't hear what he's saying. He snaps his phone shut, gets in, and slams the door harder than usual.

"Everything okay?" I ask him.

"Yeah, it's just—there's this new pharmacist and he won't give me—"

My head and ears are perked up like a deer's at hunting season. *Yessss...? He won't give you what? What won't evil Mr. Pharmacist give you, Corey, darling?*

"It's nothing," he says. "I'll come back later. No biggie."

Fack.

We are coming up on Lighthouse Road and I see a FOR SALE sign on the corner, pointing left toward that waterfront Tudor that is still sitting empty and unsold.

"Hey, turn down Lighthouse. I want to show you something really cool," I say, and I tell him about the painted ceiling and how it fools you into thinking it's real. When we get to the front door, I punch in the alarm code: 4321.

"God, are they dumb?" Corey says.

"I know, right?"

"This can't be legal," he mutters, taking off his shoes.

"We're not stealing anything," I say. "Besides, it's been empty for almost two years, and the owners adore my mom. She's brought more people to look at it in six months than everyone else combined."

We go in and I take him to the conservatory first. We look out at the darkening horizon, at the boat lights far in the distance. Then we go to the room with the painted ceiling and flip on the light.

"Wow, that's cool. Someone painted that?" Corey says, turning in a circle, looking up and around.

"Yeah, but you have to lie down and stare up at it to get the full effect."

I stretch out on the floor to stare up at it. He looks down at me like I'm nuts.

"Really, it's cool. Come on," I tell him, patting the floor next to me. He rolls his eyes and stretches out next to me and looks up at the ceiling. After two seconds he says, "I don't feel it. It looks the same."

"Give it a second. You have to relax, lose yourself a little."

Two more seconds go by.

"I still don't feel it."

I laugh and give him a shove. "You're not trying—you're distracted with thoughts of making out."

He laughs, still looking up at the ceiling. "This is true. The smell of your shampoo is killing me."

He sits up and pulls his cell and earbuds out of his pocket, "Maybe some music will help."

He unwinds the cord and sticks one end in his ear and hands me the other. Then he starts scanning files, looking for a good song.

"Something slow and trippy. Heartbreaking, maybe," I say.

"I know just the song," he says. "The guitar is killer. And her voice, the lyrics…"

He puts on a song by Aimee Mann and lies back down next to me, holding my hand, our fingers laced. The song is called "Save Me." We lie flat and relaxed, holding hands like paper cutout people. We look up at the mural and listen. As the song plays, I start to see and feel the painted light shining down on me. I look up at the sky, the trees, and the streaming light, and I get that feeling again, that feeling of being carried off into it.

About halfway through, I can tell that Corey's not looking at the painting anymore; he's looking at me. But I can't move. I'm transfixed by the light and sky above me and the beauty of the song and I feel like Corey can see right through me. I feel like he knows everything about me right at this moment, so I can't look at him.

But he can't possibly know. No one knows the secrets I keep.

Still, the song and the painting and Corey's eyes on me, and his hand on mine, it all touches me so deeply that I have tears sliding down my face and into my hair. My uneven lock is completely soaked with them.

"I think that bordered on a religious experience," he says to me on the way home.

He's staring at the road in a trancelike state, trying to take it all in. I didn't expect this night to go like this, either. Our little breaking-and-entering detour has knocked something loose in me. I can't put my finger on it, though. I smile and nod, chewing on a thumbnail.

"For real," he says. "It may sound kinda, I dunno, girly..." His face twists, like he's embarrassed to even go on. "But seriously, it was like...a moment. You know?"

He looks over at me to see if I agree. I nod my head. Then I look out the window because I don't want him to see my face when I talk.

"I know," I say. "I don't think anything bad could ever happen in a place like that, with a song like that, with someone like you. I think the earth could break apart and fall away but we'd still be there, floating in that room, listening to that song and looking up at that painting."

And I know what's been knocked loose in me now. I want to add: I LOVE YOU, COREY LIVINGSTON, but I don't dare.

We both go quiet.

"Thank you, Sid," he says, and I look at him. He blinks away the shining in his eyes and glances out his window.

"You're welcome."

After a second, he reaches over and rubs my head playfully, and then pulls me into him. "Come here," he says gently. I unbuckle and scoot in close to him. I don't care if this truck full of dials has no airbags and I get killed in a wreck. I'll die happy. He drives slow and careful and we kiss at every stop sign and red light the whole way back to my house.

~

I am lying on my bed doing some of my required summer reading: *Best Loved Poems From Around the World*. Whatever idiot invented the concept of summer reading should be shackled in the town square. They should be spit on and kicked repeatedly and heckled by passersby. Summer is for fun, end of story.

My phone rings and I can tell it's My Super Sweet Hot Boyfriend Corey Livingston because George, Paul, John, and Ringo are telling me so via poly ringtone. Apparently, Corey Livingston wants to hold my hand.

I throw the book across my bed and pick up my phone.

"Yus," I say in a pompous Mayfair accent.

"I want to take you out on Mr. D's boat for your birthday. I want to cook for you and I want us to spend the whole night together."

"Uhhh..." I say, following it up with a big chunk of dead air.

The stretching silence speaks loud and clear. It says, *I'm not ready for that!*

"Oh, no. I didn't mean that," Corey stammers. "I...I didn't mean that. Really, I meant...I just want us to be together until really late. I have something planned, but it won't work until really late."

"How late?"

"It starts at midnight. You'd be home by two at the latest."

My curfew is midnight. He always makes sure he has me home a few minutes early. He's not one of those assholes who always finds a way to screw up a girl's curfew. You know the kind—they argue or find weaselly ways to stay out later or *be* late because, well, they want what they want, and they could give two shits if a girl catches hell for it. He likes that my mom trusts him.

"What is it?"

"I can't tell you. It's a surprise."

"I guess I could tell my mom I'm spending the night at Kirsten's? She wouldn't know."

The line goes silent for a few seconds while he considers this.

"Is your mom there?" he asks.

"Yeah, she's in the kitchen, whipping up one of her big-ass mom meals." I cringe when I realize that I have spoken this out loud. I didn't mean to say it like that. Especially to him.

"Let me talk to her."

"To my mom?"

"Yeah."

"O-*kayyyyy*," I say and take my phone to her.

I try to listen but she immediately goes to her room and shuts the door. When she comes back out, she is smiling.

"What? What is it?"

"You wish, loser," she says to me.

Fack!

26

It's not technically my birthday yet, because it's only ten o'clock. Corey and I are on Mr. D's boat. He told me to eat a late lunch and skip dinner so I would be hungry again by ten thirty. Skip dinner? No problemo.

He got his boating license at the beginning of summer as part of his job. He has to have one to work at the marina. Mr. D's boat is really nice for being an older model. He keeps it clean and it has an aft cabin with a little kitchen, a booth table that converts to a bed, and then two more bunk beds. When Corey shows the beds to me, I kind of tense up, and he says, "Don't worry. Just giving you the tour. Your mom made me swear on a stack of Bibles that I wouldn't try to sleep with you tonight."

"Did you?"

"Did I what?"

"Swear on a stack of Bibles."

"I swore on the phone book."

I laugh. "So what are you saying?"

He considers this for a moment. "I told her I wouldn't try to sleep with you. I never said I wouldn't try to have sex with you."

"Oh, yeah?" I say.

I know he is joking around. He knows I'm not ready for that—he hasn't even made it up my shirt yet.

"I'm just kidding around, you know that, right?" he says, hugging me tight and kissing my cheek. "I didn't bring you here for that. I want to cook for you and give you your birthday present. That's it."

"Yeah, I know."

"And kiss you a lot." He holds my face and kisses me over and over, fast and nibbley, like he wants to eat my lips up.

"But right now, we eat," he says, pulling back.

He kisses me once more and then I watch him as he cooks me a really nice meal. He really knows his way around a kitchen—he's drizzling, he's whisking, he's chopping and sautéing. It's kind of a turn-on. I have to look away and excuse myself to go to the bathroom once so I don't start panting like Ronan does when Trixie the rottweiler strolls by. He keeps checking his watch every so often, probably to make sure he has me home by two.

"So where did you learn to cook?" I ask, sitting on the bottom bunk bed and pretending to read a boating magazine. It's in Italian, so I just look at the pictures.

"My mom, she used to cook a lot. I do most of it now."

Oooh, an opening. I pounce and run with it.

"Tell me about your mom," I say. "You never really talk about her."

He goes quiet for a second. His back is to me and he's stirring something on the stove. He clears his throat and says, "She's really an amazing person when she's not..."

He stops talking.

"Not what?" I say, trying to sound casual. My mind finishes his sentence with words like: *High? Stoned? Smashed out of her gourd?*

"Um...when she's not working. She works a lot."

I can tell he's holding back. Or lying. And I've pushed too hard. I detour us out of the awkwardness.

"Yeah, mine, too. Well, it looks like she taught you well. Whatever you're whipping up over there smells great."

"Tarragon chicken with lemon, garlic smashed potatoes, and asparagus with hollandaise sauce."

"Sounds yummy," I say.

The way he rattles off his menu combines with the smells he's making. I toss those two things around in my head, then add in the exceptionally hot way he is looking right now, and my mouth is full-on watering within seconds. I realize I'm starving. But I can't help wondering how many calories are in all of it. I'm going to be running my ass off tomorrow, but I'm going to get through this meal. And the cake. I am. He's making it for me special, and I won't let my craziness spoil it.

Dinner is out of this world. I cut it into really small pieces, because for some reason it makes things go down easier.

"This is incredible. You totally have to go to the Culinary Institute in New York. We need to start working on your application and financial aid forms and stuff."

"Yeah, I hope it works out. We have family in Brooklyn. My mom would probably move out there, too, if I got in."

"That would be great," I say, thinking more about how he just said the word *mom* again. I resist the urge to pounce, instead saying, "Yeah. I need to get busy myself. I need to pick a school already."

"Are you thinking of anywhere specific?"

"Well, I kind of would like to go away. But then I figure it's probably cheaper to just commute. If I can get into Baldwin Wallace or Case, maybe one of those."

"You should go away," he says.

I stop mid-bite and look at him; our eyes lock.

"You think?" I say, resuming eating my tiny morselettes of chicken.

I'm not sure where he's going with this. Is he trying to send me away? Is he planning on ditching me after graduation?

"Yeah. I think you should go away. You have really good grades, right?"

"Yeah. A 3.7 overall. A 3.8 if I bust my ass next year. All AP courses."

I say this calmly, but I'm starting to get upset. He's not going to wait until graduation. He's going to ditch me on my fucking birthday. At the stroke of midnight, he's going to say, *Happy seventeenth birthday, Sid! Now scram!*

"Have you ever thought about NYU or Columbia?" he asks, looking at his plate.

Things snap together in my brain; these are both colleges in New York City. He's not trying to get rid of me. He's hoping I might be near him if he gets into the Culinary Institute. I relax.

"Um, yeah. Those are places I'd like to look into; I don't know if I could get in, though. They're kind of competitive."

This is not a lie. It's the suck-ass truth of it.

He takes a bite and then sets his fork down and looks at me.

"You should go where you want to go. I'm sorry. I . . ."

He wads up his napkin and tosses it down.

"I'm beating around the bush here. I want you and me to be together. And if I don't get into the Culinary Institute, then I'll have to either get a job or try for another cooking school. Then I'll probably want you to pick some college near me wherever that is, too. I'm being a selfish dick, and we've only been dating for a couple of months. You'll probably get sick of me by then anyway."

He gets up and starts clearing dishes.

"Wait. Sit down," I say, standing up with him.

"God, I'm ruining your birthday. This is too heavy, I'm sorry." He's picking up dishes and his hands are shaking.

"Stop. Put the dishes down, Corey," I say, reaching out and touching his wrists.

He puts them down and is staring at the table. He doesn't want to look at me. Or maybe it's that he doesn't want to see me looking at him. I walk around to his side of the booth and I slide my hands under his arms and hug him. I put my head to his chest and I squeeze him.

"I want to be near you, too. I could never get sick of you. Ever."

"Good," he says, sighing. He kisses the top of my head and hugs me back for a long time. We rock and hug and I think about saying, *I love you, Corey*—but, again, I don't dare.

At eleven thirty he starts up the boat and drives us out of the marina, past Whiskey Island, and then out farther so we can look at the city. The Cleveland skyline is incredible. It's a clear, dark night with a crescent moon, and it's really, really gorgeous. He puts on *Sgt. Pepper's*.

"This is really nice," I say.

His arms are around me and we're sitting with a blanket around us on one of the wide, cushioned benches on the deck. I'm thinking this is the present—a boat ride. I wonder if it is? I don't need another present. The dinner and boat ride are enough. He could skip Christmas and Valentine's for the next ten years and still be in the black with me.

I'm all spooned up to him with my back against him, and he is kissing his favorite spot. I'm waiting for my favorite Beatles song of all time to come on, and just as it's about to, Corey reaches over and pushes the pause button on the CD Player.

"Hey, that's my favorite song. 'Lucy in the Sky with Diamonds.'"

"Every Beatles song is your favorite song," he says, checking his watch for about the hundredth time tonight.

"This is true. But that's my überfavorite."

"I know," he says, and then adds, "Look."

He points over to the far right side of the shoreline. A big chunk of city lights go off all at once. Corey releases the pause button on the CD player and turns it up really loud as my song starts up. We watch as the whole skyline goes black, bit by bit, until it's disappeared altogether.

"Hey! How did—? What just—?"

I'm freaking out. How the hell did he do that?

"It's a rolling blackout. It's been scheduled for weeks. To save energy."

"Holy crap!" I say. "That was the coolest thing I've ever seen!"

"No. It's not."

"Yes. It is."

"No. It's not. Look up."

And as John Lennon sings my favorite song in the whole world, I look up and the sky is filled with more stars than I have ever seen in my entire life. I stand up and hold my head back and look up at the stars like I used to do in my room when I was little. Only the stars are real this time. I spin around and it makes me dizzy and I feel like I'm high. My face is about to break in half from smiling. Then I look over at Corey, who is watching me with a tenderness that makes me want to crawl inside his heart, pitch a tent, and set up camp forever.

"That's the coolest present I've ever gotten in my whole life," I say.

He laughs a little, looks out at the lake, fiddles a bit with his hands.

"Yeah, well, wait till next year," he says, trying to be sly. "I've put a call in to God. Halley's Comet's gonna skywrite your name in cursive."

It's dark out, but I think he might be blushing.

I look at him. Man, he is beautiful. I walk over and sit on his lap. I kiss him long and slow and soon he shifts a little, moving himself back away from me. I lie back on the cushioned bench and pull him toward me by the shirt. I want his weight on me. I want to feel him against me. We've only kissed sitting up until now.

"Sid, I don't want you to think I did all this to . . . you know."

But I can feel him giving in; he leans down and kisses me.

"Just lay with me," I whisper. "I want us to kiss and I want us to . . ."—and I'm not really sure how to say it—". . . lay together. I want to feel you against me. I want to . . . um . . ."

"Oh," he says, his eyes getting wide. He gets it now. "Okay. Yeah," he says. "Hell, yeah."

He pockets himself in on top of me, putting his weight on his elbows and sliding his fingers into my hair. He looks at me a second and then kisses me deeply. I bend my knees and we kiss and it is delicious. That gold, rich, and melting feeling is pouring through me again. I've had it many times while kissing him, but it's never been this concentrated. The rich melted gold is pooling and I'm suddenly very glad that I went with the stretchy cotton leggings instead of the thick, sturdy jeans.

My body is telling me I'm ready for this. We kiss deeply and rock up against each other. He pulls away at one point and whispers, "Caprice." I stare at him, blinking. "My middle name," he says, catching his breath. "It's Caprice."

And we kiss more and more under the countless stars while we listen to my favorite Beatles album. I hold on to him tightly and, after a bit, he kisses my collarbone a few times and slides his weight to the side, propping himself on one elbow. He kisses me softly this time—my forehead, my cheeks, my eyelids—and I can feel him looking at me.

"Open your eyes," he whispers.

I open them. He looks right into them, with the crescent moon and stars overtop of me.

"I knew it," he says.

"What?" I say, looking up at the stars while he kisses my face.

"...You're the girl..." he says.

"...from the song..."

"...the girl with kaleidoscope eyes."

27

Making out is our new favorite hobby. It is seriously underrated as a form of contraception. If teenage couples practiced making out with the care and dedication that Corey and I do, with the keen attention to detail that it so richly deserves, then there would be no teen pregnancy problem in the world today.

Summer's almost over, and I ask him if he is getting bored with it. If he is going to eventually dump me for a skank like Starsha Lexington or someone with more skills if I don't let him get a peek or a feel of something soon. He rolls his eyes and says, "No, Sid. This is good. I can live on this for a while."

What I want to know, though, is how did I get so lucky? In January, I thought this was going to be the worst year of my life.

I seriously never thought that I would be able to come this far physically with someone. I thought I was damaged goods forever.

I'm hoping that I'll be ready for a little more soon. It's just, the idea of Corey seeing me naked or even partially naked scares me. Not because he wouldn't be great about it and gentle and all that. I know he would. But still, it scares me badly. I don't know why. I worry sometimes that I'll never be able to let someone see me naked or let someone touch me all over.

Maybe I *am* damaged goods forever.

God.

I hope not.

I am the happiest I have ever been in my entire life. So why do I still keep up with the running and the not eating and the Urge thing? Sometimes, I think I should go talk to someone. A professional someone who knows about these things. As many times as I've googled bulimia and anorexia, I've never quite found what I'm looking for. It always talks about these perfectionist girls, obsessive-compulsive girls, or athletes and models who have all these killer expectations of themselves. I'm not like that. My room is a mess half the time, and the reason I get good grades has a lot to do with natural ability and the fact that Lakewood is just a regular school. You can get a good education there, I'm not saying it's a bad school, I'm just saying that it's a really regular school. I don't think I stress about grades and perfection like some girls do. Usually I'm not grossed out by food until after I've eaten it. When it's sitting there on the plate, I want to dive in face-first. I've actually started dreaming about food, about all-you-can-eat buffets and twenty-four-hour drive-throughs. I even dreamt about an ice-cream cone that jumped into my hand and started talking. I guess it's better than dreaming about other things—much, much worse things.

I guess I know deep down why I do it. It's because of the ski trip. I never did these things to myself before the ski trip, so A plus B equals C, right? I do it because I like the way it makes me feel. When I run, it gives me this high, like a drug or something. And when I puke, it gets rid of all the nervousness that builds up inside me when I eat. When all that stuff is sitting in my stomach, churning around, the pressure builds and builds until I can't stand it anymore, so I get rid of it. It's like this release valve letting loose all the pent-up anxiety.

But...

I think, though...

I think that I also do it because... well.... I seriously can't stand the thought of having that weight on me, especially in the two places that it just *loves* to hang out—my boobs and ass. I don't want those big, double-D boobs and that bubble butt anymore. When I was at my normal weight, all "Xena-licious" or "Marilyn Juicy," as Paige liked to say, my boobs and butt were like two big blinking signs that screamed, *Grab here! Squeeze there!* So, no, I don't want that. I want to look like a normal-sized girl. I want to blend in so guys don't see me. So men don't see me. And Corey doesn't count. He's not a regular guy, he's not men—he's Corey.

So I know a lot about what's going on here. Trust me, I've analyzed myself to death. I guess what I don't know, though, is how to stop it. These feelings, the anxiety, the running, the starving, the bingeing, the puking—I've tried to stop it all, but I can't.

I don't know how.

I don't know the answer to that question at all.

28

My Super Hot Boyfriend Corey Livingston is lying on my bed playing Liam's PSP, and I'm trying to knock off this godforsaken book of poems before school starts Monday. Truly, it is a literary torture.

"I can't stand it anymore. This book sucks," I groan.

He grabs it from me and looks at it.

"Oof."

He hands it back and continues playing his video game.

I think about his being dyslexic.

"Do you have trouble reading?" I ask.

He presses away at game buttons.

"Not really, not anymore. I used to be really awful at it. I would break out into a sweat if I had to read out loud in class.

My mom finally went to the school with a note from my pediatrician that said I didn't have to read in class anymore—shit, fucker killed me again!—um, the note said it was harming me emotionally. Teacher was pissed. She was this old-school Hun who thought she could scream the stupid out of you or something. Bitch flunked me."

"Man. That's harsh. But you can read out loud now?"

"Unfortunately."

"Read to me."

"Read what? That book of cheesy poems?" He rolls his eyes, pressing buttons on the PSP.

"Nah, I was just kidding, play your game."

I roll back onto my back and try to finish the worst poetry ever put on paper. He stops pressing buttons. He snaps the PSP off and grabs the book. He looks at me through the corner of his eye, smiling devilishly, and starts reading.

"Shall I compare thee to a summer's day?"

Oh, God. He's doing the fake Professor Shakespeare thing.

"Okay, stop," I say, and I try to grab the book, but he pushes me away with one big hand and holds the book out farther from me.

"Thou art more lovely and more temperate..."

"Stop. Really, you sound like an idiot." I laugh, trying to grab the book.

"You asked for it—you're gettin' it!" he says, laughing, and goes on even louder, "...Rough winds do shake the darling buds of May!"

I almost get it from him. He jumps off the bed, and I go after him.

"And summer's lease hath all too short a date!"

He is pushing me away with one hand on my forehead, but I still get my hands on a page. It tears and we both stop and stare at it, at the corner piece of ripped paper in my fingers. Then we look back at each other. He decides he doesn't care and jumps to the other side of the room and keeps going.

"Sometime too hot the eye of heaven shines!"

I keep chasing and fighting with him, laughing my butt off. He sounds so funny. He pins me down on the bed with his knees over my arms and keeps reading, with the book in one hand and tickling me with the other hand. I scream laughing.

He stops mid-sentence at one point, lands on the word *growest* and looks at me, pinned underneath him, catching my breath.

"I think this is turning me on," he says, a bit surprised.

"Shut up!" I say, laughing, my eyes watering. I'm shaking all over.

"No, seriously, what else is in here?" He flips to the table of contents and tickles me some more. I'm laughing so hard I'm afraid I'll pee myself; I can't even make a laugh noise, which is rare for me—it's just this wheezing.

"Okay, here's one with a little more testosterone in it," he says.

He starts reading "The Spider and the Fly." I haven't gotten to that one yet; it's near the end.

"'Will you walk into my parlor?' said the Spider to the Fly. 'Tis the prettiest little parlor that ever you did spy.'"

I stop laughing. My heart seizes up. That word. That word. Where have I heard that word? The blood drains out of me.

Walk into my parlor…

"Get up," I say to Corey, but he's still going, he doesn't hear me. I can hear my dog start barking in Liam's room.

"'The way into my parlor is up a winding stair, and I've many curious things to show when you are there…'"

"Get off… meeee," I say.

I'm losing my breath, I can't breathe. Ronan is barking like mad.

"'Oh no, no,' said the little Fly, 'to ask me is in vain, for who goes up your winding stair can ne'er come down again!'"

Corey looks down at me and sees the tears streaming down my face. He can tell they are not laughter tears and I'm doing this weird convulsing thing.

He jumps off of me, panic in his eyes.

"Oh, god, I'm sorry, did I hurt you? I was just joking around. Are you okay?"

I roll off the bed and onto the floor.

"I'm… I'm…."

I scrabble upright and run out of my bedroom and into the bathroom, bent over and holding my stomach. I shut and lock the door in Corey's face. He's knocking and twisting the knob and calling my name. Ronan is butting up against Liam's door trying to get out, barking and barking. I'm on my knees in the bathroom trying to get the air back into my lungs.

Walk into my parlor... my parlor... my parlor...

I haven't really thought about him as a person in a long time. The guy, I mean. I just think of the act mostly. But now I'm thinking of him as a person, as a fellow human being. And how he really wasn't. Human, I mean. He couldn't be. How could he be human and be so calculating... so... *evil?*

I can hear Corey through the door saying that if I don't open up or speak, he's going to force the door open.

"I'm fine," I croak, "just give me a second."

There's a hissing in my ears but I think he has said the number ten. Ten seconds, he's saying. He's giving me ten seconds; he's counting, "*One, two, three...*"

Oh, god. What am I going to tell Corey when I come out of here?

I hurry up off the floor and turn on the water. I splash my face.

"I'm okay. I'm okay. Just a second," I say, wiping my face.

I throw open the door.

"It was a period cramp, I'm fine now," I say.

I walk calmly past him to Liam's door; I open it and try to quiet Ronan down, hoping it will take the focus off of me.

~

We're back on my bed. Corey is sitting with his back against the headboard and his legs stretched out straight, looking like he could cry. I'm sitting across his legs, trying to convince him that he didn't do anything wrong. Ronan is lying on my floor, snoring; it took a while to calm him down, but he's okay now.

"It was a cramp. Really," I say to Corey. I am trying to get him to look at me. He won't.

"I'm two hundred twenty pounds, Sid. I hurt you and you're lying so I won't feel bad."

His big hands are on my waist and his fingers are feeling my protruding hip bones; he is wrapping his fingers and thumbs around me, looking at his hands and thinking about my wasp of a waist, I know it.

"I'm not. I'm not lying. It was PMS."

He looks at me suspiciously before looking back down, shaking his head.

"Corey. Please."

He finally looks at me again.

"I would never hurt you on purpose, you know that, right?" he says.

I reach up and hold his face. I look into his big, sorry brown eyes.

"I know. And you didn't hurt me."

He tries to turn his face away. I pull it back. I make him look at me.

"Okay?"

He sighs and nods okay. I put my head into the crook of his neck while he hugs and strokes my back and hair. I can feel him feeling my frame, my spine, so I get up.

"Let's go make popcorn and watch sitcom reruns," I say, taking his hand.

The rest of the night, it's like I'm trying too hard to pretend it didn't happen. The more I try to be casual and light, the more I look like I'm trying. I try to make him laugh while we watch TV on the couch, and he goes along with it the best he can, but I can see he's lost in thought the whole time. I see the way he looks at me when he thinks I'm not paying attention. So I turn my back to him and nestle in, spoon into his stomach and chest, stretch out my legs on the couch and get myself into a position where he can't see my face.

He plays with my hair a little, and then, during a commercial, he presses his lips into the top of my head and rests them there.

"Sid?" he whispers, and I can feel his warm breath in my hair.

"Yeah?"

"I think you're beautiful. You know that, right?"

I stiffen all over. I know he feels me tense up, and I try to recover and relax. I pat his knee.

"Thank you," I say, sweetly.

A little *too* sweetly.

He sits up a bit, picks up the remote, and turns down the volume.

"Hey," he says, bouncing his shoulder, making my head bob a little. He wants my attention. I turn my head up and look at his mouth.

"I've always thought you were beautiful. Even before we knew each other."

I smile and nod and then turn back to the commercial, the one where the dirty mop is in love with the sparkly housewife.

Ugh. Why do we have to do this? I mean, Corey's said a lot of nice things to me, but never really anything about the way I look. And I've liked that. I want to keep it that way. I don't want to talk about the way I look. I mean, why is he saying this stuff *now*? It's because of what happened in my room earlier. It's because he thinks there's something wrong with me, that I'm too skinny or breakable or something.

Apparently, I was supposed to say something convincing back to him, because he sits up straighter, pushing my weight off of his chest. He turns to look at me head-on. I brace myself for what he's going to say next. I try hard to hide my inner wince by willing my shoulders and face to relax. *Think calm face. Soothing face. "Whatever-do-you-mean?" face.*

"You think I'm full of it," he says.

His eyes have disbelief and hurt swimming in them, so I can't look at them.

"What? No," I say and shake my head. I reach over and comb his bangs with my fingers for a second. "Of course I don't think that."

Then I put my hands in my lap. I try to look at his eyes, but my gaze keeps moving to his forehead.

"I think that about you, too, Corey. Not that you're beautiful, because, well, *that's for girls*, but I think you're hot."

Then I force myself to stare into his eyes deeply. I tilt my head slightly and add a playful grin. I'm going for a look that's suggestive, evocative, *burning*. I stare while thinking: *Just keep it going, Sid. Don't look away, stare him down, and he'll drop it. Sex sells.*

"Balls," he mutters, almost irritated.

I pull a surprised, sad face. "What? You don't think I think you're hot?"

This may work yet.

"No, Sid. Not about that. Not about me. Nice try, though, mixing a joke up with a flirty little compliment, that was slick. No, what I mean is that you think I'm making up that I think you're beautiful."

I open my mouth to argue with him, but he cuts me off.

"Not done," he says. "I've always thought it was true. Always. You know what I'm saying?"

"Yeah. I do," I say, nodding, agreeing, yep, uh-huh.

And I mean it. I know exactly what he's saying, and it's starting to piss me off, I think. It's patronizing. I make myself smile anyway. I was a cheerleader and can be a good fake smiler when I need to be. I try not to overdo it, though—just a half smile. He searches my face, studying it. I stand up and try to pull him up by the shirt sleeve.

"Come on. Let's go for ice cream," I say.

He takes my wrist gently in his hand and doesn't budge. I stand in front of him, my back to the TV, my hair all sticking up from where he was playing with it. He looks up at me.

"You don't want ice cream. You just don't believe me and you're trying to get out of talking about this."

"Yes, I do. Really, Corey, I do believe you. You think I'm beautiful. Now let's go get some ice cream. I need some serious chocolate in my life right now."

I try to walk away, but he takes my other wrist, too. Then he slides his fingers through my hands, lacing us together. He stud-ies our hands, my long pale fingers wrapped in his tan calloused ones, then he looks up at me.

"The ice cream trick isn't going to work either, okay? It's worked a couple times on me only because I let it. We'll get there and you'll eat two bites of it and try to get me to finish it for you, or you'll tell me you ate already, that you're full and changed your mind. I notice these things. And I know that you know that I notice them. I let you out of conversations you want out of, and you do the same for me—I know you do. But not this time."

Jesus. This guy sees right through me. All this time, he's seen right through me. I need to be a better liar. I sigh and smile as kindly as I can. I look him dead in the eyes and give him my best game face ever.

"Come on, Corey, you're making a big deal out of nothing."

I bend down to try and kiss him, but he turns his head away from me and leans back against the couch, still holding my hands—gently, but fixed, so I can't escape.

"So you don't want to kiss me now?" I say. *Maybe I can guilt him into dropping it.*

He lets my hands go but then leans forward and wraps his arms around my waist and pulls me into him, pressing his cheek against my stomach.

"It's just really important to me that you believe me. And that you believe it about yourself. Just sit with me for a second. Please."

I'm starting to get choked up. This is too much. I don't want to talk about this, but I don't want to push him away, either. He pulls me down to sit on his lap, to straddle him. Not tight and sexy up against his hips—more on his thighs. But I can't look at him. I'm glad my hair is messed up and in my face. My heart is beating really fast. Why does he have to talk so much? What guy talks this much? None I've ever heard of. Paige and Kirsten have no stories like this. If they did, though, they probably wouldn't tell me, I suppose. It's too private.

"I want to tell you something. About the first time I saw you."

I lay my head against his neck and he pulls me tighter. He just wants me close.

"When we were in tenth grade and none of us had cars and we had to eat at school, I saw you out on a picnic table in the courtyard. Me, TJ, and some other guys were on the roof to the service building. We would give the janitor a pack of cigarettes every couple of days to leave the door unlocked, and all of us would go up there and smoke. No one could see us because of the way the building sits. You were sitting with Kirsten and Paige and wearing your cheerleading uniform. There was this other girl there, too. She had really short black hair and all this heavy makeup. I don't think you hang with her anymore.

"Anyhow, I watched you laughing; you and the black-haired girl were throwing french fries to this seagull that was perched on the brick wall. It got brave and swooped down and started trying to snatch them off the table, out of your hands. You were screaming and jumping up and laughing really loud, and I remember thinking that you were amazing looking. Stunning. But not in the usual way. Different, you know? I watched you until the bell rang. Then I stamped out my cigarette and went back inside.

"The next week I got sent away for...well, you know...and sometimes, at night especially, when I was lying in that tiny cement room on that hard cot with no windows and feeling like I might suffocate, I would think about that cheerleader with the hair and the eyes, the redheaded angel running around and laughing in the courtyard because of that stupid seagull. I dunno, it would just make me smile, make me feel better. And when I got out, I would go to the games just so I could watch you. You were this fireball out on the field. You'd go sit with your friends at halftime and talk to kids that those other cheerleaders wouldn't be caught dead hanging out with. I never had the nerve to actually try and talk to you. Even though I knew you would talk to me back. I just, I don't know—I just couldn't do it. And I never thought I'd ever be sitting here with you like this. In my wildest *dreams* I never dreamed it. I sat in that AV room for eight weeks, watching *Deadwood* so I wouldn't have to look at you, so that I wouldn't grab you and kiss you and thank you for getting me through something that was really, really awful. I would watch you out of the corner of my eye, though. God, I wanted to kiss you so bad it hurt. I've always, always thought you were beautiful, Sid. Always."

His voice cracks, and he swallows hard. I can almost feel the lump in his throat, and I want to kiss it away. All of this makes me cry. His words are not some bullshit fiction. The black-haired girl he's talking about was Hannah Spencer; she was kind of a drama queen and spent the whole rest of the week telling people about the rabid seagull living in the courtyard that randomly attacked people. She ended up moving away. And what he said about the cheerleading is true. As soon as the cheering was over, we split like oil and water. The seven of them went one way and I went the other. And the AV room? All that time I thought he was watching *Deadwood*. Oh, god, I think this boy loves me. I think he really might love me.

"Do you believe me now?" he asks.

I sit back on his legs and look at him and nod. I wipe my eyes on my sleeve and then look at my hands, the backs of them resting on his stomach. I pick at my cuticles.

"You're beautiful, Sid," he says, pushing my hair out of my face. "And I never said it at first because it seemed so obvious to me, so easy. I didn't say it because I never wanted you to think the things I say to you are just *things*. Empty compliments to get in your pants. I wanted the things I say to you to be extraordinary, because that's what you are to me. Extraordinary. And I'm so sorry I didn't say it sooner, because I think you need to hear it. You were beautiful a year ago and you're beautiful now—"

Then he pauses, takes a careful breath, and says what I knew was coming all along.

"—but I see how much weight you've lost since last year, and it scares me."

But he's looking at me so kindly. He's not trying to be cruel or judgmental. He really means it. He's worried. I take his head in my hands and kiss his face. I kiss his cheeks and his forehead and his eyelids and his lips.

"Don't be scared, Corey," I say. "I'm fine. Everything's fine."

He shakes his head. "No, you're not fine. You're too thin; it can't be right. You need to gain some weight."

I sigh and rest my head in his neck again. We sit and hug in silence for a few minutes.

"Will you do it for me, at least?" he whispers. "So that I know you're okay?"

I pause for a second, then nod my head.

"Good," he says.

And he's better now. We sit for a bit more and then he pats my bottom and says, "Now let's go for ice cream."

And we head to Mitchell's. He orders a sin-a-chocolate eruption and I order a single dip mint chocolate chip. It's hard, but I do it. My hands shake, but I eat it. All of it.

When he drops me back home, I take a shower and go to my room. I stand for a while in front of the mirror, working up the nerve to drop the towel. Finally I do it. I haven't looked at my body or weighed myself in a long time. I haven't wanted to know. But now I look. I really, really look.

And I don't like what I see.

With the exception of the ice cream, I haven't eaten anything in two and a half days. I was actually proud. Last night and this morning, my stomach was screaming for food, and I ignored it. I thought I was being strong. Now I look at my arms and legs and I don't know this body anymore. Corey's right. And even though I don't look as horrible as the eating disorder pictures I've seen online and in health class, it's wrong. For me, it's wrong. I don't look like Sid anymore. And I don't look like a better version of me, either, like some healthy-runner-girl Sid. I passed that stage by ages ago. What I look like now is scarecrow Sid... sad, pale skeleton Sid, left out in the rain.

And yet, even after I've looked at my body and seen what I've seen, and even though I know what I know, something pulls my gaze toward the door.

There's still time to get rid of it, the voice inside me says.

But this time...this time, I don't listen. I don't want to be that girl. I've never wanted to be that girl. The girl who pukes and runs and starves herself to death because she can't deal with her pain. How did I get to this place?

I put on my pajamas and crawl into bed. I lie awake for hours. And while it takes all my mental effort just to stay put, I do it. I stay put. I reason that if I don't get out of bed, then I can't go near the bathroom, and if I stay right here, tucked under the blanket, I can't put my running shoes on and hit the pavement.

I had no idea that staying in one place could be so hard.

29

I'm sitting in the unofficial "employee booth" at The Diner—the booth nearest the kitchen, where everyone hangs out during slow spells and between shifts. The lunch shift is over and I'm adding up my tips, which consist mainly of a towering stack of one-dollar bills. I keep messing up and having to start over because I can't concentrate. I'm completely sidetracked, because one, this table is covered in crap—newspapers, abandoned cups of soured coffee, old guest checks, someone's dirty apron—and two, I can't stop thinking about Corey and what I have planned for us later today.

I have made a decision.

A big decision.

An EPIC decision.

I've decided... I'm going to let Corey go up my shirt tonight. !!!!!

I want to see him without a shirt, too. I can feel him through his clothes, and I'm thinking it's probably pretty fantastic under there. Also, it's his birthday and the last official weekend of summer. School starts Monday. Bleck.

I actually decided a few days ago that I was ready for more, but I thought I'd wait until his birthday and make it a sort of bonus gift. It's been, what, two and a half months that we've been dating? He's been a real champ about our PG-13, fully-clothed make-out sessions, but it's time for an upgrade. Plus, I've gained seven pounds back, and at least five of them are in my boobs. He'll be thrilled.

How many dollars was that? Twenty-three or thirty-three? Fack.

I start counting over again when Kirsten and Paige walk in.

"Oooh, you're rich!" Paige squeals, sliding into the seat across from me.

"Yeah, not really. It's all ones," I say, trying not to lose count. Kirsten scoots in next to Paige.

"We're going to Edgewater to tan and scope out hot guys," Kirsten says. "Wanna come?"

I seriously can't roll my eyes hard enough.

"News flash—Sid Murphy doesn't tan, she broils. Besides, it's Corey's birthday and I'm headed to the bakery after this. I need to cash out, though, and I can't count for shit."

One, two, three, four...

"Here, let me do it," Paige says. I hand the stack over to her and start cleaning up the table. I grab the coffee cups and newspaper and slide out of the booth.

And that's when I see it.

That's when everything in the world comes flying apart.

I set down the coffee cups and look closely at the newspaper in my hand, and before my brain can even register what I'm looking at, my heart and gut remember. My stomach clenches and a disconnected floatiness overcomes me as the picture and words buzz into focus.

Man Sought in Connection with Multiple Rapes.

And it's him. The face, the eyes—it's him.

I don't know if the blood is draining down into my legs or pushing up into my face. All I know is that it's not in the places it's supposed to be. My knees buckle and I slump back into the booth, completely disoriented, the newspaper rattling in my hand.

"Who?" Kirsten says, but I only half hear her question.

"What?" I say. My thoughts are dazed, muddled, and I can't stop looking at the picture. It's like I'm hypnotized by those eyes all over again.

"You said, 'It's him,'" Kirsten says more clearly.

I snap out of myself. I drop the paper onto the table, totally flustered.

"I did? I mean, no, um . . ." and I can't think of what to say.

"Hey, you okay? You look like you're about to pass out," Kirsten says, leaning over to touch my arm. Paige has stopped counting and is looking at me, her eyes like saucers.

"Who's *him?*" she says, putting the money down and picking up the newspaper. She looks at the face and then at me.

"You know this guy?" she says.

My insides twist.

"Um..." I say, and my shaking fingers reach toward my uneven lock all by themselves.

I look around The Diner, searching for something, for I don't know what, while that familiar voice rings inside my ears.

You'll be needing the lying now, Sid. You know, the lie you keep stored in that lump in your throat, that burning hot lump you like to pretend isn't there, the one that's been lodged in your neck for the better part of a year. The Fairy Tale Lie... it's right there... just push it up and out of your mouth. Say something like: "What? No, I don't know him. It looked like Corey's landscape buddy for a second. Welp, gotta run!" And then get out of here.... Get. Out.

But that's not what happens. The lie is not what comes out of my mouth.

What comes out of my mouth is a choked sob. I try not to cry, but my chin is quivering so hard, and my jaws ache from trying to hold it in. I've gone seven months and four days without telling anyone. I can do this, I can keep it in, I can keep—

"It's the guy I met," I blurt, coughing a little on my tears, "the guy from the ski trip," and my throat is on fire, my vocal cords are scorching, like I'm trying to swallow that fiery lump.

Paige looks closer at the picture. Kirsten leans in, too.

They don't get it at first. But then things start clicking in their heads as they keep reading, and their eyes get bigger and bigger.

They get it now.

"Oh, my god," Kirsten says. And she starts getting loud, "Oh, Sid...oh, god..." and I can see where she's looking. Her finger rests under the picture, right by the huge, boldfaced caption that lists his real name: TOM HAMILTON. And his alias: DAX WINDSOR.

Seeing his real name after all this time makes me cry out, and I cover my mouth with both hands. I'm going to scream. I can hear and feel the scream trying to get out. I keep my mouth covered and my eyes shut tight, stifling the scream inside me. I can't breathe. My lungs are burning. I try to think of something nice—Corey's face, his kiss—I remember that first night with him and try to breathe.

"Breathe, Sid. In. Out. In. Out....I mean, a bride needs her legs
if she's gonna walk down the aisle....You have the most
amazing laugh....It's like this light coming out of
you. I could be in a crowd of thousands
and know right where to find you....
I have wanted to do
that for so, so
long...."

The thick air streams in through my nose; it goes in and I open my eyes and look at Kirsten and Paige, my mouth still covered, squeezing, squeezing my scream. I plead to them with my eyes to say something that will erase all of this. They don't.

I take another big breath through my nose and let a long

shudder pass through me. Then I stop squeezing my mouth with my hands and roll my knuckles up and rest them against my lips in case the scream comes back. I rest my elbows on the table and breathe. I'm breathing, I'm breathing, and I think the worst might be over.

"Have you told anyone else?" Kirsten asks. "Your mom? Corey?"

I shake my head and close my eyes again. The tears roll down and splash onto the backs of my fingers and knuckles. I fold my arms over one another and put my head in them to cry for a minute. Paige comes over and kneels down on the floor next to me and rubs my shoulder. Kirsten reaches over and grabs hold of my hand. My two best friends try to comfort me, telling me over and over how sorry they are and how it's going to be okay. I listen to them while I cry and shake. And you know what's funny? I cry as quiet as I can, so that I won't cause a scene. I'm actually thinking about this little waitressing job that I love. Somewhere in the back of my mind, I am thinking about this lovely little diner.

After a few minutes, I calm down and look up. My face was on fire inside my arms and the cool air hits it and feels good. I wipe my fingers over my cheeks and eyes. I sit back and blow my hair out of my face. Some of it is stuck to my cheek from the tears. I pick it away. I think I can go on now. I grab a napkin from the dispenser on the table. I wipe my eyes and blow my nose.

"How old is he?" I say. Because I've always wondered this.

You're scaring me....Are you an escaped convict?...Not that I

know of....I'm only sixteen....But I'll be seventeen in July....
But it's just a couple of years...that's nothing....But the bar? I
mean, if you're only nineteen....Almost nineteen....Never heard
of a fake ID?...

Kirsten picks up the paper again and scans the page. She looks at me, hesitating for a second.

"Twenty-seven," she says, her eyes tearing up.

I laugh. Can you believe that? I actually laugh. It's a short bark of a laugh, but it's there. I wipe my eyes. God, I hate myself. I really hate myself.

"Come on," I say, getting up. "Not here."

We walk outside to the back alley, where Kirsten's parked, and sit against the clownmobile. And I do it. I tell them. I tell my friends the awful truth about that night, about that horrible thing that happened to me last winter, about the rape I can't remember, and at the same time, can't forget.

~

I say good-bye, the girls hug me, and then I head over to the bakery. Before I go inside, I sit in Corey's truck for twenty minutes, watching the water pour from the gutter on the florist shop next door. They have it rigged up so that rainwater runs into a barrel. For the flowers, I'm guessing. I watch the water pouring in and I think.

In movies and on TV, girls who get raped usually end up in shadowy interrogation rooms, or in courthouses filled with police officers and lawyers. There's all this talk about "evidence" and "testimony," about "he-said-she-said" and "Why didn't you report it sooner?"

I touch my uneven lock and wonder if they'll find it in his home. He cut it for a reason. A souvenir. Now it'll probably wind up sealed in a plastic evidence bag in some police station. Telling Kirsten and Paige was hard—one of the hardest things I've ever done. But telling Corey and my mom is going to be much harder. I don't know how I'm going to do it without falling apart.

I need more time. You'd think seven months and four days would be enough time, right? Enough time to work up the nerve to just open my mouth and tell them. But it's not. For me, it's not. For seven months and four days I've rolled imaginary telling fantasies around in my head, but I can never seem to make it happen. And if I'd been alone when I found that newspaper, trust me, I probably wouldn't have told Kirsten and Paige. I probably wouldn't have said a word to anyone ever. I would have suffered through it in silence and carried on with living just like I've been doing. And even though my best friends know now, I still can't muster the strength to tell my mom. And that's not even mentioning Corey. Jesus. How do you tell a boyfriend you've never even been to second base with something like that? *Oh, yeah, by the way, I was drugged and raped last winter.* Then he gets to think about it every time he touches you.

But I know that at some point, sooner rather than later, I'm going to have to tell them. I know this. And I will. But right now, right at this moment, I'm just not ready. It's too raw, and I can just *feel* this angry monster inside me, growling and throwing itself against my numb insides. The anger is shrieking to be let out, and what I want—no—what I *need* is to go somewhere right now where I can be alone and just bawl and scream and wreck myself from the inside out. I think if I do that then I will be able to pick myself up and tell my mom and Corey without disintegrating into a pile of bone and ash.

And I know where I want to go. I know where I can do that. But just as I go to get out of the truck, Corey comes walking out the back service door, and I miss my chance to take off.

"Hey, there," he says, climbing in. Then he takes a good look at me. "Sid, look at you. You're all wet and shivering."

It must have started raining as I was walking from The Diner to the bakery. I didn't even realize I was wet until now. Corey pulls off his coat and puts it over me like a blanket. He kisses my cheek and I don't say anything. I just sit and watch the water pouring into the barrel. The rain's slowing down, but it's still pouring from the gutter.

"Sid?" he says.

I don't answer him right away. I can hear him, but I can't speak.

"Sid. Hello? Anyone home?"

He starts up the truck and flips the heat on, adjusting the vent toward me. He reaches out and brushes my hair away from my cheek; he is looking at the side of my face, waiting for my answer.

"Do you love me?" I say quietly, still staring at the water.

He pauses. I turn to look at him. His eyes are soft and big and the corners of his mouth turn upward into a shy grin.

"Yeah. Yeah, I do. I was going to tell you. It's just, I've never said it to anyone, so I was...I kept..."

"I love you, too," I say, turning back to the water. But the way it comes out is like this emotionless fact, like I'm not even saying it to him directly but more to myself. I catch myself and try to say it with more meaning. I turn and look at him so he knows that I mean it.

"I do. I love you," I say.

His eyes go worried.

"Sid, what's the matter?" he says. "You look like you've been crying. Something's wrong. What is it?"

And his face is so kind and trusting. He has no idea what's coming. I try and picture what his face will look like when he is looking at me for the first time after knowing. But I don't know what it will do. I'm afraid to know that.

"Sid. Talk to me. What's going on?"

I lean in and put my head on his chest because I don't want him to see me trying not to cry. And now I need to get out of this conversation. His present. His birthday. God, how cheap and shitty.

I clear my throat.

"I'm just PMSing again," I say. "I don't know how you put up with me. I really don't. Let's open your birthday present."

I pat his chest and sit up. I start to reach into the back, to get the guitar that's sitting on the floor. It's used, but still, it's a nice instrument. He'll forget all about this conversation once he sees the guitar. But he blocks me before I can reach it.

"Wait. The present can wait," he says, looking at me, studying me.

I knew it. Here we go again. I reach back again to get the guitar.

"But you're really going to like it," I say.

"Sid. No."

He's frustrated with me now.

"The present can wait. We're not done talking. Why do you always do that? Try to distract me? We've been through this how many times? I know what you're doing. But what I don't know is why you do it. Talk to me, Sid. *Please.*"

I sit in the seat and look at him. I look at him looking at me, studying my emotions the way he always does, and something in me snaps. The anger that I've carried, the tight ball of pure hatred that I've carried around in my heart and mind and guts and in every single pore of my body for seven months and four days—anger not caused by Corey, that could never, *ever* be caused by Corey—misplaces itself. It ricochets and heads straight for him.

"God! What is it with you?" I yell. "All you want to do is talk. Talk, talk, talk! Can't you just get over shit like a normal fucking guy? Can't you just move on already? You can see I don't want to talk about it. Jesus, you and the fucking talking!"

He looks at me, speechless, and I'm glad; I want him to feel that way. It might get him off the talking for five fucking seconds.

"Don't talk to me that way," he says, looking at me like he doesn't know who I am right now.

I spew my words at him because if I don't spew, I'll cry. I will bust out crying and never ever be able to stop. And what I say next is utter viciousness; I'm setting him up for the knockout punch.

"I'm trying not to talk to you that way!" I yell. "But guess what, Corey? You keep making me! You keep making me talk about things I don't want to talk about and it's funny that you do that, you know? Because you're hiding your shit, too!"

His face twists. "What?"

"Yeah! That's right! And I've never pressed you about it. About your drug dealing and your kiddie prison and your pothead *mother*! You never want to talk about any of those things, do you?"

And I've hit my mark. Corey's face looks like I've decked him. And what's horrible is that it feels good somehow. Dear god, what's wrong with me? I *want* to deck him. I get out of the truck before I actually *do* deck him.

He comes after me in the parking lot. He takes me by the elbow and I turn to look at him. I've never seen him this upset. He looks like he could slap me. So I slap him first, before he gets the chance. I slap him hard.

He flinches, and his other hand goes to his face.

"You hit me?"

He says it like a quiet question, like he can't believe it. He's not even angry now. He's in complete shock. So I slap him again to snap him out of it. I try to slap him a third time but he catches my arm, pushes it down to my side and then spins me around into a bear hug. He squeezes me snugly so I can't move. Not hurting me, but still. I'm immobilized completely in under a second.

"Let go! I wanna leave!" I yell, trying to buck him.

"Like hell you're leaving! You don't get to say that shit to me, hit me, and walk off. You want to know about my mother, Sid? You want to know about my drugs? Well, now you're gonna hear it. You're gonna hear the whole damn story."

I squirm and fight, but he has me good and he's not even trying. His words come out like darts into my neck.

"My mom is sick, Sid. Got it? Sick!"

He turns me around to look at him and he is holding me by the shoulders. Firm, like he held my wrists that day of the fight in school. Only this time when he's looking at me, he hates me. His eyes are tearful and wounded, but angry, too. He wants to shake me; I can feel him wanting to shake me. But he doesn't. Because he is a person who would never do that.

"She has MS. Multiple sclerosis? I'm sure you know what that is, Miss College Prep 3.7, smart-ass, know-it-all grade point average, but let me enlighten you further. MS is a life of never knowing if your next step is going to be your last. It's never knowing if you're going to wake up one day and be blind. It's a life of *endless, excruciating* fucking pain that *never* goes away. And the only thing that makes it bearable? The only thing that gives you any relief at all? Well, it just so happens to be illegal in Ohio. So that's why I grew it! That's why I *still* grow it! Because she needs it. And I'm going to keep growing it if it means I can make her life bearable. She smokes it and it makes her life bearable! And that's why I don't want you to come over—I don't want you involved. I don't want you to be there if the police come busting my door down again. I don't want you to be locked up like I was!"

Oh, god.

What have I done? Someone please tell me why I've done this? Why have I said these terrible things? It's unforgivable, what I've said, and I want to take it all back. I need to tell him I'm sorry, tell him everything. I'm going to tell him everything.

"Corey, I..."

He releases my shoulders. He holds up his hands and shakes his head. "Don't. Just don't. I don't wanna hear it. The talking is over, Sid. You win. No more talking. We're done."

I am left standing in the parking lot, watching Corey's truck get smaller and smaller.

I want to run, but something in me just can't do it anymore. Plus, it hurts. Did I mention that? That I have to go to bed with frozen peas on my shins? I just lay there while my shins throb and throb under the bags of frozen peas.

I can't run anymore. Running's out. No more running.

So I walk.

I walk and walk and walk.

30

It's still unsold. This beautiful house on the lake, and nobody wants it. I'll take it. I'll take this house on the lake with a ceiling that points the way to heaven. I thought I would get here and be able to expel that voice, that angry voice, that ball of hatred and shame and despair that haunts me, even in my sleep. I thought I would scream my head off, pull my hair out, and tear my own skin off.

But that's not what's happening. What's happening is something quiet and unimaginable, something wonderful. I lay and look up at the painted sky, and the rage just dissolves; it just drifts out of me. This peaceful feeling overcomes me, and I feel soft and still inside. I look up at the painted ceiling and remember that night.

I'm standing in the condo kitchen. Rapist Tom Hamilton is asking me about cheerleading. The cheerleading is fascinating him. I am telling him about camp and how awful it was and he's laughing and I really think he likes me. I think I'm being a regular laugh-riot comedian. Then this strange sort of giddiness washes over me. I look down at the glass and there are three of them in my hand. I try to tell Rapist Tom Hamilton that I feel dizzy, but I can't move my mouth. He smiles at me just as my fingers go limp and the glass slips out of my hand. Down the glass goes in slow motion, crash, all over the tiles. And I'm falling into nothingness.

I lay here and remember that feeling, that sensation of falling and floating, of giving in and sliding under. But it's not scary and horrible under this painted sky. Because this time, before the darkness comes, something new and amazing occurs to me.

Tom Hamilton did his worst to me, and I'm still here.

I'm still here.

I can shut my eyes without fear now. For the first time since last winter, I welcome sleep. Because I know that when I wake up, I'm going to text my mom to come and get me. I'm going to tell her everything. Then I'm going to call Corey and tell him everything, too.

I don't know how long I sleep. My body can't tell time. It feels like it did that night, like nothing and everything all at once, like a spark of a moment stuck inside forever.

Until I wake up.

No—until I'm *woken* up.

Someone is shaking me by the shoulders, saying my name,

saying it loud. But I'm not afraid, because I know that voice. I'd know that voice anywhere. I could pick that voice out of a crowd of thousands. I open my eyes and see him—Corey is looking down at me. His eyes are red; he's been crying.

"Are you okay?" he says, pulling me up and toward him.

I nod my head and blink. I can tell from the heartbreak in his eyes that he knows.

"You know about me," I say, fighting back tears.

He nods and then pulls me into him, hugging me close. After a moment, he pulls back and looks at me very hard.

"You could have told me," he says, his eyes filling up. "I want you to know that you could've told me. Because it doesn't change anything. For me, it doesn't change a thing. Okay?"

I nod, and the tears spill out. This time, I don't fight it. I let them fall.

We hug each other and cry.

"And we couldn't find you," he says, sobbing into my hair. "Oh, god, your mom and Kirsten and Paige, we looked everywhere and couldn't find you. I'm so sorry I left you in the parking lot. I'm so sorry."

We hold on to each other and he tells me how he found out. He knows because Kirsten and Paige told my mother, and she told him. When I didn't come home from work, my mother called Kirsten's house, and even though I swore them to secrecy, they still told. They told because they know my mom and they know me and they knew it was the right thing to do.

I have good friends.

The best.

After a while, Corey pulls back again and smooths the curls out of my face. I study his eyes. I study what his face is doing now that he knows. I search my mind for the emotion that will describe the way he is looking at me. And it reveals itself to me: *Assurance.* Corey will pull through for me. He will love me in the exact same way. I know this now.

"I'm sorry I hit you," I say. "I'm sorry for what I said about your mother."

"I know. I know you are," he says.

"I need to call my mom."

"She's on her way. We've all been driving around Lakewood for hours. I called her from outside. I saw your shoes at the steps."

We hug some more and say nothing else for a long time. The silence is comforting, all by itself. After a while, I hear my mom and Liam coming through the house.

"In here," Corey calls out. My mom rushes in and kneels down next to me. She takes my face into her hands. She looks at me closely, her swollen eyes purposeful.

"You're going to get through this. We are going to get through this. You hear me?"

I nod and our eyes cry out to each other with such relief. She kisses me and hugs me tight.

"Why is everyone crying?" Liam asks quietly, carefully crouching down to look at us. "We should play Tinker. That'll make everyone feel better."

Corey gets up and takes Liam by the hand.

"Come on, buddy. Let's go to the truck. Everything's fine. Your mom and Sid need to talk for a little bit."

After they leave, I look at my mom.

"It was you I wanted to tell," I say. "I don't know why I didn't. I just...I'm sorry."

"It's okay. You don't have to be sorry. Ever," she says. "I'm here now, we're all here, and it's going to be okay. You're going to be okay."

I tell her what happened. All of it. And when I'm done and we've cried ourselves out, she says it again, with renewed intensity: "You're going to be okay."

Then she stands up and stretches out a hand to me and leads me through the house to the conservatory. We stand together, looking out at the lake, for a long time, watching far-off boat lights flicker on, one by one, in the dusky light. After a while, my mom runs her hand gently over my hair, and then walks outside to wait for me.

I stay a moment longer.

I step up to the wall of windows and press my fingertips against the cool glass, my mother's words echoing in my heart and mind. *You're going to be okay.* I watch as the endless ribbons of water rock and swell under a quiet, cobalt sky, and I choose to believe. I choose to believe that I will be okay.

Acknowledgments

I'd like to thank God. Cliché? Probably. But it's how I feel and what I know to be true and right. I firmly believe that whatever creative gifts I have, they have been given to me by God, so I thank Him. Forever and ever, I thank Him. I'd like to also thank my first family: a father who provided me a safe and loving home to grow up in and a mother who has always believed in me and who, in my adulthood, has become my dearest friend. Thanks also to my brother, Randy Clayton, and my sister, Irish twin, and other dearest friend, Stacey (Clayton) Reynolds. Love and gratitude to my second family: my husband, Ray, who has loved me for going on twenty years now; my bright, beautiful daughter, Mary; and my strong, patient son, Ryan.

If praise were an actual physical object, I'd get a shovel out and start heaping it onto the members of Team Sid. My amazing agent, Alyssa Reuben, who took a chance on this big old nobody from Ohio and worked tirelessly for over two years on my behalf and on behalf of this book. My wonderful editors at Poppy, Pam Gruber and Elizabeth Bewley, who took a good story and made it great, and my copy editor, Martha Cipolla, who took a great story and made it flawless. This book would not be what it is today without the input of these incredible women. Also, much thanks to my cover designer, Liz Casal, who captured the essence of Sid so, so perfectly.

I would also like to mention and thank my first reader, Dr. Rosemary D'Apolito (Rosebud). I was a former social worker, a stay-at-home mom, and a dog-walker when I met her nearly a decade ago. (Also, I occasionally liked to write stuff down....) I used to walk her dogs—bearded collies named Lily and Frasier. Rosebud was the first person to ever read my work, and she helped me to realize that my "midlife crisis" was actually an attainable dream.

I want to give special thanks to my friend Alyssa Brugman, an Australian author whose exceptional way with language and voice motivated me early on in my writing journey. Her young adult novels made me want to be a better writer. While I thank her for being such an inspiration, I mostly want to thank her for writing me back. About three years ago, I was feeling pretty down and riding full-blast on the "query-go-round" of rejection when I wrote her a fan letter. It meant the world to me when she replied back with the kindest e-mail.

Thanks also to my thesis advisor, mentor, and good friend, Christopher Barzak, who leads the way for all of us living and writing in Youngstown. I'd like to thank the academic community at Youngstown State University, specifically Dr. Gary Salvner, Dr. Rebecca Barnhouse, Dr. Patricia Hauschildt, and Terry Benton, who all believe in the importance of writing for and about young people. Also, big thanks to Noelle Bowles, Reginald McKnight, and Karen Boyle, who all saw this story in its earliest stages and encouraged me to keep going. Thanks to my awesome writing group, Invisible Ink, which includes my partner in crime, Kelly Bancroft, as well as James Hain, Annie Murray, Christopher Lettera, and Mindi Kirchner-Greenway. Thank you to my other supporters: Gabrielle Mullins, Bob Reynolds, Alyssa Clayton, Jo Ann Hylton, Victoria Dippolito, Caitlyn Ryan, Candace Shives, Christina Meeker, Christine Rasey, Lisa Squiric, Maegan Riley, Jess Nash, Joe Alesnik, Renate Prescott, Bob Pope, Mack Hassler, Jill Sommer, Kim Zander, Hollie Slusarczyk, Traci Purdum, and the Znidarsic Ladies: Marlene, Lynnette, and Melissa.

I want to acknowledge the musicians mentioned in this novel, especially the lovely Fiona Apple. I cannot imagine a world without her music in it. For over fifteen years, she has provided me with a personal soundtrack for meaningful living, and for that I am ever grateful.

Lastly, I want to thank the city of Lakewood, Ohio, and its schools for providing me with such a rich landscape in which to set this story.... I may have fudged some of the details, but hopefully I captured the heart of your wonderful city. And more broadly, I'd like to thank the cities of Cleveland and Youngstown. I'm a rust belt girl through and through and am so utterly proud to call these places my home.

Where stories bloom.

poppy